When it comes to impressing his new in-laws, poor John Pickett hasn't a "ghost" of a chance!

"Look here, Mr. Pickett," said the squire, closing the door against any curious eavesdroppers, "if you're going to be one of the family, you might as well make yourself useful."

It was not the opening Pickett was expecting, but he was not about to let pass the opportunity to redeem himself, if possible, in his father-in-law's eyes. "If there is anything I can do, sir—"

"I believe there may be. It's my wife, you see. She's got the idea the house must be haunted."

"Haunted?" Pickett echoed. "Begging your pardon, sir, but what would have put such an idea into her head?"

"She claims she heard footsteps walking about the house last night." Sir Thaddeus appeared to struggle with himself, and when he spoke again, it was as if the words were dragged from his unwilling throat. "Oh, the devil! In for a penny, in for a pound, I suppose. If you must know, Lady Runyon is persuaded she knows the identity of this particular spirit."

"Does she?" Pickett asked, but even before Sir Thaddeus answered, he knew what was coming.

The older man sighed. "My wife believes she heard the ghost of Claudia, our elder daughter."

THE JOHN PICKETT MYSTERIES

PICKPOCKET'S APPRENTICE
(A John Pickett novella)

IN MILADY'S CHAMBER

A DEAD BORE

FAMILY PLOT

DINNER MOST DEADLY

WAITING GAME
(Another John Pickett novella)

TOO HOT TO HANDEL

FOR DEADER OR WORSE

For Deader or Worse

Another John Pickett mystery

Sheri Cobb South

Stop right there!

Yes, you. Before you begin reading *For Deader or Worse*, you might be interested to know that there's a new John Pickett short story available for free download. Chronologically, it falls between *Too Hot to Handel* and *For Deader or Worse*—in fact, it takes place about two days after *Too Hot to Handel* ends—and although it's certainly not necessary to read it in order to understand this book (it's only about 2,000 words, or 7 typed double-spaced pages), it does offer readers a brief glimpse of what happens to the very newly married John and Julia after the last page of *Too Hot to Handel* is turned. Download your free copy of "I'll See You in My Dreams" in EPUB, MOBI, or PDF formats at http://dl.bookfunnel.com/aipv9hyob5

Ready? Okay, *now* you can turn the page . . .

PROLOGUE

Which Finds a Lady in Distress

May 1796
Somersetshire

H is lordship paused in the doorway of the drawing room, observing with a critical eye the beautiful young woman sitting on a striped satin sofa and making minuscule adjustments to the tea tray and the sumptuous tower of cakes which filled the small table conveniently placed at her elbow. Any other man might have taken pleasure in the sight of the lady's golden beauty, but his lordship, noting the second cup and plate, scowled his disapproval.

"Entertaining visitors to tea, Claudia?" he asked, his tone cautioning the lady to answer in the affirmative at her peril.

"Yes, my love. Won't you join us?" The endearment was strictly a matter of form, for any affection she had once felt for his lordship had not long survived the marriage vows.

"It depends. Who, may I ask, is honoring us by accepting our hospitality?"

The lady colored slightly, but answered in a voice that was clear and strong. "Jamie Pennington is to return to Oxford tomorrow, so I thought—"

"Damn Jamie Pennington!" his lordship exploded. "Are we never to see the back of that whelp?"

"I can hardly cut the acquaintance when Jamie and I have been friends since we were both in leading strings," she protested in coaxing tones.

"It is not your childhood friendship, but your present one which troubles me."

His lordship's chiseled countenance darkened ominously and her ladyship, recognizing the warning signs, made haste to placate him. "Recall, my dear, that Jamie is to have the living at Norwood Green when his father retires. Am I not even to entertain the vicar without provoking your jealousy?"

"Jealousy?" scoffed his lordship. "Why the devil should I be jealous of a cub still wet behind the ears? But I tell you this, Claudia: I will not stand idly by while my wife plants cuckold's horns on my head under my own roof!"

At the injustice of this charge, her ladyship's spirit, still not entirely quashed after two years of marriage to a highly volatile man almost two decades her senior, overcame her fear, and she shot to her feet. "Oh, how dare you?"

"I might ask you the same, madam! Do not think I have not noticed the way you encourage that young man's infatuation, all in the name of a childhood friendship which he would have outgrown long ago, did you not constantly feed the flames." His gaze flicked from her face to her abdomen, which had not yet begun to swell with the advent of his lordship's heir. "And what of my son, Claudia? May I expect him to have ginger hair?"

It was too much to be borne, this final insult not only to herself, but to one who was entirely innocent of the sordid charge laid at his door. White to the lips, she picked up the silver teapot and flung its steaming contents over his lordship's immaculate shirtfront. With a roar of rage, he sent tea table, cups, and cakes scattering with one sweep of his arm. In the next instant he was upon her, raining blows down upon her face, head and shoulders, while she huddled lower and lower in an attempt to shield the child she carried. At last, having reduced his lady to a quivering heap upon the floor, his lordship administered a swift kick to her ribs, then turned on his heel and left the house, slamming the door behind him.

Her ladyship lay there for some time after he left, sobbing softly as she considered her husband's accusations. Had she indeed encouraged Jamie to dangle after her? It was true that she had known he loved her, had done so ever since he had returned from Eton. There had been no talk of marriage between them, however, for at eighteen he had been much too young to support a wife and she, not quite seventeen, had entertained too many hopes of a brilliant season in Bath to consider an early marriage to the vicar's son, however sincere her affection for him. Yes, she could see how there might have been some grain of truth to her husband's claims; still, her actions had not been from any intention of playing her husband false, but rather a futile attempt to return to those happier, more innocent days when she had been the belle of Norwood Green, before she had married his lordship and the scales had been ripped from her eyes.

The long-case clock in the hall began to chime the hour, and her ladyship wiped her eyes with her sleeve, flinching at the pain. Jamie would arrive at any minute, and she must not let him see her like this. She must get up the stairs to her room, closing the drawing room door behind her lest he see the wreckage of the tea things littering the floor and draw his own conclusions. Although she had not yet surveyed her reflection in a looking-glass, she was certain that cosmetics could not disguise her husband's handiwork; she would have to instruct the butler to deny her, saying she was unwell. It would be no less than the truth; she only hoped she could reach the privacy of her own bedchamber before she vomited all over the carpet.

She pushed herself upright to a sitting position, and felt such a stab of pain in her side that she was temporarily deprived of breath. Steeling herself against the agony she knew would follow, she forced herself to stand on legs that balked at supporting her. With her left hand pressed to her ribs, she managed to reach the nearest wall, and by bracing herself against it contrived to trace the perimeter of the room to the door. In the same manner she circled the hall until she reached the foot of the stairs, noting that the servants had all disappeared, as was their usual habit when the master and mistress quarreled. Her split and bloodied lower lip twisted in a cynical travesty of a smile. God forbid that they should be called upon to defend her against his lordship's wrath.

By the time she reached the staircase, the last of her strength was exhausted. When she released the wall in order to grasp the banister, her legs buckled and she fell to her knees. She tugged her skirts out from beneath her and began, slowly and painstakingly, to climb the stairs on all fours. All too soon, a knock sounded on the door.

"Jamie," she murmured. She looked up and found that, although it felt as if she had been climbing forever, she was only halfway to the landing. At this rate, she could not possibly reach her bedchamber in time. Perhaps, if she could get as far as the landing, she might turn the corner and be out of sight. Perhaps the butler would refuse to come out of hiding, and Jamie, receiving no answer to his knock, would go away . . .

The knock sounded again, more insistently this time, and her ladyship dragged herself up one more step. Four more to go . . . Three . . .

The door swung open hesitantly, and a familiar voice called cheerfully, "Hullo? Is anyone home? Claudia? *Claudia!*"

A red-haired young man of twenty-two crossed the hall in three strides, then took the stairs two at a time until he reached her. Jamie Pennington dropped to one knee beside her, taking in at a glance her bloodied lip and rapidly swelling eye.

"Claudia, what's happened?" he demanded, his face

11

turning pale beneath its scattering of freckles.

"It's nothing," she insisted feebly, turning her face away. "His lordship—we—we quarreled—"

" 'Nothing'? My parents quarrel every now and then, but Papa has never once blackened Mama's eyes!"

"It's not usually this bad," she protested feebly. "I brought it on myself. I provoked him—"

"The devil you did!" He stood upright and glanced swiftly around the hall. "Where is his lordship?"

"I—I don't know. He stormed out right after—after—"

She broke off as Jamie retraced his route down the stairs. Instead of departing the way he had come, however, he stopped before the massive hall fireplace, standing on tiptoe to take down one of the two crossed swords mounted above it.

"Jamie, what are you doing?"

He wheeled about to confront her. "Do you think I haven't noticed all those Sundays you've come to church with a black eye or a swollen lip? Cover them with cosmetics all you like, Claudia, and joke about your own clumsiness in tripping over the carpet. You can fool everyone else in Norwood Green, but you can't fool me. I should have killed the bastard years ago."

"No, Jamie!" She raised a trembling hand in supplication. "No, you mustn't!"

"You would defend him?" Jamie's wrath faded, replaced by bitter envy that one so undeserving should command such loyalty. "You would plead for his life after the beating he gave you?"

"No," she said, her voice faltering until only a whisper remained. "But if he were to kill you, I should have no one."

"Your parents—"

She shook her head. "I can't tell them. Mama would never understand." Her lower lip twisted, her upper one being by this time so swollen as to make movement impossible. "Mama is very big on a woman doing her wifely duty."

Jamie, coming to a decision, let out a sigh and returned his weapon to the mantelpiece. "Very well, then. Have you a shawl anywhere?"

"In the drawing room," she said, indicating its direction with a vague gesture that made her wince. "Jamie, what are you going to do?"

"I'm getting you out of here before he kills you!"

Ignoring her faint protest, he strode across the hall to the drawing room, his copper-colored eyebrows arching upward at the sight of the wreckage which was all that remained of the repast to which he'd looked forward for days. He snatched up the large paisley shawl draped over the back of the sofa, and returned with it to the staircase. He draped it over her head like a hood, the better to protect her poor battered face from curious eyes, and then lifted her in his arms.

"Am I hurting you?" he asked, hearing her sharp intake of breath.

"Yes." Her voice was barely a whisper, but she clung to his lapel with all the strength she could muster. "But please don't let go."

13

"I'll never let you go, Claudia," he said, and the words carried all the weight of a sacred vow.

1

Which Finds John Pickett
Embarking Upon a New Mission

March 1809
London

T he bells of St. Mary-le-Strand woke him. This in itself was not unusual, for the bells of the old church at the foot of Drury Lane had been tolling the hour for almost a century, and had summoned John Pickett to Bow Street every morning for the last five years.

But he was not going to Bow Street today. The realization of what he was to do instead propelled him from the warmth of the bed, and he stepped barefooted onto the rag rug that afforded the only protection from the cold wooden floorboards. He stirred the banked coals of the fire and set a kettle of water to heat, then picked impatiently over a breakfast which had been sent up by his landlady, and for which he had no appetite. Pushing the bowl of porridge away, he set about his morning ablutions without waiting for the water to heat fully. After washing with water that could only charitably be described as tepid, he shaved with more than usual care. Staring back at him from the mirror mounted on the wall over the basin was a rather pale young man of almost five-and-twenty whose brown eyes held an expression of nervous anticipation not unmingled with stark terror. Having managed to eradicate his faint beard without accidentally slitting his throat, he dressed in a snowy white shirt, breeches, stockings, and shoes before tying his starched cravat with fingers that shook. He brushed his rather wild brown curls into submission and tied them back at the nape of his neck with a black velvet ribbon before putting on the white brocade waistcoat and dark blue double-breasted tailcoat that had been sent over from the tailor only the day before.

He patted the inside coat pocket (quite unnecessarily, for he knew very well what it contained), then packed his shaving kit into the battered valise standing open in the corner. He closed it and fastened its worn leather straps, then paced the floor for the next ten minutes, until a knock on the door put an end to his perambulations.

"Good morning, Mr. Pickett," said the grinning individual standing just outside, a stout fellow wearing the striped waistcoat and caped driving coat of the town coachman. "Whenever you're ready, we'll be on our way."

"Good morning—Jervis, isn't it?" Pickett said, trying to recall the man's name. The conveyance was courtesy of his magistrate, Mr. Colquhoun, who had made many of the arrangements, up to and including the clothes on Pickett's back. And perhaps it was just as well, Pickett thought, for today's mission was quite outside his own experience. "I'm ready, so let's be off."

He bent to pick up the valise, but the coachman waved him away. "I'll just get that for you, shall I?"

Pickett nodded, still uncomfortable with the idea of letting servants do for him what he was quite capable of doing himself. As Jervis hoisted the bag to his shoulder, Pickett cast a long look back at the two-room flat that had been his home for the last five years, then followed the coachman out of the room and down the stairs into the crisp March air. Once in the street, he reached for the door of the carriage, only to fall back in some chagrin when Jervis rather pointedly cleared his throat. He allowed the coachman to open the door, then climbed inside.

The distance from his own lodgings in Drury Lane to his destination in Curzon Street was a scant two miles—less than that as the crow flies—but there were far greater differences than could be measured in linear dimensions. As the unrefined bustle of the Covent Garden district gave way to the elegant shops of Piccadilly and finally to the manicured residential squares of Mayfair, Pickett fell victim to increasing doubts as to his ability to succeed in the approaching endeavor. By the time the carriage rolled to a stop, his state of mind had deteriorated to a condition approaching panic. Granted, Mr. Colquhoun seemed to think his future at Bow Street was bright, but before that he'd been a collier's apprentice and, before that, a juvenile pickpocket. There was nothing in his past—nor his present either, for that matter—to render him in any way qualified for what he was about to undertake. Who was he to think he could succeed where another, far more advantaged than he, had failed? Who was he to—

"Curzon Street, number twenty-two," trumpeted Jervis, flinging open the carriage door and putting an end to Pickett's self-disparagement.

The time had come. Pickett disembarked, then took a deep breath, gave a tug to his waistcoat, and mounted the shallow stairs to the front door. He was obviously expected, for no sooner had he lifted the knocker and let it fall than the front door was thrown open.

"Mr. Pickett, sir!" exclaimed the butler, beaming at him. "Do come in."

"Rogers."

Pickett returned the butler's greeting with a nod, but retained his hat and gloves, for he would not be staying long. He followed Rogers down a short narrow corridor to a drawing room at the rear of the house. The butler opened the door to this chamber with a flourish.

"Mr. Pickett, my lady—er, madam," he announced, then fell back to allow Pickett entrance.

At the butler's announcement, a woman rose from her chair before the fire, a beautiful golden-haired lady wearing a high-waisted gown of light blue silk along with a radiant smile.

"John!" she exclaimed.

At the sight of her, all his misgivings fell away. He was the luckiest man in the world, and it was a wise man who did not question his good fortune, however undeserving of it he knew himself to be.

"Well, my lady?" he asked, regarding her with a quizzical smile. "Are you ready to marry me?"

* * *

In fact, they were already married, and had been since the previous October, when an expedient yet innocent masquerade as man and wife while in Scotland had resulted in their finding themselves legally wed according to the laws of that country. The annulment process was already well underway when Pickett had been seriously injured in the line of duty, and Lady Fieldhurst had taken it upon herself to nurse him. That had been two weeks ago, and while he had lain unconscious, her ladyship had decided (as his magistrate said) to keep him. In a way, Pickett supposed he owed his attacker a debt of gratitude. For the last week, he had been recovering from his wounds and, if he were honest, he had to admit that not all his time in bed had been spent sleeping. Today's wedding ceremony was not strictly necessary, since their irregular marriage was perfectly legitimate, but a practical measure to prevent the lady's aristocratic in-laws from challenging and perhaps invalidating the union. Lady Fieldhurst—how long would it be, Pickett wondered, before he was able to think of her as Julia?—had left their Drury Lane love nest only the previous afternoon, when her friend Lady Dunnington had appeared at the door, announcing her intention of dragging Julia back to Curzon Street, where she might prepare for the wedding and pack her bags for the journey to Somersetshire that would immediately follow the ceremony. When he had tried to protest this high-handed kidnapping of his bride, Lady Dunnington had insisted that it was not at all the thing for a bride to spend the night before the wedding with her husband—an exercise in logic so convoluted that by the time he had deciphered it sufficiently to form a rebuttal, she had already borne Julia off in her barouche.

Now her ladyship—no, *Julia*, he reminded himself— gave her footman instructions for the hiring of a post chaise while the butler stowed her portmanteau on the boot of the magistrate's carriage. Pickett looked on, suddenly self-conscious and a little embarrassed at being for the first time in public (and fully clothed) with the lady who had occupied his bed in a delightful state of undress only thirty-six hours earlier. It was a relief when he climbed up into the vehicle behind her and Jervis closed the door, leaving the two of them in relative privacy.

"How did you sleep last night, John?" Julia asked demurely as the carriage lurched into motion. "I hope your injury did not pain you overmuch?"

"I slept well enough," he said, although in truth he had been obliged to dose himself with laudanum, less for relief from the dull headache that still troubled him from time to time than for help falling asleep in a bed which suddenly seemed much too empty. "And you?"

"My dear John, surely you jest! For the first time in a fortnight, I had a large, well-heated room and a nice thick mattress all to myself." She tucked her hand into the curve of his arm and lowered her voice to a conspiratorial whisper. "I hated it."

The trip to Mr. Colquhoun's residence did not take long, and soon they entered the magistrate's house, where the guests were already assembled. These were of necessity few, as Pickett had no family save for a ne'er-do-well father in Botany Bay, and the only relatives of Julia's who resided in London were actually her late husband's kin and vehemently disapproved of the match. Although Lady Dunnington could not entirely applaud Julia's choice, she was there to stand up with her friend nevertheless, along with Lord Dunnington, and of course Mr. Colquhoun, Pickett's magistrate, who along with his wife was hosting the wedding breakfast. Julia's parish priest, whom Pickett had met while investigating Lord Fieldhurst's murder, was to perform the ceremony, and had arrived just ahead of the bridal couple.

What can be said about a wedding that has not been said before? It was exactly like every other wedding with its vows to love, honor, and obey, and yet uniquely their own. There was an awkward moment when Pickett stammered blushingly over the line that states "with my body I thee worship" (just as if he had not been worshipping quite devoutly for the past week), but save for Lady Dunnington, who was obliged to hide her smile behind her gloved hand, it is doubtful that anyone but the bride and groom noticed.

Then, too, when the priest instructed the bridegroom to put the ring on her finger, Julia tried her best to frown him down, determined to spare Pickett the embarrassment of confessing the lack of a wedding ring. But it was perhaps just as well that she failed to catch the clergyman's eye, for to her great surprise, Pickett reached into the inside pocket of his coat and withdrew a small circlet of gold.

And suddenly the thing was done. The company repaired to the dining room for the wedding breakfast, and amidst the confusion of congratulations Mr. Colquhoun drew Pickett aside and handed him a folded paper which, when opened, proved to be a bank draft made out for a sum that made Pickett's eyes all but start from his head.

"I—I can't accept this, sir!" he protested.

"And why the devil not, pray?" demanded the magistrate, scowling fiercely.

"You've done so much already—"

"Let me be very clear. This is not a personal gift, but your share of the reward promised by the Princess Olga Fyodorovna for that little business at Drury Lane Theatre."

"Then everyone on the Bow Street force received cheques in this amount?"

"Everyone received something, but yours is rather larger than the others'."

"But why should it be? If you will recall, I was unconscious during most of the investigation."

"Oh, I recall—better than you do, I daresay! I recall that you were very nearly killed for your part of the investigation, and if it hadn't been for that, we might still be trying to solve the thing. Take it, John. God knows you've earned it."

Pickett struggled with himself. He didn't like the idea of being paid for work he hadn't really done (and he did not believe getting himself coshed over the head counted, no matter what Mr. Colquhoun might say to the contrary), but he could not deny that he needed the money. He had reluctantly allowed his wife to pay for the post chaise that would shortly convey them to Somersetshire, telling himself this was an acceptable use of her money since the entire purpose of the trip was to allow her to introduce him to her parents, but the fact of the matter was that he didn't have a choice. The purchase of her wedding ring had severely depleted his meager savings, and although he certainly did not begrudge that expenditure, it had left little to spare for a wedding trip.

"Yes, sir," he said with a sigh, and tucked the cheque into the inside pocket of his coat where Mrs. Pickett's ring had so recently resided.

"Good man," Mr. Colquhoun said, nodding his approval. "Now, tell me about this honeymoon. How long do you expect to be in the West Country?"

"Two days to get there, and another two for the journey back to London—as far as how long we stay in Somersetshire, I suspect it depends on the reception we get from Sir Thaddeus and Lady Runyon." He grimaced. "I may be back at Bow Street within the week."

"I won't insult your intelligence with assurances that your mama- and papa-in-law will be thrilled with the match; still, I don't doubt they'll find that you improve upon closer acquaintance. But take as much time as you wish. You need not hurry back to Bow Street."

"Oh, but I must. After all," he added with a rather fatuous smile, "I have a wife to support."

Mr. Colquhoun cleared his throat. "Look here, John, I know the two of you haven't had much time to talk about the future, but I think you should ask your wife—"

"Begging your pardon, sir," the butler murmured discreetly, tapping Pickett on the shoulder, "but the post chaise is at the door."

"Thank you," Pickett said, grateful to the man for having the tact to inform him—rather than his wife, who had paid for its hire—of the vehicle's arrival. Turning back to the magistrate, he said, "Well, I guess I'd best collect Mrs. Pickett, and we'll be on our way. As for everything you've done, sir, I can't thank you enough—"

"Never mind that," protested Mr. Colquhoun, waving away Pickett's half-formed expressions of gratitude. "Only be happy, and that will be thanks enough for me."

A burst of feminine laughter drew Pickett's attention to the opposite corner of the room where Julia stood, engaged in lighthearted conversation with Lady Dunnington and Mrs. Colquhoun. "Be happy, sir? How can any man who is loved by such a woman be otherwise?"

"How, indeed?" grumbled the magistrate some minutes later, as he and his wife stood on the front stoop with the other guests, waving their handkerchiefs as the yellow-bodied post chaise bowled away.

"Beg pardon, love?" asked Mrs. Colquhoun, a plump, good-natured woman who, having reared four children and buried three others, had accepted without question her husband's deep and fatherly affection for the young man he'd rescued from a life of crime a decade earlier.

"I was only thinking of our newly wedded pair," he said with a sigh. "I hope they will be happy."

By "they," of course, the magistrate meant "he," and Mrs. Colquhoun knew her husband well enough to understand the concerns he did not express. "Why should he not?" she countered. "One has only to see them together to recognize the depth of their affection for one another."

"Yes, but I've only just discovered that Mr. Pickett expects to support his bride on his earnings."

"And so he should do! What is wrong with that?"

"While he lay unconscious, I learned from the lady herself that her widow's jointure will not end with her remarriage. In fact, if she intends to live in the manner to which she is accustomed, it is she who will be supporting him, not the other way 'round."

"Oh," said Mrs. Colquhoun, rather daunted by this revelation. "But surely you must have misunderstood, my dear. If, as you say, they have lived together as man and wife for the past week, they must have talked about it by now."

He turned to regard her somewhat sternly, but beneath his bushy white eyebrows, his blue eyes held a twinkle. "My dear Janet, has it really been so long since we were first wed? Whatever they may have done for the past week, I can assure you that *talking* has not been a priority."

* * *

As the post chaise rattled westward, Julia held out her left hand, the better to admire the simple gold band on her third finger.

"You didn't have to do this, John."

25

"Yes, I did." There would be many, many things that her first husband had given her which he would never be able to match, but he had no intention of conceding defeat before the ink on the marriage lines was even dry. "Believe me, I did."

Julia, having a very fair idea of the direction his thoughts were taking, bent a keen gaze upon him and said, "You're not in competition with Fieldhurst, John. It wouldn't be fair." She laced her fingers through his and gave his hand a squeeze. "Poor Fieldhurst wouldn't stand a chance."

He smiled at that, as she had intended, so she pressed on. "But how did you manage it?"

He shrugged. "I had a little money put back from that business with Sir Reginald Montague."

"No, I mean how did you *manage* it? You never left the flat!"

"Oh, that. Mr. Colquhoun acted as my deputy." He grinned at her. "It made a welcome change."

"I do like your magistrate."

"He thinks very highly of you, too."

It was another unexpected benefit of his being injured, the discovery that while he had lain unconscious, the two people he loved best in the world, who had previously regarded one another with mistrust (if not outright hostility) had apparently bonded over his inert body.

They broke their journey for the night at a posting inn at Reading, which was not as romantic an experience as might have been expected in a newly wedded couple; six hours of being bounced over bad roads in a poorly sprung chaise had caused Pickett's half-healed injury to make its presence felt with a vengeance. Julia waited only long enough for him to procure a room from the innkeeper before bearing him off to this chamber, dosing him with laudanum, and putting him to bed.

They set out once more at first light, and although Pickett was in agony after three hours, he resisted her efforts to medicate him as long as possible, determined to be awake and alert when he made his bow to the squire and his lady. Julia at last prevailed by offering to slide to the end of the seat and let him rest his head on her lap. It made for a tight fit, with his bum wedged against the outer wall of the carriage and his long legs stretched out on the seat opposite, but he rather liked the warmth of her thigh beneath his cheek, and there was something wonderfully soothing about the rhythmic caress of her fingers as she stroked his hair. . .

Thus it was that, when the post chaise turned off the road onto the long drive to Runyon Hall, Julia was obliged to shake her husband by the shoulder in order to rouse him.

"John? Wake up, darling, we're almost there."

"What?" Pickett sat up, frantically straightening his cravat and raking his fingers through his untidy curls. "You should have wakened me an hour ago!"

"Nonsense! You needed the rest," Julia insisted.

And so it was that Pickett descended the post chaise a short time later flushed and disheveled from sleep. Furthermore, as he helped Julia disembark, he noticed on her skirts a small damp spot which he very much feared was his own drool.

"The squire is going to kill me," he muttered under his breath.

"I beg your pardon?"

He shook his head. "Never mind."

She sailed up the front stairs with the ease of long familiarity, then raised the iron door knocker and let it fall.

"Good evening, Miss Julia," said the butler who answered, opening his eyes wider at the sight of the recently widowed daughter of the house arriving with a tall young man in tow.

"Good evening, Parks," she replied. "I trust Mama and Papa received my letter?"

"Indeed they did." The butler inclined his head. "Your lady mother ordered dinner to be held back for your arrival."

"Excellent! Are they in the drawing room, then? We shall go to them at once. You need not announce us."

Since he could not have announced them in any case without first being informed as to her companion's designation, Parks merely bowed his acquiescence. Julia took Pickett's arm and steered him across the hall, stopping in the doorway of a cheerful salon decorated for comfort as well as fashion, with a sofa and two overstuffed wing chairs arranged about an Adam fireplace over which hung a rural landscape executed by the hand of a skillful amateur.

"Mama! Papa!"

At the sound of her voice, the squire (whom Pickett recognized from their brief meeting in London almost a year earlier) cast aside his sporting journal and rose to welcome his adored child, his jovial greeting dying on his lips as he realized she was not alone. In the chair adjacent, a frail little woman laid down her embroidery and regarded her daughter with an expression of bewildered disbelief that exactly mirrored her husband's.

Julia took a deep breath. "Mama, Papa, I should like you to meet Mr. John Pickett"—her fingers, which had been tucked into the curve of Pickett's elbow, slid down his forearm to cling tightly to his hand—"my husband."

2

In Which John Pickett Fails to Impress

A moment of stunned silence greeted this pronouncement. Pickett, finding himself the object of two penetrating and far from admiring gazes, addressed his beloved under his breath.

"You didn't tell them?"

"I thought it would be better done in person," Julia murmured.

"But you wrote a letter—"

"I told them I was bringing a surprise," she offered, half hopefully and half apologetically.

Pickett sighed. "I suppose that's one way of putting it."

Lady Runyon, whose cool composure few circumstances had the power to disturb for long, found her tongue at last. "Well, Julia, this is very sudden," she said in a voice that shook only slightly, as she crossed the room to kiss her daughter's cheek.

To her new son-in-law she offered her hand, and Pickett, correctly surmising that any attempt to raise it to his lips would be seen as either toad-eating or impertinence, contented himself with pressing her fingers with what he hoped was the correct degree of respectful deference.

"Damme, I know who you are!" exclaimed Sir Thaddeus, who up to that point had been puzzling over where he might have seen this vaguely familiar young man before. "You're that fellow from Bow Street!"

"Yes, sir," Pickett said, sketching a bow. He would have expressed his pleasure in meeting Sir Thaddeus under happier circumstances, but his tongue was bridled by the realization that Sir Thaddeus was unlikely to view his daughter's unequal marriage in such sanguine terms.

Whatever his bride's parents might have said in response to the squire's discovery was forestalled by the arrival of Parks with the announcement that dinner was served.

"Oh, but we aren't properly dressed," Julia protested, glancing down at her elegant traveling costume, its skirts now sadly creased. "Perhaps just a tray in our room—"

"I daresay we can dispense with dressing for dinner, since you've only just arrived," Lady Runyon said with the air of a monarch granting an undeserved dispensation. "Mr. Pickett, if you will be so good as to give me your arm?"

He did so, albeit not without a glance at Julia which held more than a little of stark terror. Julia accepted her father's escort, and they fell in behind as Lady Runyon led the way to the dining room on Pickett's arm. For the first several minutes, while footmen proffered dishes and filled wineglasses, the conversation was limited to platitudes regarding the weather and the state of the roads. Once the last of the servants had withdrawn, however, Lady Runyon turned to regard her daughter.

"Now, Julia, perhaps you will explain to us how this 'marriage' "—she all but shuddered as she spoke the word—"came about."

And so Julia did, beginning with their first meeting over Lord Fieldhurst's dead body and continuing through their further acquaintance in Yorkshire, their fateful sojourn in Scotland and, finally, the visit to Drury Lane Theatre that had almost put a period to Pickett's existence. On one step in their journey to the altar, however, she remained determinedly silent. She said nothing of the night in Pickett's flat when they had abruptly abandoned the annulment proceedings into which so much effort had already gone. That night was theirs and theirs alone, an experience far too precious to offer it up for her parents' condemnation.

"But enough about John and me," she said at last, seeing at last an opportunity to turn the subject. "You must tell me all the news from Norwood Green! How are Mr. and Mrs. Pennington? Do they ever hear from Jamie?"

"The vicar and his wife are both quite well. As for James, it is a curious thing that you should ask, for he has only recently returned from the Continent. It seems he has inherited Greenwillows from his Aunt Layton, and has come to inspect it and meet with an estate agent about putting it on the market. It is quite a pretty property, so he should be able to get a good price for it."

"He doesn't intend to return for good, then?" Julia

asked, her brow creasing.

Lady Runyon shrugged her narrow shoulders. "I fear I am not in his confidence. You may ask him yourself, for we are invited to dine at Brantley Grange, and I am sure he will be in attendance. Oh dear, I suppose I must let Mrs. Brantley know that you are not alone, so that she may prepare for an additional guest."

"I—I don't want to put anyone to any trouble—" Pickett began.

"If Mrs. Brantley finds she cannot extend hospitality to Mr. Pickett, then I fear I must offer her my regrets," said Julia, with steel in her voice.

Lady Runyon frowned. "I see no reason why she should not do so, Julia. I hope you do not intend to fly up into the boughs at every perceived slight. However, I must caution you to brace yourself for a shock, my dear. Lord Buckleigh has remarried."

Now that he was, thankfully, no longer the cynosure of all eyes, Pickett found his mind beginning to wander, for there are few things more tiresome than to listen to others exchange reminiscences about a set of persons with whom one is unacquainted. But at the suggestion of a rival for his wife's affections, his attention was once again fully engaged.

"Lord Buckleigh, remarried?" echoed Julia, turning rather pale. "When did it happen, Mama?"

"Several months ago—October, I believe. They have only recently returned from their wedding trip."

"You never mentioned it in your letters."

"You had enough sorrow of your own to deal with—or

so I thought," Lady Runyon added darkly, glancing at Pickett.

"What is she like, Mama? Have you met her?"

"I saw her at church last Sunday—a very young woman, and pretty enough, I suppose, if one admires that type. But we have not yet been introduced. As I said, Lord and Lady Buckleigh have only just taken up residence at Buckleigh Hall."

Julia winced at the sound of the lady's title, and Pickett feared the worst. Seeing his stricken expression, she explained hastily, "Lord Buckleigh was married to my sister."

Pickett had not known until that moment that she had a sister, but Lady Runyon clearly did not wish to discuss the matter further. She laid her napkin beside her plate and rose from the table. "If you will come with me, Julia, we shall leave the men to their port."

Something in the lady's expression gave Pickett to understand that Julia would not enjoy her *tête-à-tête* with her mother any more than he would his own discussion with her father. They exchanged a glance of mutual sympathy, and Julia followed her mother from the room.

* * *

As the ladies left the dining room, the butler slipped inside and fetched two glasses and a decanter of ruby-colored liquid from the sideboard, placing them at Sir Thaddeus's elbow before quietly effacing himself. Alone with his new son-in-law, the squire filled both glasses and pushed one across the table to Pickett.

"Now that the womenfolk are gone, let's have the truth with no roundaboutation," Sir Thaddeus said brusquely. "How much do you want?"

"I—I beg your pardon, sir?"

"What is your price?" Sir Thaddeus asked by way of explanation. "How much will it take to persuade you to return to London and make no further claims on my daughter's affections?"

Pickett could only stare, appalled. "I have no price, sir, but if I could be persuaded to do as you suggest, you may be sure that it would require more than you or any other man could offer."

"You—you scoundrel!" Sir Thaddeus exclaimed, turning quite purple with rage.

"Sir Thaddeus, I'm afraid you are laboring under a misapprehension. Your daughter and I are married—married twice over, in fact, once in Scotland and once in England. The marriage has been consummated," he added for emphasis, willing himself not to blush. "If I were to abandon her as you suggest, you would condemn her to a life of loneliness, for there can be no undoing it, not at any price."

"Misapprehension, eh? Oh no, sirrah, I understand perfectly!" The squire set his glass down with such force that the liquid sloshed over the side, leaving a blood-red stain spreading over the immaculate white of the linen tablecloth. "As for her being lonely, I'm not sure but what I wouldn't rather see her living in adultery with a gentleman who is her equal, than legally wed to the sort of fellow who would take advantage of her gratitude and her generous nature in order

35

to coerce her into a union that any fool must see is unworthy of her!"

"There was no coercion, sir. The decision was a mutual one. As for the suitability of the match, I can assure you that no one is more aware of my own unworthiness than I am. But while there may be any number of men more deserving of your daughter's hand, I defy any of them to love her more than I do."

Sir Thaddeus studied him for a long moment, then let out a heavy sigh. "I can't deny you were indispensable to her during that business with Lord Fieldhurst," he conceded grudgingly.

"If that is true, it was because I loved her even then, and considered it an honor to be of service to her. Believe me, sir, the idea that I might profit from my efforts on her behalf never entered my mind."

" 'Profit'? An interesting choice of word, Mr. Pickett," Sir Thaddeus barked, scowling at his son-in-law. "I must tell you that I don't think much of any man who is content to live as a petticoat pensioner."

"No, sir, neither do I," Pickett said, relieved to find one point, at least, on which they could agree. "I have twenty-five shillings a week on which to support a wife. I have been sending half of that to my father in—to my father, but I intend to write him that I can no longer do so now that I have taken a wife."

"Is your father retired, then?"

Pickett nodded. "In a manner of speaking." He supposed being arrested for petty thievery and transported to

Botany Bay constituted retirement, of a sort. "I know my earnings do not amount to much by the standards to which your daughter is accustomed, but there are also the occasional compensations for criminals convicted, as well as private commissions, and I intend to do all I can to rise in my profession. My magistrate seems to feel my prospects are good."

"You appear to have it all worked out," scoffed the squire. "With twenty-five shillings a week, I suppose my Julia's four hundred pounds per annum hardly weighed with you at all."

Pickett frowned in confusion. "Begging your pardon, sir, but—what four hundred pounds?"

"Her widow's jointure amounts to four hundred pounds annually."

"But surely that must have ended with her remarriage," Pickett pointed out with growing unease.

"Aye, in the normal way of things it would have. But in the marriage negotiations with Fieldhurst, I insisted that in the event of his lordship's early demise, she should be free to marry again without penalty. Don't know what I was thinking—I suppose it seemed like a good idea at the time, given the difference in their ages—but you may be sure that I had no thought of enabling her to throw herself away on the likes of you!"

Pickett hardly heard this unflattering speech, so perturbed was he at the revelation that he had married a lady of independent means. "Sir Thaddeus, may I—may I be excused?" He had no idea if such an abrupt departure from the dining room was proper, and he didn't really care; he wanted to have a word with his wife, and that as soon as possible.

"What, already? Well, if you've finished"—the squire's frowning glance took in Pickett's untouched wine-glass— "we'll rejoin the ladies."

The two men rose from the table, but as they approached the door, Sir Thaddeus laid a restraining hand on Pickett's arm. When he spoke, it was in a much altered tone.

"One more thing, Mr. Pickett," he said, his voice almost timid. "When we met in London, you were made aware of certain—activities—of mine. I would be obliged to you if you wouldn't mention them to Julia."

Pickett did not have to ask for an explanation; he well remembered his interview with Julia's father in the days following the murder of Lord Fieldhurst, when he'd discovered that Sir Thaddeus, who had ostensibly hurried to London in support of his daughter, had in fact already been in Town for the purpose of procuring at a price those feminine attentions of which his wife's uncertain health had in recent years deprived him.

"I may not have a gentleman's education, sir, but I am well aware of the difference between facts uncovered in the performance of my duty and appropriate topics of drawing room conversation. As for my mentioning such a thing to your daughter, even in private, I can only say that if you believe me capable of revealing to her information which could only cause her pain, well, I can understand your revulsion at the idea of her being married to me."

The squire looked a bit shamefaced, but his embarrassment was leavened with relief. "That's all right, then," he said, and led his son-in-law to the drawing room where the ladies waited.

* * *

Having reached the drawing room, Lady Runyon sank onto the sofa with a sigh of bombazine skirts and looked up at her daughter with reproachful eyes. "And so you are married again—to a Bow Street Runner, no less!—with poor Fieldhurst hardly cold in his grave," she chided gently. "Really, Julia, what were you thinking?"

Julia took a seat at the opposite end of the sofa. "I was thinking that I love Mr. Pickett and want to spend the rest of my life with him," she said, lifting her chin defiantly.

Lady Runyon sighed. "Oh, he's a good-looking boy, I'll grant you that."

"He is much more than a 'good-looking boy,' Mama! How can you say such a thing, after hearing how he saved my life on more than one occasion? And I did not even tell you the whole, in order to spare his blushes, but he rescued us both from the Drury Lane fire by fashioning a rope from the curtains and climbing down from a third-tier box while carrying me on his back."

Lady Runyon appeared a bit nonplussed by this revelation, but rallied quickly. "I'm sure no one is questioning the young man's bravery. Still, I can't help thinking poor Fieldhurst never would have allowed you to become embroiled in so dangerous a situation."

Julia plucked at her skirts, a nervous gesture which

betrayed her growing agitation. "No, for it never would have occurred to Frederick that I might have insights from which he might benefit—which was Mr. Pickett's whole purpose in inviting me to accompany him to the theatre in the first place."

Lady Runyon cast her eyes heavenward. "Next you will tell me this Mr. Pickett loves you for your mind."

"Yes, he does!" Julia snapped, along with the last fraying edges of her temper. "For my mind, and my face, and my character, and—"

"And your four hundred pounds per annum?" her mother asked with deceptive sweetness. "What does he think of that?"

This simple question had the effect of stealing the wind from Julia's sails. "I—I'm not sure if he even knows about them," she confessed, casting her mind back to the meeting with her husband's solicitor during which Lord Fieldhurst's will was read. To be sure, John—Mr. Pickett, as she had thought of him then—had been present for part of that interview, but she was not certain if he would have heard about the dispensation of her widow's jointure, nor remembered it even if he had.

"And it never even occurred to you to wonder? Really, Julia, how could you be so foolish?"

"Pray do not speak to me as if I were a child, Mama! Recall that I was married for six years. I am quite old enough to know what I want!"

"What you *want?*" Lady Runyon echoed scornfully. "A fine world this would be if young girls went about marrying whomever they wanted!"

" 'Young girls'? Mama, I am twenty-seven years old!"

"Are you indeed?" Lady Runyon asked in mild surprise. "I suppose you must seem younger when you throw a childish tantrum."

Julia closed her eyes and took a deep, steadying breath. "I beg your pardon, Mama."

"But as I was about to say, you cannot only consider what you want, Julia. You have a responsibility to marry wisely."

"Have I, indeed? To whom, pray?"

"Need you ask? Any children born of such a union as yours must surely suffer for their father's inferior status—"

"There won't be any children, Mama," Julia said in a flat voice. "In six years with Frederick, I never showed the least sign of—of being with child."

"Very well, then don't think of children. Think instead of your upbringing, of your lineage, of what is due your name—"

"Are you telling me to think of *you*, Mama, that it is my responsibility to please *you* in my choice of a husband? I have done that once already, when I married Frederick. Is that not enough?"

"Julia, my dear, you wound me to the quick!" cried Lady Runyon, pressing one arthritic hand to her heart. "Next you will be saying I coerced you into marriage with Lord Fieldhurst!"

Julia sighed. "No, for I was dazzled with his rank as only a nineteen-year-old girl can be. But I have paid for my mistakes—paid dearly for them!—and I expect to do better this time. I knew you could not approve of John, at least not until you have come to know him better, but I had hoped you would at least try to be happy for me."

Lady Runyon pulled a lace-trimmed handkerchief from her sleeve and dabbed at her eyes. "My dear child, I do so want you to be happy! You are all I have left in the world."

"I know, Mama," Julia said gently, patting her mother's hand. "I miss her, too. But Claudia has been gone these dozen years and more, and I must live my own life, for I can't live hers. No one can."

"I'm usually not such a watering pot," observed Lady Runyon, unfolding her handkerchief and refolding it to expose a dry surface. "I sometimes go whole days without thinking of poor Claudia at all. I suppose it is Lord Buck-leigh's bringing home a new bride that has made me feel it so keenly. That, along with Major Pennington's return."

"Oh, is Jamie a major now?" asked Julia, eager to give her mother's thoughts a happier direction. "He must be doing very well in the army."

Lady Runyon gave a disdainful sniff into her handkerchief. "He has certainly prospered, but I cannot pretend to like him. I will always believe that he knew more about Claudia's disappearance than he ever let on. Why else, pray, would he have left Oxford so precipitously to run off and join the army? And less than twenty-four hours after she was last seen!"

"Mama, you cannot mean to suggest that Jamie would—would do her an injury! Why, he adored her! Had it not been for Lord Buckleigh, he might have married her."

"But who is to say that love cannot turn to hate, once it is rejected?"

"If Jamie had any such inclination—which I do not believe, not by a long chalk!—surely he would not have waited until two years after the wedding to act on them."

"Yes, dear, but—"

Before Lady Runyon could voice her rebuttal, the door opened and Sir Thaddeus entered the room, followed by his new son-in-law. Pickett's expression held so much of dazed consternation that Julia wondered exactly what her father had said to him. His eyes met hers in a silent plea, and she deemed it high time he was rescued from her less than welcoming family. Fortunately, she had the perfect excuse ready to hand.

"John, is your head troubling you? Perhaps you should seek your bed early tonight. Mama, Papa, may we please be excused? We left Reading very early this morning, and Mr. Pickett's head injury was aggravated by the indifferent state of the roads."

"I had no reason to suppose you were not coming alone, Julia, so I didn't have a second bedchamber made ready," Lady Runyon fretted. "I've put you in your old room, but if you can wait, Mr. Pickett, I will have the housekeeper prepare another."

"Thank you, Mama, but we shall do very well in one," Julia said, and bore her grateful husband out of the drawing room and up the stairs.

No sooner had they reached the second-floor bedroom

and closed the door than Julia turned and buried her face in his chest. "Hold me, John."

Pickett, nothing loth, wrapped his arms around her, his own concerns temporarily forgotten. "Was it as bad as all that?"

"Worse." She let out a long sigh. "I know I should have written and told them but, well, I didn't want to give Mama an opportunity to prepare her arguments. Heaven knows she was bad enough without the benefit of advance warning."

Whatever his shortcomings, Pickett was not stupid, and he knew he must tread lightly. Unlike the Fieldhursts, whom he knew she took a certain satisfaction in thwarting, the squire and his lady were her own flesh and blood. He did not want to be the cause of a rift between his wife and her parents; in fact, he was not at all certain that, if he said anything against them, she would not feel compelled to come to their defense. And so he said nothing at all, but led her to the wing chair before the fire (which had already been lit in preparation for their—rather, for *her*—arrival), sat down, and settled her on his knee, whereupon she leaned against him and put her head on his shoulder.

"Papa treats me as if I were still nine years old, and that is bad enough," she complained, while he took her hand and kissed each fingertip in turn, "but with Mama I find myself *acting* as if I were still nine years old, which is infinitely worse, and—John! You aren't listening!"

"Yes, I am. I heard every word. You were saying your mama makes you act as if you were still nine years old." He frowned down at the hand he still held. "Now you've made me lose my place. I shall have to start over again," he said, and did so.

"She doesn't *make* me, exactly, for it is my own fault. It is only that Mama—that Mama—that she—oh, *bother* Mama!" she exclaimed and, snatching her hand from his, pulled his head down to hers so that his kisses might land on her lips, where they belonged.

It was not until quite some time later, after the candles were snuffed and they lay cocooned together in the bed she had slept in as a girl, that Pickett recalled the question he had meant to ask.

"My lady," he murmured against her hair, "is it true that you have an income of four hundred pounds a year?"

"Mm-hm," she mumbled, barely awake.

He twisted one of her golden curls around his finger, considering her answer for a long moment before posing another question. "Would you still have married me if—"

She stirred in his arms, making a little snuffling noise which gave him to understand that she was already asleep. And perhaps, he thought, it was just as well. Maybe it was better not to ask questions for which he might not like the answers.

* * *

Pickett did not sleep soundly that night, due in large part to his determination to wean himself off the laudanum that had been his constant companion since the night of his injury. Had he taken another dose before retiring to bed, as Julia had urged, he probably would not have heard the noise at all. But having at last drifted off without narcotic aid, he was abruptly awakened by a faint click. His eyes flew open but, as some instinct warned him to keep still, he made no movement but for the slightest turn of his head to ensure that his lady still slept. His gaze darted about the unfamiliar room in search of the sound's source, but even as he told himself without conviction that he must have dreamt it, the noise was repeated and the door began, ever so slowly, to open.

As the hammering in his heart began to subside, his ire increased. He was prepared to make a great many allowances as far as his in-laws were concerned; in fact, knowing himself to be no one's ideal candidate for their daughter's hand, he was not without a certain amount of sympathy for them. Still, certain things were sacred, or ought to be, and the privacy of the marriage bed was one of them.

His mind made up, he threw back the covers and, sliding his arm gently from beneath his wife's head, he slipped out of bed and crept slowly across the unfamiliar room, taking particular care to avoid barking his shins against the furniture in the dark. Upon reaching the door, he grasped the knob and flung it wide—and found himself staring into an empty corridor. He stepped out of the room and looked up and down the passage in both directions, but saw nothing, not even the faint glow of a candle disappearing in the distance. He sniffed the air, but detected no acrid scent of a light recently extinguished.

A dream, he decided, no doubt the result of a guilty conscience. Surely it could not be right to exercise his conjugal rights under the very roof of his wife's disapproving parents. He thought of that fellow whom Lady Runyon had mentioned at dinner, the lord who under different circumstances would have been his brother-in-law, and who had just returned from his wedding trip; he hoped his lordship's honeymoon had been more satisfying than his own promised to be.

Heaving a sigh, he padded back across the room and slid beneath the covers.

3

Which Tells of a Girl and a Ghost

May 1796
Somersetshire

J amie strode down the stairs and across the hall with Claudia in his arms, then kicked the front door open and carried his precious burden around the north end of the house to the stables beyond.

"Higgins!" he bellowed for the groom. "Higgins! Where are you?"

A lanky young man very nearly Jamie's own age came out of the farthest stall, his eyes goggling at the sight of the mistress in the arms of the vicar's son, whose horse he'd just unsaddled.

"Tom! Where is Higgins?" It occurred to Jamie that the absence of the groom might be a good thing; the stable hand Tom, having less responsibility and substantially smaller wages, might feel less of an obligation to report the incident to his lordship, particularly if Jamie made it worth his while to hold his tongue. "Never mind, it doesn't matter. Saddle up my horse, and her ladyship's mare, too."

Claudia made a faint noise of protest. "Jamie, no—I can't—"

"It's all right, Claudia," he said soothingly. "I don't expect you to ride."

He turned back to the stable hand, who was still staring slack-jawed. "You can tie the mare's rein to my saddle. Get going, man, don't just stand there!"

The stable lad tugged his forelock in acknowledgment, then set about his task.

When Tom had finished, Jamie set Claudia on her feet and bracketed her waist with his hands. "I'm sorry, but this is going to hurt."

She gave him a brave little smile. "I don't mind."

He lifted her onto his own horse, noting her sharp intake of breath, and then swung himself up into the saddle behind her.

"Now," he said, reaching into his pockets for a handful of coins and tossing them down to the stable hand, "I suggest you forget everything you've seen here today."

"I don't remember nothing, sir," Tom replied promptly, stooping to pick up a silver shilling that had slipped through his fingers.

"Good man!" said Jamie, and urged his mount forward.

He did not set off down the long tree-lined drive which eventually gave out onto the main road, for he dared not run the risk of encountering anyone who might report their flight to his lordship. Instead, he took a less-traveled path that skirted the home wood before crossing the meadow where a flock of sheep grazed, oblivious to human suffering.

As the distance between themselves and his lordship's magnificent Palladian mansion increased, Claudia began to relax against Jamie's shoulder. When at last they descended the ridge that hid the house from view, she never looked back.

* * *

March 1809
Somersetshire

"I thought I would show John about the house and gardens today," Julia told her parents at breakfast the next morning. "That is, if you have no objection, Mama."

"None at all," Lady Runyon assured her, taking what comfort she could in the fact that the evil hour in which her lowborn son-in-law would be thrust upon the unsuspecting neighborhood would be delayed, and with it the public knowledge of her daughter's precipitous descent in the eyes of the world.

The foursome exchanged labored platitudes for the next twenty minutes, until at last Julia turned to Pickett. "If you are finished, John, I shall take you upstairs and show you the schoolroom, where Claudia and I used to plague our governess."

"I'm sure Claudia never did any such thing," protested Lady Runyon, "She was always such a well-behaved child."

"You notice that Mama makes no such claims about me, however," Julia said, forcing herself to smile. In the thirteen years since her sister's death, Claudia had grown more and more saintly in her mother's eyes. Julia had loved Claudia deeply, but if her sister had been half the paragon their mama claimed, Julia was quite certain she would have detested her.

As Pickett rose to follow his bride from the table, Sir Thaddeus cleared his throat. "A word with you first, Mr. Pickett, if you will."

Pickett agreed, albeit without enthusiasm. He had not forgotten that door creaking open in the night, and he still thought Sir Thaddeus was the most likely culprit. He gave the slightest of reassuring nods to Julia's questioning look, and allowed Sir Thaddeus to lead the way to his study.

"Look here, Mr. Pickett," said the squire, closing the door against any curious eavesdroppers, "if you're going to be one of the family, you might as well make yourself useful."

It was not the opening Pickett was expecting, but he was not about to let pass the opportunity to redeem himself, if possible, in his father-in-law's eyes—provided, of course, that the means did not impinge upon the sanctity of the marriage bed. "If there is anything I can do, sir—"

"I believe there may be. It's my wife, you see. She's got the idea the house must be haunted."

"Haunted?" Pickett echoed. "Begging your pardon, sir, but what would have put such an idea into her head?"

"She claims she heard footsteps walking about the house last night." Sir Thaddeus hesitated as a possible explanation for this phenomenon occurred to him. "I don't suppose you, or Julia—?"

"No, sir." Recalling the bedroom door opening in the wee hours, he asked, "I gather you weren't wandering the hallways, either?"

Sir Thaddeus shook his head.

"Did you hear any such footsteps?" Pickett continued.

"Didn't hear a sound." The squire looked a bit sheepish. "Had more than a drop of brandy before I retired, and slept like a babe newborn."

Pickett nodded in understanding. What the squire meant, of course, was that the news of his daughter's disastrous marriage had driven him to the bottle. But at least he could acquit his father-in-law of spying.

Supernatural occurrences were outside his purview, but Pickett suspected the explanation for Lady Runyon's mysterious footsteps was rather more mundane. Based on his own brief experience working incognito in the servants' hall of a Yorkshire manor house, he thought it very likely that some footman or chambermaid had recalled a duty left undone, and had sought to rectify the omission before it could be discovered in the morning. Pickett considered it a professional courtesy, of a sort, to protect the unknown domestic who had, after all, meant no harm, and whose own interrupted sleep would probably be punishment enough to render a repeat performance unlikely.

But it would not do for him to appear too cavalier in dismissing Lady Runyon's concerns. "I believe it is not unusual for stately old houses like this one to claim restless spirits," he observed. "As I understand it, some families are actually quite proud of them. Have there been no rumors of hauntings before?"

"No, none at all." Sir Thaddeus appeared to struggle with himself, and when he spoke again, it was as if the words were dragged from his unwilling throat. "Oh, the devil! In for a penny, in for a pound, I suppose. If you must know, Lady Runyon is persuaded she knows the identity of this particular spirit."

"Does she?" Pickett asked, but even before Sir Thaddeus answered, he knew what was coming.

The older man sighed. "My wife believes she heard the ghost of Claudia, our elder daughter."

* * *

The words still rang in Pickett's head a short time later as he stood with his bride in the third-floor schoolroom, a rather barren apartment whose utilitarian furnishings of table, chairs, bookcase, and globes were brightened by a number of colorful if inexpert watercolors pinned to the walls.

"That one is Claudia's, as are most of the better ones," Julia said, gesturing toward a large landscape of Runyon Hall and its grounds executed in the brilliant greens of springtime. Seeing him pause before a slightly lopsided charcoal portrait of a young woman whose chin was propped in hands with short, stubby fingers, she added, "I always preferred drawing people to scenery, but my governess complained that I could never get the hands right. As you see, she was quite correct."

It was not his wife's artistic ability, however, that

interested Pickett at the moment. "You never told me you had a sister."

"The subject never arose," she pointed out. "If you have any siblings, you've never mentioned them, either."

"I believe my father could be a very charming man when it suited his purposes. For all I know, I may have half-siblings scattered all over London. But no, I have no brothers or sisters that I'm aware of. Tell me about Claudia, though—that was her name, was it not?"

Julia nodded. "She was older than me by six years, and I adored her. And pray do not believe everything Mama says about her, for she was not at all the paragon of perfection that Mama tries to make her out to be!"

"How did she die?"

A shadow crossed Julia's face. "I don't know all the details, for I was only fourteen years old at the time, and no one would tell me anything! I do think it is a mistake to keep children in the dark, for their imagination only makes things worse than if they had been given an honest answer, do you not think so? But to answer your question, I don't believe anyone knows for sure, not really. She was Lady Buckleigh by then, for she had married Lord Buckleigh two years earlier, when she was eighteen. One day she went out riding in the Mendips, and her horse came back without her."

She walked slowly across the room to gaze out the window toward the Mendip Hills away to the east, as if still watching for her sister's return. "Lord Buckleigh organized an extensive search, in which Papa naturally took part, but Claudia's body was never found. As I said, neither Mama

54

nor Papa would answer my questions, but from little things they let drop, and from things the servants said, I gather the searchers found her shawl clinging to a bush in a gorge deep in the hills. There was a great deal of blood on it, as well as on the ground nearby, by which they assume"—her voice cracked on the words—"they assume a wild animal must have got her."

"A terrible way to die," Pickett noted sympathetically.

Julia sighed. "Yes, and there is more, although I set no store by ugly rumors."

"Rumors?"

Julia forced herself to say the hateful words. "It is known that Jamie Pennington, the vicar's son, was expected to tea that afternoon, and in fact tea things for two people were found scattered all over the drawing room floor. And the following day, Jamie did not return to Oxford as planned, but ran off and joined the army. The next we heard from him, he was in the Low Countries with the seventh cavalry."

"And the rumors suggest that he killed her?"

She arched her left eyebrow. "Who wants to know? John Pickett my husband, or John Pickett the Bow Street Runner?"

"Maybe a bit of both," he acknowledged. "I don't like unsolved mysteries, particularly unsolved mysteries that trouble the woman I love."

He punctuated this statement by putting his hands on her shoulders and kissing her gently but firmly on the lips. She allowed herself the luxury of leaning into him for a moment before taking up the thread of her narrative.

"To answer your question, yes, there were rumors that Jamie had killed her, but I don't believe them. Why, he adored Claudia! On his school holidays, he would come to visit and the three of us would go out riding together." She smiled at a half-forgotten memory. "He used to give me tuppence to ride ahead so that he might be alone with her."

"He must have taken it hard when she married this Lord—Buckleigh, was it?"

She nodded. "I daresay he did not know about it until well after the vows were said, for he was away at Oxford at the time. He was only a year older than she, and so was not yet old enough to support a wife, although nineteen seemed quite grown up to me at the time." She frowned at him. "If you are subscribing to the popular theory and thinking he killed her in a fit of jealousy, let me assure you that he could not have done so! Jamie wouldn't harm a fly!"

"Far be it from me to argue with you, my lady, but if he has seen action on the Continent as you say, it is safe to assume that he has harmed much more than flies."

"Yes, but this is not at all the same thing. Why, Jamie was almost like family! I was only twelve years old, but I was so certain he and Claudia were meant to be together that I was quite annoyed with her for accepting Buckleigh's suit. I was persuaded she should wait until Jamie came of age, and marry him instead." She grimaced. "Then again, given my own choice of husband, perhaps she was right to ignore me."

"That's put me in my place," said Pickett with deceptive meekness.

"John, how can you?" Julia exclaimed, trying not to laugh. "I was speaking of Frederick, and you know it!"

"I rather hoped you were," Pickett confessed, and gave himself up to the pleasant task of allowing her to soothe his supposedly wounded feelings.

Still, her recollections had given him sufficient food for thought. Granted, when he had met her, Lord Fieldhurst already lay dead at her feet—but what if fate, or destiny, or a mischievous Providence had brought them together earlier? It was bad enough believing, as he had then, that he could never have her, but at least he had been spared the agony of knowing she belonged to another man. Was it possible that after two years of seeing the woman he'd hoped to marry as Lord Buckleigh's wife, Jamie Pennington had finally cracked under the strain?

No, Pickett thought, he could not believe it any more than Julia did. Under similar circumstances, he might have thought longingly of killing Lord Fieldhurst, especially given the fact that his lordship had made his viscountess's life a misery. But Pickett could not imagine any situation that would have induced him to lay violent hands upon the woman he loved.

"John?" asked Julia, regarding him with a puzzled expression. "What are you thinking?"

He smiled tenderly down at her. "I was just thinking that I concede Jamie's innocence."

After they left the schoolroom, Julia pointed out rooms as they traversed the corridor. "That room belonged to my governess, Miss Milliken. She still lives in the village. I must take you to meet her someday. And this"—she hesitated before the door at the end of the passage—"this is the nursery," she said, and pushed the door open.

It seemed like a harmless little room; certainly there was nothing in it to put that stricken expression on her face, or to make her hand tremble on the doorknob.

"My lady?" Pickett asked softly, seeing her distress.

She shook her head. "It's nothing, it's only—the cradle there"—she nodded toward the opposite wall, where a small wooden bed on rockers held pride of place, its frame elaborately carved with cherubs which, presumably, would appear to watch over any infant who lay therein—"it was commissioned by my grandparents when Mama was born, and Claudia and I each slept there in our turn. It was always understood that Claudia and Buckleigh's child would use it someday, or mine and Fieldhurst's." She gave a sad little sigh. "Poor Mama."

Pickett suspected that it was not her mother she was thinking of. He said nothing, but put his arm about her and gave her shoulder a little squeeze.

Her next words proved him correct. "John"—she turned within his arm to look up at him with solemn eyes—"you know, don't you, that there will be no children for us?"

He knew. For himself, he considered it a small price to pay to have her for his wife, but he also knew she would not see it that way. "Have you considered that maybe it's better that way?" he pointed out gently. "With a viscountess for a mother and a Bow Street Runner for a father, the poor child would be neither fish nor fowl."

Again, that wistful sigh. "Yes, I suppose so. If you're ready, we'll go back downstairs." With a brightness that seemed somewhat forced, she added, "Did you notice the suit of armor in the hall? When I was little, Claudia and Jamie used to tell me it came to life at night and prowled about the corridors. I was terrified of it!"

Pickett, eager to give her thoughts a happier direction, expressed his interest in being shown this object of her childhood nightmares, and they prepared to head back downstairs. As he turned away from the nursery, however, the morning sunlight struck the bare floorboards—children, it seemed, did not warrant such luxuries as carpet, no matter how wealthy their parents—and he noticed a curious sight.

"Do you know if anyone uses the nursery anymore?" he asked as they descended the stairs.

"No, but I doubt it." She wrinkled her nose. "I daresay it is not even cleaned with any frequency. Did you notice the dust on the floor?"

He had indeed. And he had also seen, in the shaft of sunlight, a path of footprints crossing the room, leaving shiny spots on the floor where the dust had been disturbed.

Apparently the Runyon ghost was fond of children.

4

In Which John Pickett
Makes His Bow to the Local Gentry

I 'm afraid I shall have to beg off, my lady," Pickett apologetically informed his wife later that evening, after they had retired to their room to prepare for dinner at nearby Brantley Grange. "My head . . ." He raised one hand to his temple and tried to look pathetic.

In fact, his head was not troubling him at all, but he wanted to explore the nursery more thoroughly without having to explain his actions to Julia or her parents. The injury he had sustained a fortnight earlier seemed as good an excuse as any to avoid a dinner he had no desire to attend in any case.

Displaying a shrewdness that he found disconcerting, Julia regarded him with one eyebrow skeptically raised. "Your head, is it? When it has not troubled you all day! Confess, John, you are fighting shy of being paraded before Somersetshire society!"

"Well, now that you mention it—"

"It won't be so bad, I assure you. They are not the sort of aristocracy one might meet in London, but only country gentry, most of whom I have known all my life."

He shook his head. "I wouldn't want to embarrass you—"

"Do you think I am ashamed of having married you?" she demanded, with the light of battle in her eyes. "Nothing could be further from the truth! Why, after Frederick was murdered, you cut quite a romantic, even a heroic, figure. You would not deprive me of the opportunity to show you off just a little, would you?" she added coaxingly.

Privately, he doubted her friends and neighbors would be very much impressed, but when she looked at him like that, he could deny her nothing. "Very well, then, if you insist," he said with a sigh, abandoning at least for the nonce his plans for laying the Runyon ghost.

"I knew you would not fail me," she said, and stood on tiptoe to give him a quick kiss before turning to the evening garments spread out on the bed. "Now that that's settled, we'd best hurry. Papa has ordered the carriage for seven o'clock and he hates for his horses to be kept standing."

Pickett tugged his cravat loose and tossed it onto the bed. "Far be it from me to offend your father any more than I've already done," he said, unbuttoning the placket of his shirt and pulling it over his head.

Julia, having put on fresh stays, clutched this undergarment to her bosom and turned her back to present the laces to her husband. "Darling, would you?"

In a week and a half of marriage, Pickett had acquired a

layman's knowledge of ladies' clothing. He began lacing the strings, while Julia issued instructions.

"Tighter . . . tighter . . . no, that's *too* tight! I can hardly breathe!" She looked over her shoulder to regard him with mock severity. "It seems to me that in a very short time you have become far more adept at taking them off than putting them on."

"What can I say?" Pickett pondered mournfully as he tied the knot at the proper tension. "My heart isn't in my work."

"Wicked man!" she chided him playfully. "And I supposed you to be all innocent and unspoiled. Never was I so deceived in anyone!"

The mention of deception wiped the smile from his face. She had not deceived him, exactly, but her jesting accusation was sufficient to recall her undisclosed fortune to his mind. "My lady, when were you going to tell me you have an income of four hundred pounds a year?"

"Then you did not know after all?" She turned to face him, pleased out of all proportion by his ignorance and wishing only that her mama might have been present to witness it. Then again, considering the fact that he stood before her in nothing but his smallclothes, and she in only her petticoat and stays, Lady Runyon's absence was probably a good thing. "But surely you must have done! You were present when Frederick's will was read, were you not?"

"Yes, but I didn't remember all the details. I never dreamed they would affect me beyond my investigation into Lord Fieldhurst's death." A new and horrible thought occurred to him. "My lady, you cannot think I married you for such a reason as that!"

Seeing his distress, she was quick to reassure him. "Of course not! You married me for the same reason I married you: because neither of us could bear the prospect of being parted from one another again." She lifted the flounced hem of the gown lying on the bed and disappeared headfirst into its silken folds. When her head emerged, she found him still staring at her with the same stricken expression on his face. "Darling, don't take it so much to heart. It may have been my money before, but it became yours by law the moment we were wed. Does it really matter where it came from?"

"Yes, it does," he insisted. "A man wants to believe he can support his wife. Your father accused me of being a petticoat pensioner, and it appears he spoke no less than the truth. It's—it's emasculating."

"If that is your only concern, I will be more than happy to address it after we return," she said with a coy smile. "In the meantime, we are due at Brantley Grange within the hour. Pray don't let's quarrel on the very night we are to make our first social appearance as man and wife!"

Pickett sighed. "It is not my intention to quarrel with you at all." He turned away to pick up a clean shirt, muttering under his breath, "But I won't touch a farthing of what is rightfully yours."

In spite of his misgivings, Pickett took some comfort in the knowledge that no fault could be found with his appearance as, clad in his wedding finery, he followed the squire and his lady into the Brantley domicile with Julia on his arm. If he was lucky, he reflected, Julia's former brother-in-law would be in attendance with the new Lady Buckleigh and, in the flurry of congratulations that were sure to follow, no one would take any notice of his own humble self at all.

Alas, these hopes were soon dashed. "Sir Thaddeus and Lady Runyon," the butler announced, "and Mr. and Mrs. John Pickett."

The effect on the occupants of the room was immediate. At the mention of the newly married Picketts' names, the smiles which had greeted their appearance froze on the faces of some half-dozen couples, who now stared open-mouthed at the new arrivals. The spell was finally broken when the hostess came forward to welcome them. Sizing her up at a glance, Pickett saw a woman of late middle age, built along formidable lines which dwarfed the frail Lady Runyon and, indeed, all the other women present and not a few of the men.

"Lady Runyon, Sir Thaddeus," she boomed, "always a pleasure! And my dear Julia, it has been far too long since you graced Norwood Green with your presence."

"Thank you, Mrs. Brantley. Please allow me to present my husband," said Julia, gesturing toward Pickett. "I appreciate your allowing me to bring him on such short notice."

"Not at all, not at all," Mrs. Brantley assured her, the inconvenience of having to rearrange her table at the eleventh hour more than compensated by the realization that her dinner party would be the talk of the neighborhood for at least a month. "I fear you young people may find us very dull, however. I did not arrange for dancing, since you were in mourning—or so I thought," she added, with a darkling glance at Pickett.

Having progressed so far without being thrown out on his ear, Pickett was now obliged to run a veritable gauntlet of ladies and gentlemen, their facial expressions ranging from shocked disbelief to thinly veiled condemnation, as he bowed, shook hands, and tried to fix names with faces. This process was perhaps mercifully interrupted by a new arrival, a man in the scarlet regimentals of the cavalry officer, whom Pickett had no difficulty identifying even though he'd never set eyes on the fellow. Although Jamie Pennington must have been in his mid-thirties, his ginger hair was untouched by gray and his smile appeared curiously boyish. After exchanging greetings with his hostess, the man made a beeline for Julia.

"Little Julia, all grown up!" he exclaimed.

"Jamie!" she cried joyfully.

She offered her hand and, although he took it in both of his own, he did not raise it to his lips, but pulled her toward him and kissed her heartily on both cheeks. Releasing her, he turned to Pickett and held out his hand.

"So this must be the luckiest man in London."

Pickett grinned and shook his hand, liking the man in spite of his earlier misgivings. "And fully aware of my good fortune, I assure you."

"My husband, John Pickett," Julia said by way of introduction. "Mr. Pickett is the Bow Street Runner who came to my rescue after Frederick was killed. John, this is

Major James Pennington, a very dear old friend. But Jamie, how did you know I was married again?"

Was it his imagination, Pickett wondered, or did Major Pennington check ever so briefly before shrugging his epaulet-adorned shoulders? "News travels quickly in the country, you know. We none of us keep our secrets for long."

"I am glad to know that you, at least, do not hold it against me that I remarried before the year of mourning was through," Julia said.

"You forget that I have been fighting on the Continent for the past decade," Jamie reminded her. "War has a way of stripping life down to its bare essentials. On the battlefield it is not unusual for war widows to remarry immediately, rather than face the rigors of attempting to return to England alone. As long as you and your husband are happy, what has anyone else to say to the purpose?" He turned to glare at Pickett with exaggerated sternness. "You *will* make her happy, will you not?"

"I'll do my best, Major," he promised with a smile.

The conversation was interrupted by a pair of new arrivals. The butler entered the room to announce a distinguished-looking silver-haired man of about fifty, accompanied by a very young lady whose light brown hair was her only identifiable feature, as she kept her gaze fixed firmly on the carpet at her feet. Pickett, assuming she must be the man's daughter and nervous at making her own social debut, fully entered into her feelings of discomfiture.

Then the butler made his pronouncement. "Lord and

Lady Buckleigh."

Pickett heard a sudden intake of breath, although he could not have said whether this came from Julia, who turned pale and clutched his arm, or Jamie Pennington, whose jaw clenched. Lord and Lady Buckleigh made their way slowly about the drawing room, his lordship presenting his bride to each of the other guests in turn, until at last they reached Julia.

"My dear little sister," said Lord Buckleigh, taking her hand and raising it to his lips with practiced grace. "May I present my new bride? I know you are too kind to hold it against her that she takes the place once held by your poor sister."

Julia forced a smile. "Of course not. Pray accept my sincerest felicitations on your marriage, Lady Buckleigh."

She was rewarded with a murmured thanks and the briefest of glances from wide hazel eyes before Lady Buckleigh's gaze once more sought the floor.

"But I have recently remarried as well, my lord," Julia continued. "Allow me to present my husband, Mr. John Pickett."

"Mr. Pickett." His lordship nodded in Pickett's direction. "I hope you will not think me presumptuous in welcoming you to a family of which I am no longer a member, save for the bonds of affection."

"Thank you, my lord," Pickett said, returning Lord Buckleigh's nod. He noticed his lordship made no attempt to offer his hand, but Pickett's welcome thus far had not been so warm that he could afford to read slights where perhaps none were intended.

"Major Pennington," continued Lord Buckleigh, nodding curtly at Jamie.

Jamie's demeanor, so warm and friendly with Pickett, had undergone a dramatic transformation. "Your lordship," he responded with the merest jerk of the head.

"I confess I am surprised to see you here," observed Lord Buckleigh. "I had believed you fixed on the Continent with your regiment."

"Did you indeed? But then, life is often full of surprises, is it not?"

Lord Buckleigh's smile, already far from warm, seemed to freeze on his face. "I fail to take your meaning, sir. Would you care to explain yourself?"

Jamie seemed to consider the question for a long moment. "No," he said at last. "No, I don't believe I would."

Lord Buckleigh's countenance turned dark, but before he could reply, the butler returned to announce dinner. Jamie immediately turned to Julia, his sunny temperament apparently restored. "Julia, may I have the honor of escorting you to dinner?"

"Indeed, you may," she declared, and took his proffered arm.

Pickett, who had been warned in advance by his bride that married couples would not be seated together at table, turned to the only person present who seemed to share his own discomfort.

"Lady Buckleigh, will you do me the honor?"

Startled hazel eyes flew to his, and a strained silence

descended upon the room, broken only by a short bark of laughter from Mr. Brantley, who was shushed immediately by his wife.

"I say, Mr. Pickett," put in Jamie, pitching his voice so that the whole room might hear, "I suppose it's dashed unsporting of us to cut out our elders by laying claim to the most charming ladies in the room. If you will surrender Lady Buckleigh to our host, I shall relinquish your wife to my father. Papa, will you serve as my deputy in taking Mrs. Pickett in to dinner?"

There followed a series of complicated maneuvers which Pickett could never afterwards recall, but which resulted in his offering his arm to a spinster lady of advanced years and bringing up the rear of the promenade into the dining room. Here he found Mrs. Brantley's dinner both plentiful and palatable, but he could not enjoy it as he might have hoped. Painfully aware of having committed some ghastly *faux pas* (although he was not at all certain of the exact nature of his crime), he was terrified of embarrassing his wife with some further infraction, and so sat between his elderly dinner partner on one side and Mrs. Pennington, the vicar's wife, on the other, wishing the floor might open up and swallow him.

It did not, which proved to be a great pity. For the conversation at length turned to the impending retirement of the vicar, an occasion which had been delayed many years ago when his son, who was to have succeeded him, had abandoned his studies at Oxford and chosen the army instead.

"What do you intend to do with your time, Mr. Pennington," asked a woman whose name Pickett could not recall, "once you no longer have to write sermons and visit sick parishioners?"

"Oh, I daresay I shall continue to study the scriptures and visit the sick," confessed the vicar. "After all, the habits of forty years are not so easily forsaken. As for the rest . . ." he shrugged his shoulders, clearly at a loss.

Sir Thaddeus spoke up from his position at his hostess's left. "Perhaps Mr. Pickett might have some suggestions. I believe his father is retired, is he not?"

"In a—in a manner of speaking," said Pickett, squirming in his chair.

"Is he indeed?" The voice was the vicar's, and kindly enough, but it seemed to Pickett as if every eye at the table was suddenly fixed upon him—and that he had forgotten to put on his clothes.

"Er, yes sir."

"Pickett . . . Pickett . . ." His host, Mr. Brantley, pondered the name from the opposite end of the table. "I once knew a Gerald Pickett in Wells. I don't suppose you have family in Somersetshire, young man?"

Pickett shook his head. "No, sir."

"Mr. Pickett hails from London," his father-in-law explained. "That's where he met my girl. Daresay his father still lives there, is that right?"

The fear that, upon his next visit to London, Sir Thaddeus might feel an obligation to make his father's acquaintance prevented Pickett from agreeing and thus putting an end to an uncomfortable line of questioning. "No, sir. That is, my father is originally from London, but now he is—is farther east."

"Kent, then?" the vicar guessed. "Ah, the garden of England!"

"No, sir," said Pickett, sliding lower in his chair. "Still—still farther east."

Mr. Pennington chuckled. "I wasn't aware that one could go farther east than Kent and still be in England— unless, of course, you refer to the coast of Suffolk, or perhaps Norfolk."

Afterwards, Pickett was to wonder how differently the evening might have ended, had he seized upon this explanation. But he had no idea what connections in these counties his father might be supposed to have had, and so he elected to stick to the truth, so far as he was able.

"There's the thing," Pickett confessed. "He's—not in England anymore."

"Dangerous time to be traveling abroad, what with Boney running amok," observed Sir Thaddeus, scowling. "Come, man, don't be mysterious! If not in England, where *is* your father?"

"Botany Bay," Pickett said miserably.

This pronouncement had the effect of reducing the party to silence. "Do you mean to tell me," Sir Thaddeus began, his face turning purple with suppressed fury, "that my daughter is married to the son of a common felon?"

Quite unexpectedly, Pickett was filled with a perverse pride in his shameless sire. Throwing caution to the wind, he sat up straighter in his chair. "Not at all, sir. By all accounts, my father was rather an *un*common felon." He turned to face his host. "Have you a safe, Mr. Brantley? If I were a betting man, I would lay you odds that I could have it open in less than a minute—less than thirty seconds, if I were not so out of practice. I learned the skill at my father's knee at an age when your own sons were no doubt still in the schoolroom."

Across the table, Jamie Pennington chuckled. "Oh, well done, Mr. Pickett!" he murmured under his breath.

"A wager!" exclaimed Sir Thaddeus, his anger over-shadowed by some vague notion of salvaging his family's honor, or his natural love of sport, or perhaps a combination of the two. "I'll wager you he can do it within thirty seconds, Brantley. Name your stake!"

To Pickett's dismay, every male member of the party quickly chose sides, and they rose as one and fetched their champion along to the study where he might put his skills to the test, leaving the ladies behind in sole possession of the dining room. Lady Runyon, blushing scarlet, regarded her ashen-faced daughter with an expression that did not bode well for Julia upon their return to the Runyon abode.

From her own end of the table, Mrs. Brantley spoke down its deserted length with determined cheerfulness. "Tell me," she addressed what remained of the party, "how long do you suppose we can expect the mild weather to hold?"

* * *

The drive back to Runyon Hall was accomplished in strained silence, broken only once by Sir Thaddeus, who rubbed his hands together gleefully and exclaimed, "Twenty-seven seconds, by gad!" before encountering a quelling look from his lady and clamping his mouth shut. Upon their being admitted to the house, Pickett, pleading a headache which by this time was quite real, stumbled up the stairs before the front door was closed behind them. Sir Thaddeus gestured toward the door of his own study, made some vague reference to brandy, and disappeared. Alone with her mother, Julia had not long to wait before the inevitable recriminations began.

"Well, Julia, I hope you are happy with your choice now!"

"My sentiments toward Mr. Pickett have undergone no change, Mama," she declared. "Why should they have done?"

Lady Runyon lifted her eyes heavenward. "Why, indeed? I vow, Julia, I was ready to sink!"

"Nonsense! Did you never make a misstep when you were first introduced into Society? I know I did—more than one, in fact! In any case, I thought Jamie covered beautifully for him."

"Oh, if claiming Lady Buckleigh for dinner were all—! But then to announce in front of all our neighbors that his father was nothing but a common criminal—"

"And what was he supposed to do? It was Papa and the other men who kept pressing him for specifics when he tried his best to be discreetly vague."

"Julia Runyon! Have you the effrontery to try and blame your father for this—this debacle? You have done this Mr. Pickett of yours no favors, my dear. The young man is completely out of his depth—and he is well aware of it, even if you are not. Why, he even calls you by your courtesy title!"

Julia's cheeks burned at the memory of a certain verbal exchange between herself and Mr. Pickett during their masquerade as man and wife, never dreaming that under Scottish law such a representation might result in a legal marriage.

You must call me Julia, she'd insisted then. *If I were really your wife, you wouldn't call me 'my lady.'*

No, he'd said rather wistfully. *If you were really my wife, I would call you* my lady.

"I suppose it must sound that way," she admitted to her mother. "But it is actually a—an endearment, of sorts."

"I see." Lady Runyon's lips thinned. "In that case, perhaps you should give him a little hint that such intimacies are best indulged in private."

Julia dashed a hand over her eyes. "Oh, where is the use in talking? Poor John can do nothing right, so far as you are concerned."

She did not wait for an answer, but climbed the stairs wearily to her own bedroom. There she found her husband, who had shed his coat and waistcoat and now, clad only in shirt and breeches, sat slumped in the wing chair while he stared morosely into the fire.

"John?" she called softly to him.

"I'm so sorry," he said without looking at her. "I never meant to embarrass you."

"You didn't embarrass me." She crossed the room to

74

stand before his chair, then cradled his head against her bosom and pressed her lips to his hair. "I had the best man there. Twenty-seven seconds? I should like to see any of them match that!"

He relaxed into her embrace with a half-hearted smile. "I'm glad your father was pleased, at all events. But I'd already put myself beyond the pale long before that, when I offered to escort Lady Buckleigh to dinner. Apparently it was the wrong thing to do."

She sighed, searching for words that would explain the proper protocol without sounding insulting. "Sometimes dinner partners are assigned, but Mrs. Brantley's party was not so formal as all that. Still, it is understood that ladies of higher rank are partnered by gentlemen of similar status."

"Brantley was a mere 'mister,' too," Pickett pointed out.

"Yes, but he was our host. It was his privilege—or responsibility, depending on how one looks at it—to escort the highest ranking female, just as Mrs. Brantley, the hostess, was escorted by Lord Buckleigh, the highest ranking male."

"I didn't know," he confessed. "Poor little Lady Buckleigh just looked so uncomfortable that I felt sorry for her. I knew the feeling," he added drily.

She leaned away from him, cupping his face in her hands and tipping it back so that he looked her squarely in the eye. "You made a mistake because you have a kind heart," she informed him. "That is more important to me than any amount of social aplomb. Besides, Jamie managed to set everything to rights, so pray think no more of it."

"Ah yes, Jamie. A good sort of fellow, if only he didn't take such an interest in my wife."

"Jamie's only interest in me stems from a long-ago desire to be my brother-in-law, so you need not concern yourself there. As I see it, there is only one thing to worry about."

"And what is that?"

"I only hope Mr. Brantley's safe is not robbed before we return to London. Twenty-seven seconds? My dear, we would never persuade a jury of your innocence!"

He liked that "we." He liked it very much. For the first time since the disaster in the dining room, Pickett smiled, realizing that Mr. and Mrs. Brantley, Lord and Lady Buckleigh, Jamie Pennington, and even his mother- and father-in-law were surprisingly unimportant. "I love you, Julia Pickett," he said, then pulled her down onto his knee and kissed her quite thoroughly.

If the Runyon ghost prowled the halls that night, Pickett never noticed.

5

In Which a Pleasant Sunday Outing
Takes a Most Unpleasant Turn

U ndisturbed as he was by any supernatural visitations, Pickett slept quite soundly until morning. With the dawn, however, his peace was at an end, for it was Sunday, and he and Julia would naturally be expected to accompany her parents to the morning service.

As the day was fine, the four set out on foot, and by the time they reached the ancient stone church it was clear that those present at Mrs. Brantley's dinner, both guests and servants, had not been idle. Every neck craned as churchgoers strove to obtain a view of little Julia Runyon and her shockingly *outré* new husband. Even those gentlemen who had profited handsomely by Pickett's lock-picking skill had been suitably chastised by their wives for their part in the disaster, and now acknowledged the newest member of the Runyon party with the curtest of nods—a cold reception made all the more noticeable by the deference with which Lord Buckleigh and his bride were greeted only a few minutes later.

All in all, it was a relief to Pickett when they entered the box pew that had provided seating (and, perhaps more important, privacy) to the Runyon family for generations. Once they were safely ensconced away from prying eyes, they had not long to wait until the vicar rose to begin the service, and all eyes were, thankfully, drawn to the tall, thin man in the pulpit.

"As many of you know," the Reverend Mr. Pennington announced, "my son James has returned from the hostilities on the Peninsula, however briefly. I appreciate your prayers for him, and indeed for all our young men fighting the French. I've asked him to read the lesson today, which will be taken from the Apostle Paul's first letter to the Corinthians."

Jamie took his father's place at the pulpit with a curiously combative gleam in his eye. "Thank you, Papa, but I have changed my mind. I shall be reading from the second chapter of James's epistle instead." He took a deep breath, and launched into the writer's scathing denunciation of Christians who fawned over the wealthy in their midst while dismissing the poor as beneath their notice. Julia, realizing exactly what he was doing, took Pickett's hand beneath the prayer book they shared and gave it a squeeze.

Jamie's point was apparently well taken, for after the service Pickett's welcome to the neighborhood, if not precisely enthusiastic, was at least somewhat warmer, and those who had shunned him earlier had the grace to look ashamed. As he escorted his wife across the churchyard,

Pickett observed, "I think Major Pennington was right not to take holy orders after all."

"Do you?" Julia asked, looking up at him from beneath the brim of her bonnet. "Why do you say that?"

He gave her a rather sheepish smile, not quite certain whether to be grateful for the major's intervention or embarrassed by it. "It seems to me he's a bit too fond of setting the cat amongst the pigeons. Don't tell me he didn't enjoy that little demonstration, for I won't believe it!"

She chuckled at that. "Well, yes, you're probably right. Jamie doesn't have much patience with perceived injustices. It is one of his more admirable qualities, although I don't doubt he's come to grief over it more than once."

"My dearest Julia!" cried a quavering female voice, and both Picketts turned to discover an elderly female picking her way across the churchyard as quickly as her tottering steps would allow.

"Millie!" Julia exclaimed, and hurried to meet the woman, whereupon both ladies embraced warmly. "John, you must allow me to make you known to Miss Milliken, my former governess."

Behind her half-moon spectacles, the governess's rheumy blue eyes darted from Julia to Pickett and back again. "I am so glad you escaped your ordeal unharmed, Julia—you must know I followed the news most diligently, although any word from London was of necessity several days old by the time it reached Norwood Green—but are you sure it was wise to remarry so soon after being widowed?"

"Pray meet my husband, and decide for yourself," Julia

urged. "Miss Milliken, may I present Mr. John Pickett? John, Miss Milliken was once charged with the impossible task of educating my sister and me."

Miss Milliken inclined her head. "Mr. Pickett," she said warily, her doubtful glance taking in every detail of his black tailcoat's indifferent tailoring.

Sensing her governess's disapproval, Julia hurried to explain. "Mr. Pickett, you must know, is the Bow Street Runner who proved my innocence in the matter of Frederick's murder."

The difference this knowledge made in Miss Milliken's demeanor was astounding. To Pickett's dismay, the little lady cast herself onto his chest and threw her arms around him. "My dear boy! Pray forgive an old woman's prejudices! I can never, *never* thank you enough for what you have done for my little Julia!"

"The—the honor was all mine, ma'am," Pickett protested, wondering how he might extricate himself from Miss Milliken's embrace without giving offense. Thankfully, the matter was settled by the lady's need to fumble in her reticule for a handkerchief with which to wipe her eyes. Pickett, relieved to find himself freed, was only too glad to offer his own.

"I beg your pardon, Mr. Pickett," said Miss Milliken, her voice muffled by its folds. "You will think me a foolish old woman, I know, but with no children of my own, I have always thought of the Runyon girls as my own dear daughters. To lose poor Claudia in such a way, and then to be faced with the prospect of losing Julia as well—"

Overcome with emotion, she sought recourse to the handkerchief once more.

Julia, glancing about, realized that they had attracted considerable attention. Correctly guessing her husband's embarrassment (no great mental feat, as his blushes gave him away), she lost no time in making their excuses.

"I see Mama and Papa waiting for us, so I fear we must go now, Millie, but I should like to bring Mr. Pickett to tea one day, if I may."

"Oh, certainly, certainly!" exclaimed Miss Milliken. "Your dear papa was so kind as to give me a positively *lavish* pension, you know, so I was able to hire a lovely little cottage only a short walk from the village."

There followed a rather lengthy description of the agreeable location of this residence, along with its many amenities, but at last, after promising to come to tea in the very near future, Julia and Pickett were able to make their escape. They quickened their steps in order to catch up with Julia's parents, and found Lady Runyon gazing wistfully across the green at a young woman leading a little girl by the hand. The woman was obviously a farmer's wife, her plump cheeks rosy from exposure to sun and wind, and her Sunday best gown clean and neat, yet far from fashionable. The child was quite another matter. She was about three years old, with wide blue eyes and red-gold curls that glinted in the sun, and she wore a white frock worked with fine embroidery about the neck and hem.

"What a beautiful child," Lady Runyon sighed mournfully. "She reminds me so much of Claudia at that age."

Since Claudia's blonde hair had held no trace of red, Julia glanced at Pickett and rolled her eyes. "Mama, how can you say so? She is certainly a beautiful child, but she looks nothing like—"

She broke off abruptly as Jamie Pennington stopped to speak to the young mother. He tweaked one of the child's curls playfully, and the little girl hid her face in the woman's skirts, then peered timidly out at the vicar's son.

Julia froze where she stood, pressing her hand to her heart, which had begun to race alarmingly. But for the girl's shyness, the child might have been Jamie's daughter.

"My lady?" Pickett murmured. "Are you all right?"

"Jamie—and that little girl—"

She had not expected him to mourn Claudia forever; for all practical purposes, he had lost her two years before her death, when she had married Lord Buckleigh. Still, Julia had difficulty reconciling the memory her sister's ardent young admirer with the image of a cavalry officer of thirty sowing his wild oats willy-nilly amongst the women of the local yeomanry.

Pickett followed her gaze, and arrived at a very fair estimation of his wife's thoughts. "Major Pennington has been fighting on the Continent for the last several years, has he not?"

"Yes," Julia said slowly. "Still, I suppose he must have come home on leave sometime."

There was nothing Pickett could say to that. Sir Thaddeus addressed some question to his daughter, and conversation became more general. They soon reached

Runyon Hall, where after a cold collation as befitted the Sabbath, Lady Runyon declared her intention of lying down for a nap. Sir Thaddeus patted his belly and declared his need for exercise, then turned to his son-in-law and offered to show him about the place. Pickett was pleased to accept, until he was given to understand that this expedition would not be made on foot, as he had supposed, but on the back of a horse.

"I've never ridden before," Pickett protested.

"No time like the present, I always say," insisted the squire. "Mind you, it's better to start young. I put my Julia on her first pony when she was only four years old, and now I'll wager she's got the prettiest seat in the county."

Pickett, having recently become intimately acquainted with the seat in question, could find nothing to dispute in this assessment, but quite aside from the realization that he and his father-in-law were thinking of two entirely different things, he bethought himself of another reason that he should be excused from the proposed outing.

"I haven't any riding clothes."

These objections, too, fell on deaf ears. His own wife betrayed him with her assurances that his brown coat would serve very well, and Sir Thaddeus went so far as to offer him the loan of a pair of riding boots. These proved to be a bit small, but by this time Pickett had recognized the futility of argument, and resigned himself to pinched feet. He only hoped that he might escape the outing with no greater injuries.

"Tom!" Sir Thaddeus bellowed for the groom as they

approached the stables. "Tom, where are you?"

A moment later the broad stable door opened, and a strapping youth still in his teens emerged into the sunlight.

"Will, where's Tom?" Sir Thaddeus demanded.

The stable boy shrugged. "Dunno, sir. He hasn't been in all morning."

Sir Thaddeus muttered a curse under his breath. "Drank himself into a stupor last night at the Pig and Whistle, I'll be bound! Will, I need you to saddle up my roan, her ladyship's mare, and"—he studied Pickett appraisingly—"what are you, about twelve stone? Will, fetch Lucifer for Mr. Pickett here."

Sir Thaddeus followed Will into the stable, and Pickett turned to regard Julia with a look of abject horror. "Your father is going to put me on a horse named Lucifer?"

"It isn't as bad as it sounds," she assured him hastily. "He was given the name as a colt, because of his beautiful black color. He's a sweetheart, really."

She turned as Will emerged from the stable leading a sleek black horse. "You wouldn't hurt a fly, would you, Lucifer?" She took the rein from Will, and stroked the animal's velvety nose. "You'll take good care of my darling, won't you?"

"I'll try," said Pickett, giving his mount a dubious look.

"I was talking to the horse," Julia said, then gave him a wink and turned to allow her father to boost her into the saddle.

For the first several minutes, Pickett had no thought but maintaining his balance in a saddle that seemed impossibly high off the ground. As he grew accustomed to the horse's gait, however, he began to relax and was able to look about at his surroundings.

"It's a pretty place your father has here," he observed to Julia, who had drawn up alongside him.

"I have always thought so," she agreed. She might have added that, since the property was unentailed, it would all be his someday, married as he was to Sir Thaddeus's only surviving offspring, but she wisely refrained from making this revelation just yet; the four hundred pounds per annum had been enough of a shock to him for the nonce.

As they skirted a copse of trees, Pickett noticed a small stone cottage nestled in the woods.

"Who lives there?" he asked Sir Thaddeus, nodding his head in the direction of the house without releasing his white-knuckled grip on the reins.

"No one, now," was his father-in-law's answer. "It's actually the gamekeeper's cottage attached to Greenwillows, the old Layton estate—the woods there mark the southern boundary—but old Mrs. Layton didn't hunt, so the place has stood empty for years."

Pickett had been almost certain he'd seen a curl of smoke rising from the chimney, and started to turn in the saddle for a closer look. Lucifer, however, had no very high opinion of this maneuver, so he was obliged to abandon the attempt.

"Mrs. Layton," echoed Julia. "Isn't she Jamie's aunt, the one who died and left her estate to him?"

"Aye, she was the vicar's sister. Since she and Layton

85

never had children of their own, she left everything to Jamie. All this belongs to him now."

"It's a pity he intends to sell it," Julia said. "I should have thought he would want to sell his commission and settle down here someday."

Sir Thaddeus cleared his throat with the awkward air of a man fighting his own emotions. "Maybe he finds it too painful. After all, your sister . . ."

Determined to give his thoughts (and indeed, her own) a happier direction, Julia said brightly, "Come, Papa, let's race! John, you don't mind, do you?"

Pickett shook his head. "So long as I am not expected to participate, no."

"Very well, Papa, let us race to that tree." She raised her crop and pointed it in the direction of a single oak crowning a distant hill.

Sir Thaddeus agreed readily, and they were off. Pickett had a bad moment or two with Lucifer, who was much inclined to join in the fun, but having at last gained control of his mount, he proceeded at his own pace and reached the tree some minutes later.

"Who won?" he asked cheerfully.

Julia, still on horseback, turned to regard him with an expression of such horror that the smile was wiped from his face.

"My lady?"

He clambered down from the saddle none too gracefully, and hurried toward her. She kicked her foot free of the stirrup and slid off the sidesaddle and into his arms.

"Oh, John! Oh, John!" she cried, burying her face in his chest.

"Sir Thaddeus?" Pickett turned toward his father-in-law, who was bending over a large rock which proved, on closer inspection, to be no rock at all.

"It's Tom, my missing groom," Sir Thaddeus said. "He's dead."

6

*In Which John Pickett Pays a Call
and Discovers a Clue*

P ickett gently but firmly set Julia aside and joined her
father beside the body. At first glance Sir Thaddeus's
groom appeared to be the happiest corpse Pickett had ever
seen; a closer inspection, however, revealed that the man's
hideous grin was actually a gash: his throat had been slit
from ear to ear, and the gaping wound was caked with blood.
In fact, blood was everywhere. It covered the corpse from
chin to chest, and soaked the ground where the body lay.
Pickett stooped and swiped a finger across the man's throat,
but found nothing save for a few tiny reddish-brown flakes;
clearly, the groom had lain here for some time if such
copious amounts of blood had had time to dry. With his
other hand, Pickett withdrew a handkerchief from the inside
pocket of his brown serge coat and wiped his finger clean.

He rose and turned to his father-in-law. "Sir Thaddeus,
if you will take Julia back to the house—"

"No, John, please don't send me away," she protested.

"I am quite all right, now that—now that you are here. Please let me stay. I promise I won't faint on you, or have hysterics, or anything of that nature."

He smiled at her. "No, you won't, will you?" he noted with more than a trace of admiration. It was not the first time she'd come face to face with death—nor the second, for that matter—and although she had not been bred for such grim scenes, she had risen to the occasion every time, even being of enormous assistance to him more than once. "Very well, my lady, you may stay if you wish."

The matter being settled, Pickett turned his attention back to the issue at hand. He studied the ground around the body, and circled the tree, pausing occasionally to nudge a large leaf aside with the toe of his borrowed boot.

"You are looking for the knife," Julia guessed.

"Yes, or any other weapon that might have produced such a result," Pickett said. "Probably a knife, but I can't rule out a hatchet, or a sword, or anything else with a sharp edge."

Having completed his circuit of the tree without success, he arrived back at the body, and looked down at it for a long moment. "I should think it unlikely that he fell on top of it, but I can't ignore the possibility. Sir Thaddeus, if you will assist me?"

Sir Thaddeus stepped forward at once to take the dead man's legs while Pickett lifted his shoulders. Together they moved the man out of the dried puddle of his own blood, but it was as Pickett had expected. They found no knife, or indeed any other weapon, lying beneath him on the ground.

"And you say he was your groom?" Pickett asked his father-in-law. "Do you know if he had a quarrel with anyone? Or any reason why someone would want him dead?"

Sir Thaddeus shook his head. "Not that I ever heard. A bit too fond of spending his evenings at the Pig and Whistle for my liking, but not so much that it interfered with his work. I'd have thrown him out on his ear if it had," he added darkly.

Having discovered all he could from the site, which was little enough, Pickett turned his attention to the body itself. He folded back the front of the blood-encrusted coat, plunged his hand into the pocket, and withdrew his clenched fist.

He opened his hand, and let out a low whistle. "You must pay your staff well, sir," he remarked to his father-in-law.

"Well enough to prevent anyone else from making them a better offer," Sir Thaddeus admitted. " 'The laborer is worthy of his hire,' and all that, you know. What makes you say so?"

Pickett held out his hand to reveal a pile of coins, including a number of golden guineas.

The older man's eyes bulged. "I don't pay them as well as all that!"

"Have you any idea how he might have come by such a sum of money?"

The squire shook his head. "No, none."

"Are you aware of any ways a groom might earn such a

sum on the side in ways that were perhaps less than ethical?"

Sir Thaddeus frowned as he considered the matter. "I suppose he might pocket a bit under the table in illicit stud fees."

"How so?" asked Pickett.

"Someone who wanted to breed my Lucifer there, for instance, with one of his own mares might slip Tom a tidy sum to allow Lucifer to escape into his own pasture while his mare was in season."

"Do you know of anyone who might have offered Tom such an arrangement?"

"Well, there's Griggs whose property borders mine to the south. He's had his eye on Lucifer for his Andromeda for years, but I'll have none of it, and so I've told him more than once. His Andromeda is as sway-backed a nag as I've seen in many a long day. Any offspring of hers would be no credit to Lucifer."

"Have you any reason to believe this Griggs might have offered Tom such an arrangement as you describe?"

Sir Thaddeus shook his head. "Griggs is no judge of horseflesh, but I've never heard anything said against his morals." He paused and gave a discreet cough. "I don't suppose he could have done it himself?"

Pickett, correctly assuming this question to refer to Tom rather than the absent Griggs, looked down at the body. "I should have thought anyone trying to commit suicide in such a way would lose consciousness before he could make a cut so wide, or so deep. And then there's the money. That means something; I'm sure of it. Why would a man who'd just come into a windfall suddenly decide to do away with himself?" He frowned thoughtfully. "I suppose the coroner will have to be called, and the—tell me, Sir Thaddeus, who is the local Justice of the Peace?"

"That would be Lord Buckleigh. Good thing he's back from his honeymoon, what?"

"Indeed it is, although it's not much of a start to his married life." Pickett sighed. "Mine either, for that matter."

"I expect I should be the one to break the news to Tom's wife," Sir Thaddeus said with all the eagerness of a man about to have a tooth drawn. "His being in my employ and all."

Pickett would have preferred to perform this task himself, for a great deal could be learned about the state of a man's marriage by his widow's reaction to the news of his death. But he suspected his father-in-law was correct in claiming a sort of *noblesse oblige* where this somber task was concerned, so he merely nodded in acknowledgement and turned to his wife.

"My lady, will you return to the house with your father and send word to Lord Buckleigh and the coroner?" Anticipating her objection, he added, "I promise, I will be fine. It won't be the first time I've been alone with a body."

She gave him a rueful smile, and allowed him to make a stirrup of his hands and toss her into the saddle. A moment later, father and daughter were cantering away across the downs, and Pickett was left alone to examine the site where the groom had met his death. Apart from the spot where the body had lain, there was very little blood, and this in itself was surprising; whoever had done the deed must have been liberally splattered, and although Pickett did not expect him to leave a trail which might be followed—in his experience, murderers were rarely so obliging—there would certainly have been bloodied garments to be disposed of. Pickett paced off an ever-widening circle, searching the ground for some sign of a hole having been dug, or a ditch which might have been invisible from the spot where the murder had occurred. He found neither, but he did identify one feature that he had not noticed before: just over a ridge to the east he could glimpse the slate tiles of a roof. The scene of the crime was not quite so isolated as he had first imagined.

He glanced uncertainly back at the body. He disliked leaving it there, but he wanted to do a little investigating before word of the groom's death spread throughout the neighborhood like wildfire—which it would do, he had no doubt, as soon as Julia and Sir Thaddeus reached Runyon Hall with the news. Taking the horse Lucifer by the reins, he heaved himself into the saddle (an ungainly process he was only thankful his wife and her father were not present to witness) and set out for the house below the ridge.

He found it strangely quiet. A very pretty residence built during the previous century of golden stone from the nearby Cotswolds, it seemed somehow frozen in time, with no signs of life anywhere. Pickett directed his borrowed mount to the stables behind the house and, when no stable hand came forward to meet him, called for assistance. No one answered.

"Well, Lucifer, it looks as if it's just you and me," he

muttered under his breath.

He dismounted with relative ease, having gravity on his side, and led the horse from the pale sunshine of early spring into the shadowy gloom of the stables.

"Hullo?" he called. "Is anyone here?"

There was no reply, and as his eyes adjusted to the darkness, he realized the stalls were empty. Now that he thought of it, the building lacked the odors of horse and fresh hay that had assailed his nostrils at Sir Thaddeus's stables. Apparently there had been no horses stabled here for some time. Seeing he could expect no assistance from a stable hand, Pickett looked about for something to which he might tether Lucifer's reins, and his eyes alighted on a pile of clothing in one corner.

Dropping the horse's reins, he went to investigate, and found a caped greatcoat liberally splashed with blood. The dark patches were stiff, but when he raised the garment to his nose, he found the metallic scent still strong; although the blood had had sufficient time to dry, it was a fairly recent addition. Perhaps even more interesting, however, were the cut and cloth of the garment. They were not at all what one might expect a groom or stable boy to wear, but the fine wool and skillful tailoring typical of a gentleman's wardrobe. And while he knew from his aristocratic bride that servants sometimes were given their masters' or mistresses' castoffs, this particular garment appeared too new to have been already replaced.

He let the greatcoat fall, then rose and turned his attention back to the horse, only to find himself alone in the stable; Lucifer, it seemed, had abandoned his unfamiliar rider and bolted. Resigning himself to a long walk back to the Runyon property, Pickett decided to delay this exercise until after he'd made inquiries at the house. Forsaking the stable, he walked to the front door, and found the iron knocker wrapped in the black crape indicative of mourning. He rapped sharply on the wooden panel.

After several long minutes, during which Pickett began to wonder if the house were as empty as its stables, the door swung open with a creak of neglected hinges, and an ancient butler rasped, "Yes, sir?"

"I should like to speak to the master or mistress of the house, if you please," Pickett said.

"So should I," the butler replied, sizing up at a glance Pickett's brown serge coat and borrowed boots. "Unfortunately, Mr. Layton has been dead for this decade and more, and Mrs. Layton followed him just after Twelfth Night."

Pickett glanced past the butler, and found confirmation of his words in the white Holland covers draped over the hall furnishings, giving the room a ghostly appearance. "Then the house is empty?"

The butler inclined his head. "But for myself, sir, yes."

"And the stables?"

"As Mrs. Layton rarely left the house after the master's death, the horses were sold years ago."

"I see," said Pickett, his mind working rapidly. It appeared that the Layton stable would be an excellent place to hide incriminating clothing; had it not been for his own presence in the neighborhood and his knowledge of criminal investigations, the telltale garment might have lain there undiscovered for years. "Are there no visitors to the house, then?"

"None, sir," said the butler, shaking his head. "Only the young master."

"The young master?"

"Young Mr. Pennington," the butler explained. "He was the mistress's nephew and godson. He inherited the estate upon her death."

With a sinking heart, Pickett wished his wife were not quite so fond of Major Pennington. For if this was Jamie Pennington's house, then it was also Jamie Pennington's stable—and, quite possibly, Jamie Pennington's greatcoat, hidden in the corner and drenched in blood.

* * *

Upon entering her parents' house, Julia headed straight for the writing desk in her father's study. Lady Runyon, hearing footsteps in the hall, followed the sound and discovered her daughter, quill pen scratching urgently over paper.

"Have you returned already?" Then, seeing her pale face, "Why, Julia! What has happened? Where are your father and Mr. Pickett?"

"Papa and Mr. Pickett are quite all right, Mama. In fact, there has been a—an accident. Your groom, Tom, is—is dead, and Papa has gone to break the news to his wife."

"And you?" Lady Runyon asked, her gaze shifting to the half-finished letter on the desk.

"I am writing to Lord Buckleigh—and to the coroner."

Lady Runyon nodded slowly. "It is very thoughtful of you to notify Lord Buckleigh, since poor Tom was once his stable boy. But why the coroner?"

"Because," Julia took a deep, steadying breath. "Because Tom's death was not—not an accident, precisely."

"Julia!" exclaimed Lady Runyon, her meager bosom swelling. "Has that boy exposed you to violent death *again?*"

"First, Mama, Mr. Pickett is not a 'boy,' and second, he did not 'expose' me any more than Papa did! In fact, I was in Papa's company when we discovered the—the body. We were racing to the old oak at the corner of the Layton property—you remember the one, it stands all by itself at the top of the ridge—and when we got there, well, there was Tom." She grimaced at the memory. "Or all that was left of him."

"So, if you are here writing letters, and your papa has gone to Tom's house, then where, pray, is this Mr. Pickett of yours?"

"He stayed behind to investigate." Seeing disapproval writ large upon her mother's countenance, she added hastily, "You must agree that there is no one in Norwood Green more qualified to do so."

"I must do nothing of the kind! Your Mr. Pickett should remember that he is a guest here, and behave accordingly. Norwood Green has both a Justice of the Peace and a coroner. He should allow them to do their jobs."

"They can hardly do so until they have been notified, can they?" Julia said, and turned back to finish her correspondence with shaking hands.

An uneasy peace reigned while the footman was dispatched to deliver these messages. When they were alone again, Lady Runyon picked up the thread of the unfinished conversation. "I don't mean to criticize, my dear. Perhaps it is unfair, but I can't help comparing your new husband"— she all but shuddered on the word—"with poor Fieldhurst. *He*, I know, would never have embroiled you in such an unsavory business."

"You are right about one thing, Mama: it *is* unfair! Frederick would never have 'embroiled' me in a murder investigation, for it never would have occurred to him that I might have opinions, or insights, or indeed any other function beyond the purely ornamental."

"Well, but Julia, my dear," protested Lady Runyon, whose own views of the matter were far more closely aligned with her late son-in-law's than with her daughter's.

"And on the subject of 'poor Fieldhurst,' there is a great deal you never knew about him." And sparing no detail, Julia catalogued first husband's sins, beginning with the opera dancer he had taken under his protection shortly after their honeymoon and ending with her own lady's maid, and all the other women (at least, all the ones she knew of) in between.

"My poor Julia!" her mama exclaimed at the end of this recital. "I wish you had told me earlier!"

"Why?" Julia asked bitterly. "What difference would it have made?"

"To him, none," Lady Runyon admitted. "But I should

have asked you to consider if you were doing all you might to make him comfortable, to—"

"Mama!" exclaimed Julia, listening to her mother in growing indignation. "Do you mean to suggest that Frederick's infidelities were my fault?"

"Of course not, my dear. But men feel differently about these things. Depend upon it, these little *affaires* in no way detract from a man's feelings for his wife. Why, your own Papa makes two trips to London a year for that very purpose, and always returns to me more affectionate than ever."

Julia stared at her mother with stricken eyes. "Do you mean to say that even *Papa*—?"

"Come, Julia, you are not a child! You must know that in recent years my health has not been what it once was. But it is a wife's duty to see that her husband's needs are met, whether that entails meeting them herself, or turning a blind eye while he seeks satisfaction elsewhere." She added, more gently this time, "Sexual congress is not only about pro-creation, you know. To a man it often represents youth and virility. Could I really be so cruel as to deny your papa that reassurance?"

Julia, stunned, could not speak. Quite aside from this entirely unexpected facet of her father, she realized that perhaps she had not been entirely fair to her husband. Not Fieldhurst—no indeed, for she was quite certain she had nothing with which to reproach herself where he was concerned. But for the first time it occurred to her that she might have done John Pickett a disservice. Caught up in newly discovered feelings of love and uncertain if he would survive his injuries, they had consummated their accidental marriage without much thought for the future; in fact, the present had been too precious, and too precarious, to waste a moment in thoughts of what might never come to pass. Now, however, her mother's words brought new and unwelcome questions to mind. At four-and-twenty, he need have no concerns about lost youth, and however inexperienced he might be, she could testify as to his virility. Procreation, on the other hand . . . In six years of marriage to Frederick, Lord Fieldhurst, there had been no sign of a pregnancy, and the physician who had tried his best to treat this condition had made it clear that the situation was unlikely to change. This, in fact, was what had driven the final wedge between herself and her first husband. Although he hadn't Lord Fieldhurst's urgent need for an heir, surely John Pickett would desire children no less than her first husband had done. Might he someday come to regret the hasty consummation that now bound him to a barren woman in a childless marriage?

"Mama," she began slowly, only to be interrupted by a scratching at the door.

"Begging your pardon, ma'am," began the butler, entering the room.

"Yes, Parks?" asked Lady Runyon. "What is it?"

"It's Lucifer," he said. "He's come back to the stable."

Lady Runyon smothered a sigh at the return of her son-in-law. "Very well, you may inform Mr. Pickett that we shall join him in the drawing room directly."

Parks gave a discreet little cough. "There's the thing, ma'am. The horse has returned without its rider."

7

Which Describes Various Encounters,
Both Human and Spectral

U pon leaving the Layton house, Pickett returned to the spot where Tom's body lay. The coroner had not yet arrived, nor had Lord Buckleigh in his rôle as Justice of the Peace. There was nothing he could do, therefore, but wait and think—and it was perhaps inevitable that his thoughts returned to the cottage on the edge of the wood, from whose chimney, he could have sworn, a plume of smoke had risen. His father-in-law had said the house was empty, but in view of the fact that a gruesome murder had been committed nearby, he would be a fool not to investigate. Grimacing at the prospect of making such a trek in his too-small borrowed riding boots, he steeled his resolve and set out.

He reached the house ten minutes later, limping toward it on feet upon which more than one blister was already beginning to form. As he approached, he looked up at the chimney; if there had been a fire in the grate before, it had been put out, for no smoke curled up from the stone flue

101

now. He walked up to the door and knocked. There was no answer. He knocked again. Still no answer, but was that a faint scuffling sound from within, or simply the sigh of leaves in the trees?

He made up his mind to find out. He rattled the doorknob, and was not surprised to find it locked. He groped in his pockets for some tool he might use to force the lock, and was pleased to discover one of his wife's hairpins. It was one of the unforeseen small pleasures of marriage, he'd found, these constant little reminders of his lady that were wont to turn up unexpectedly in apparently random places.

Turning his attention back to the matter at hand, he dropped to one knee before the door and inserted the hairpin into the lock. A moment later there was a click, and the knob turned in his hand. He stood and pushed the door open, and the pale spring sun spilled into the dark cottage, casting dappled shadows into the bare little room.

"Hullo?" Pickett called, stepping gingerly inside. "Is anyone there?"

There was obviously no one in the room in which he stood, for the space was too sparsely furnished to provide a hiding place. A scarred deal table and two chairs were positioned against one wall beneath the window to catch the afternoon sun, and a worn sofa faced the fireplace where, presumably, the gamekeeper and his wife had once sat on cold evenings.

The fireplace . . .

Pickett crossed the room to the hearth, then bent and held one hand over the partially burned log resting on cast iron firedogs. It was warm, so warm that he was forced to withdraw his hand. There was no fire now, but there certainly had been one, and not very long ago. Whoever extinguished it could not have gone far. He glanced at the staircase—little more than a ladder, really—that led to a loft where the gamekeeper must have slept. Whoever might be waiting at the top would surely have the advantage of anyone approaching from below. Did he dare climb it?

A month earlier he would not have hesitated, but now he had a wife to consider. He did not flatter himself that she would miss his lost earnings, should he be killed in the line of duty, but he realized he was not ready to give up his new-found happiness, and he had every reason to believe she felt the same. He reminded himself of his charge to protect the King's peace, and acknowledged that he had a further obligation, however vague, to investigate a murder that involved his wife's family, albeit indirectly. He took a deep breath and began, slowly and quietly, to mount the stairs.

His foot was on the fourth tread when a shadow fell across the room, blocking out the light from the open door. He wheeled about and found Jamie Pennington standing in the doorway.

"Mr. Pickett?"

Pickett nodded. "Major Pennington."

"May I ask what you are doing on my property?" The engaging vicar's son of the morning was gone, and it was the military man who regarded him with a look of such sternness that for the first time in many years, Pickett felt like the fourteen-year-old pickpocket who had been hauled before the magistrate.

"I was riding past with my wife and her father when I thought I saw smoke coming from the chimney," he explained. "Sir Thaddeus had said the house was empty, so I thought I would investigate."

Jamie smiled, and Pickett had the impression that he was feigning a carelessness he did not feel. "Very conscientious of you, Mr. Pickett, but I should not want to trouble you with such things while you are on your honeymoon. A message sent to me at the vicarage would have sufficed, and I would have looked into the matter myself. Ah well, no harm done. Come along, and let us find Julia!"

Pickett gestured toward the fireplace. "Major, there was a fire lit here until quite recently. Someone has been in the house—and may still be here, for all we know."

"It was probably old Wilson, the butler," Jamie said with a dismissive wave of one hand. "He's been looking after the place since my aunt died."

"He didn't mention it when I spoke with him earlier," Pickett observed.

"Perhaps he didn't consider it any of your business," suggested Jamie, and his smile held more than a hint of steel. "I appreciate your concern, but I really must insist that you leave this house."

Thus adjured, Pickett had no choice but to descend the stairs and exit through the door Jamie held open for him.

"Now then, Mr. Pickett, let's find Julia," Jamie said in something approaching his usual manner.

As they walked away from the house, Jamie flung an

arm across Pickett's shoulders, a companionable gesture that did not deceive Pickett for a minute. Clearly, the major had no intention of allowing him to search the house the moment his back was turned. Who—or what—was he trying to protect, and why?

Jamie would have steered Pickett back in the direction of the Runyon estate, but here he underestimated his man. Ignoring the pressure of Jamie's hand on his shoulder, Pickett turned instead toward the place where Tom's body lay, leaving the major no choice but to follow.

"Tell me," Pickett said as they emerged from the woods, "what do you know of Sir Thaddeus's groom?"

"Very little," Jamie said with a shrug which seemed to Pickett a bit too offhand. "I had a nodding acquaintance with him when he was a stable hand at Buckleigh Manor, but then, I have been out of the country for these last dozen years and more. Why do you ask?"

Pickett pointed toward the ridge. "See that tree? Tom, or what's left of him, is lying there with his throat slit."

"Dear God!" As a soldier, Jamie was surely no stranger to violent death, but at this revelation his countenance assumed a greenish cast. "Is it true?"

"Do you know of any reason why I should lie about such a thing?"

Jamie shook his head. "No, but—does Julia know?"

Pickett nodded. "She and her father found him."

"Am I to understand, then, that you intend to investigate? You are a long way from Bow Street, Mr. Pickett."

"True, but I feel some obligation to do what I can, given

that my wife's family is involved."

"And how do you figure that, Mr. Pickett?" Jamie's voice had grown cool again, and his hand on Pickett's shoulder stiffened.

"Need you ask? Besides the fact that Sir Thaddeus was the fellow's employer, he and Julia found the body."

"Of course." Jamie gave a shaky laugh. "You must forgive my obtuseness. It's—it's rather upsetting news."

"And yet as a military man, you must be accustomed to violent death, Major."

"One would suppose so, but this—murder in the wilds of Somersetshire"—he shook his head in bewilderment—"it is a very different thing, and one that isn't supposed to happen here."

"One might argue that such things aren't supposed to happen anywhere," Pickett pointed out. "And yet they do. Have you any idea why anyone might want Tom dead?"

"Look here," Jamie said testily, "haven't I just told you I've been out of the country? How the devil should I know?"

"Very well, then, let's try another question: whose blood-stained greatcoat is hidden in the stables at Green-willows—a property, I believe, which you have recently inherited?"

Jamie's face darkened with anger, but any reply he might have made was interrupted by the thunder of hoof beats. Pickett turned and saw, not Lord Buckleigh or the coroner, but a mare being ridden hell-for-leather over the downs by a hatless female in a red velvet riding habit whose skirts billowed out behind her. Even as he started in her direction, she reined in her mount and slid from the saddle.

"My lady?" Pickett began. "What—?"

Julia, who had, over the last twelvemonth, narrowly escaped the gallows, discovered more than one dead body, and faced down formidable social censure (to say nothing of her own mama), now saw her husband apparently healthy and unharmed, and fell completely apart. She picked up her skirts and ran the last few yards, finally hurling herself against his chest. "Oh, John! The horse—Lucifer—he came back without you—it was just like Claudia all over again!"

"Hush, love," crooned Pickett, taking her tearstained face in his hands and raining gentle kisses over it. "I'm quite all right—just forgot to tie up the horse. Nothing is wrong with me but a few blisters and my own stupidity."

However unfounded her fears, the act of soothing them required some time and not a few murmured endearments punctuated by still more kisses; consequently, it was some time before Julia looked beyond Pickett and discovered Jamie standing just beyond him, regarding her with the rather self-conscious expression of one who finds himself the unintentional witness to an exchange of intimacies best expressed in private.

"Jamie? What are you doing here?"

"I was in the area looking over my inheritance when I ran across your Mr. Pickett," he answered.

It was, Pickett knew, rather less than the truth, but he could not fault the man for his discretion; until he could prove either Jamie's guilt or his innocence, he thought it was probably wisest not to reveal every detail of the encounter to his wife.

They had not long to wait until they were joined by a cavalcade comprising Sir Thaddeus, Lord Buckleigh, a frail elderly man who could only be the coroner, and several laborers riding on the back of a farm wagon, which would be used for bearing the dead man's body home.

"Mr. Pickett," said his lordship, offering his hand, "I am sorry to meet you again under such circumstances. And Major—"

"Buckleigh."

The two men did not shake hands, but gave one another the curtest of nods. If looks could kill, Pickett thought, they would have needed a bigger wagon.

Pickett waited while Julia and her father explained how they had discovered the body and then, after Julia moved aside to speak with Jamie, approached the Justice of the Peace.

"I've taken the liberty of conducting a brief examination," he told Lord Buckleigh. He gave a short accounting of the contents of the dead man's pockets, but for reasons he could not explain, he made no mention of his visit to the Greenwillows stable and the remains of the fire in the supposedly empty cottage.

Buckleigh nodded. "I see. Yes, an unusual sum for such a man to have in his possession, to be sure. But that was all? There was no paper—a note or a letter, perhaps, or a bill of sale—to suggest how he might have come by it?"

Pickett shook his head. "No, nothing."

"I am obliged to you, Mr. Pickett," said his lordship. "It

is fortunate that a man of your expertise was on hand, however regrettable that your honeymoon should be interrupted by this unpleasantness."

"No more than yours, my lord. I understand you have only just returned from your own wedding trip." He hesitated a moment before adding, "With your permission, sir, I should like to investigate this case."

"I thank you for the offer, but I would not like to impose."

"No imposition at all. The man was my father-in-law's servant." Seeing his lordship was not convinced, he urged, "Surely you would not deprive me of the opportunity to assist my wife's family."

A hint of a smile lightened Lord Buckleigh's rather severe countenance. "And yet I suspect, Mr. Pickett, that it is not assistance that concerns you, but redemption. In fact, you hope that by bringing their servant's killer to justice, you may win your in-laws' approval."

"I don't hold out for miracles, my lord, but I suppose it can't hurt," Pickett acknowledged, answering his lordship's smile with one of his own.

Lord Buckleigh gave him a long look. "How old are you, Mr. Pickett?"

From anyone else, the question would have been an impertinence, and regardless of its source, Pickett felt the familiar annoyance at the unspoken assumption that his lack of years equated to incompetence. Still he understood that, right or wrong, his lordship's title gave him the right to take certain liberties that would be offensive in a man of lower status. Since he had no desire to offend the very one from whom he was asking a favor, Pickett stifled a sigh. "Twenty-five, my lord," he said, although he was in fact anticipating his natal day by a week and a half.

Lord Buckleigh nodded, frowning at the ground where the elderly coroner made his fumbling examination of the body. "Rather young, but age, as we know, is no guarantee of expertise." He turned back to Pickett. "Very well, Mr. Pickett, the case is yours. But you will, I trust, keep me informed as to the progress of your investigation."

"Of course." This was his opportunity to describe his discovery of the bloodied greatcoat in the stable, as well as his suspicion that someone had taken up residence in the empty gamekeeper's cottage. He did so, concluding with his determination to have a closer look at the cottage in the not too distant future.

"And the property, of course, belongs to Major Pennington," observed his lordship, his eyes narrowed in suspicion. "Interesting, but hardly surprising, when one considers the matter."

"Indeed?" Pickett's eyebrows rose. "Why not?"

"Because," Lord Buckleigh said with great deliberation, "I have every reason to believe that Major Pennington killed my first wife."

* * *

Julia, meanwhile, had moved apart from the little group with Jamie.

"Jamie, what I said a moment ago—about Claudia—I am sorry you had to hear that. I know you loved her, too."

110

Jamie nodded in understanding. "I'm glad you found your Mr. Pickett unharmed, in any case. I confess, when I first heard you had married a Bow Street Runner, I feared the fellow must have coerced you in some way. If I had not already come to the conclusion that I was mistaken, that little demonstration would have been sufficient to inform me of my error."

"No." She blushed very becomingly, as befitted a bride. "No coercion on his part was necessary. But on a related subject, you must allow me to thank you for standing up for him at the Brantley dinner last night, and again at church this morning. It was very kind of you."

Jamie dismissed his own gallantry with a wave of his hand. "It was nothing. As it happened, I was well compensated for my efforts."

"Indeed?" Julia cocked her head inquiringly. "In what way?"

"I had four guineas on your husband's ability to open Brantley's safe within the allotted time. Although," Jamie added with a twinkle in his eye, "now that his credentials are established, I wouldn't be a bit surprised if, after your departure for London, your Mama makes a point of counting the silver."

"Very likely." She made a moue of distaste. "I fear I did not help matters, for I neglected to tell Mama and Papa of. my marriage until we arrived. You are well enough acquainted with Mama that I am sure I need not explain the omission."

He gave a shout of laughter, then remembered his

surroundings and lowered his voice. "Indeed not! But perhaps your parents will come about in time. Your Mr. Pickett seems to be a good man. Perhaps—" A shadow crossed his expressive countenance, and he added under his breath. "Perhaps a bit *too* good."

Julia, thinking her ears must have deceived her, asked, "Too good? What do you mean?"

Jamie shook his head as if to banish whatever thought had clouded his brow. "Never mind."

She would have pressed him for an explanation, but before she could do so, they were joined by the subject of the conversation himself, along with Lord Buckleigh and the coroner.

"Bad news, my lady," Pickett said, taking her hands and giving them a reassuring squeeze. "The coroner has ordered an inquest for Tuesday morning, and since you and your father discovered the body, you will both be expected to give evidence."

"By gad, Mr. Hughes," Sir Thaddeus expostulated, addressing himself to the elderly coroner, "I don't see why you must needs drag my daughter into this. I was the first one on the scene. By two lengths, in fact," added the sportsman with some satisfaction.

"Nevertheless, you will both be needed to corroborate one another's account," insisted the elderly lawyer.

"And Mr. Pickett?" asked Julia, glancing from her husband to the coroner.

"His presence will be required as well. Although I understand he didn't arrive at the scene until some minutes later, he might, given his background, have noticed something the two of you missed."

"It isn't the same as a trial, you understand," Pickett added hastily, knowing the horror she'd once felt at the prospect of standing trial for her first husband's murder. "No one is being judged, least of all you. In fact, you don't have to answer any question you don't wish to."

Julia drew a ragged breath. "It's all right, John." She turned to the coroner with head held high. "Of course, Mr. Hughes. I will do whatever I must to see that justice is done."

* * *

The rest of the afternoon passed in a blur. The groom's death had cast a pall over the house on a day when, due to the Sabbath, activity was already restricted, and it was with a shared sense of profound relief that, shortly after dinner, the Runyon family dispersed to their separate bedrooms for the night.

"Not that I shall get a wink of sleep," Julia observed, "for every time I close my eyes, I will see that poor man lying beneath the tree with his throat—"

"Try not to think of it, my lady," Pickett urged, knowing even as he said the words that she would find it impossible to follow this advice. He thought briefly of giving her thoughts another, more pleasant direction, but given the circumstances, it seemed somehow inappropriate. He gave her a rather perfunctory kiss, and snuffed the candle.

In spite of her declaration that she would not be able to

shut her eyes, Julia fell asleep quickly but, whether from a lack of laudanum or a mind weighed down by the day's events, Pickett lay awake at her side for the long watches of the night.

And so it was that, in the wee hours after midnight, he heard the soft sound, scarcely more than a vibration, of footsteps overhead. The Runyon ghost, it seemed, was restless. Pickett could relate; he was more than a little restless himself. He slid out from under the bedclothes as quietly as possible, but as he reached for his breeches, Julia rolled over.

"John? Where are you going?" she asked sleepily.

"I, er, your father asked me to look into something," was his evasive reply. "With everything that happened today, I almost forgot."

She raised herself up on one elbow. "You will be careful?"

"My lady, you grew up in this house," he pointed out. "What do you think is going to happen to me?"

"I—I don't know." Until he had been injured, it had never occurred to her that what he did was dangerous, that in pursuing justice he might be putting his life at risk. It was a new and unwelcome realization which had only been strengthened that afternoon when the horse Lucifer had returned to the stable without him. "Promise me you'll be careful."

"If I see your father coming after me with a cricket bat, I promise I'll run," he said, then leaned over the bed to kiss her lightly. "Go back to sleep, my lady. I'll be back shortly."

He did not take a candle, nor did he put on his shoes, for he wanted no light or sound to betray his presence. With one hand against the wall for guidance, he padded bare-footed down the dark corridor and up the stairs to the floor above. This, it seemed, was the same one his wife had shown him the previous morning: there was the schoolroom, with the governess's bedroom beyond, and there at the end of the hall was the nursery, the faint glow emitting from the open door suggesting the existence of a midnight visitor. Slowly, so as not to make any noise, he paced with measured steps down the passage until he reached the nursery door.

He drew up short on the threshold. A single candle had been lit and set on a chest of drawers, whence its flickering light illuminated the slender, golden-haired form of a woman. *Julia?* She stood with her back to him, one hand resting on the elaborately carved cradle and rocking it gently. He had no idea how she had contrived to reach the nursery ahead of him, but surely that was less important at the moment than comforting her for the barrenness which, it seemed, had not been entirely banished from her thoughts, even by the grisly events of the afternoon.

Soundlessly, he crossed the room to stand behind her, then slipped one arm about her waist and dropped a kiss onto her golden curls.

Her reaction astounded him. She tore herself away from him, then whirled and slapped his face. Stunned, they stared at one another, and Pickett found himself confronting a stranger, a woman of at least thirty whose wide blue eyes regarded him with consternation. Before he could question this apparition, she picked up her skirts and her candle, and disappeared through the wall. Or so it might have appeared, had Pickett's own brief stint as a footman not acquainted him with the hidden stairs that allowed the staff to move virtually unseen between the servants' hall and the family's rooms. He moved quickly to the jib door that concealed these stairs, but by the time he found the hidden catch and flung the door open, the woman was gone. No light from her candle illuminated the descent, and although Pickett could hear her footsteps echoing far below, he knew better than to attempt to go plunging down the narrow steps in the dark.

And so there was nothing he could do but stand looking down into the darkness, rubbing his stinging cheek and muttering, "I think I just kissed a ghost."

* * *

He returned to the bedroom to find Julia asleep, and for this he was grateful; he had not yet decided how much, if anything, to tell her of his night's wanderings. He did not climb back into bed at once, but sat in the chair before the long-dead fire, pondering this latest discovery and what it might mean. After several minutes, he moved to the writing desk and lit a candle, then positioned the embroidered fire screen to prevent the light from falling on his wife's face and disturbing her slumber. He fumbled in the desk drawer for paper, pen, and ink, and sat down to compose a letter to Patrick Colquhoun, Esquire, of the Bow Street Public Office at Number 4 Bow Street, London.

Dear Sir, he wrote, *it appears that I am in no danger of being dispatched back to London with the haste which I had originally feared. In fact, my father-in-law's groom has been murdered. I hope to find his killer and thus win some measure of respect from Sir Thaddeus and Lady Runyon, although I do not flatter myself that this would win their whole-hearted approval of me as a husband for their daughter. I hope you will pardon my presumption in asking for your help in this matter. I hesitate to ask, since you have done so much for me and Mrs. Pickett (oh incredible words!) already, but I know of no other way to obtain the information I require. I wonder if you will be so good as to make inquiries at the Horse Guards on my behalf and discover anything you can about a Major James Pennington, familiarly known as Jamie, of Norwood Green, Somerset-shire, who is known to have served in the Low Countries with the seventh cavalry in 1796, and more recently in the Peninsula. In particular, I wish to know if a woman has been following the drum under Major Pennington's protection. I dare offer no further explanation here, lest this letter fall into indiscreet hands before I am prepared to voice suspicions which may yet prove to be groundless, but please believe I would not make such a request without just cause. Until my return to Bow Street I remain, as ever,*

Your most grateful servant,
John Pickett

8

Which Finds John Pickett's
Investigations Underway

May 1796
Somersetshire

Having reached a deep gorge safe from prying eyes, Jamie judged it time to call a halt. Claudia drooped against him and, much as he treasured the feel of her light, warm weight against him, he could not like the way she bent forward almost double over his arm, clutching her abdomen and moaning piteously. He had cracked a couple of ribs himself once, when in his younger days he had fallen out of a tree in the orchard adjoining the vicarage, but although it had hurt like the very devil, he could remember suffering none of this groaning agony. At last, he reined in his horse along a stream and dismounted, then lifted Claudia down.

"I need to water the horses," he told her apologetically. "If you don't mind waiting—"

She nodded. "I'll be all right."

She removed her shawl and began to fold it. Jamie, seeing what she was about, took it from her trembling hands and made a cushion of it, then placed it on the ground and settled her on it.

"I'll be right back," he said, and turned to the horses.

He untied Claudia's mare from his saddle and, after allowing the horse to drink its fill, gave it a slap on the rump that sent it back the way they had come—back, in fact, to Buckleigh Manor, where its appearance would no doubt raise the alarm, if Tom the stable boy had not already done so. Having seen his own horse watered, Jamie withdrew a handkerchief from the pocket of his tailcoat and plunged it into the cool stream. He wrung out the excess water, then carried the wet handkerchief to where Claudia sat and dropped to one knee before her.

"I'm sorry, but we can't wait any longer," he said, tipping her chin up with one hand while he bathed her poor battered face with the other, dabbing away the dried blood caked about her nose and the corner of her mouth. "We must reach Bristol before nightfall. Once there, we should be able to lose ourselves easily enough in the city."

"Jamie, I can't ask such a thing of you," Claudia protested weakly. "You were to have succeeded your father as vicar of the parish. You can hardly do so while keeping a mistress."

"*A mistress?*" Jamie scowled at her as fiercely as ever his lordship had done, but Claudia was unafraid. "Do you honestly believe I could ever think of you in such sordid terms?"

She gave a feeble smile, a grotesque twisting of her unblemished lower lip. "It is what I shall be, whether you choose to think of it that way or not."

"Claudia, all I want is to get you away from that bastard before he kills you. As for—the other part—we need not—that is, I won't—what I mean is, you don't have to do anything you don't want to. It will be enough for me, just having you with me."

"I could not be so cruel as to deny you, after all you have given up for me. Besides"—coloring rosily, she looked down and began plucking blades of grass with great concentration—"there have been times of late, with Buckleigh, when I—I would close my eyes and—and try to imagine it was you."

"My darling!" He cradled her head gently against his shoulder, and pressed kisses into her bright hair.

"Oh Jamie, I was such a fool for marrying Buckleigh!" she cried, giving in at last to the tears she had held back so bravely for so long. "Can you ever forgive me?"

"There's nothing to forgive, sweeting," he insisted.

"But your career—your future—"

In fact, this was a subject that had preyed heavily upon his mind ever since they had made their escape, but he could not burden her with this knowledge on top of everything else she had suffered. "I daresay I should have found the church deadly dull work, anyway," he said with a shrug.

"But what will you do? How shall we live?"

"Papa had just given me the bank draft that was to cover my tuition at Oxford," he said, patting his breast pocket. "It should cover an ensign's commission just as well. Would you be willing to follow the drum with me, Claudia? It would not be a luxurious existence—not by any means—but we would be together, and no one need know that we are not truly man and wife. The enlisted men wouldn't care in any case, while as for the officers—well, since Lord Buckleigh never took you to London, the likelihood of encountering anyone who would know the truth would be slight. Will you come with me?"

"Yes, Jamie, with all my heart," she said, eyes aglow beneath their bruises.

He took her left hand and slid his lordship's wedding ring off her finger, then withdrew the signet ring from his little finger and with it replaced the other. "I, James Matthew Pennington, cannot take thee, Claudia Elizabeth Runyon Buckleigh, as my lawfully wedded wife, but I promise nonetheless to love you, comfort you, honor, and keep you in sickness and health; and, forsaking all others, to keep only to you so long as we both shall live."

Her fingers tightened about his. "I, Claudia Elizabeth Runyon Buckleigh, cannot make to you vows which I have already made to another, but I promise that I shall love you as well as any wife could ever love her lawful husband, and that I shall never, ever give you cause to regret the sacrifices you have made for me."

"As if I ever could!" said Jamie, and sealed his vow by kissing her with as much feeling as he dared, given the condition of her abused lips.

At last they broke apart, and Jamie rose reluctantly to

his feet. "I wish I might allow you to rest longer, but I dare not linger. At any moment, Lord Buckleigh may realize you have flown and set out in search of us."

He took her by the arms and lifted her to her feet, then stared with horror at the shawl on which she had been sitting. A bright red stain, dotted with clots of a darker red, spread across the green and gold paisley print. He looked behind Claudia, and saw the stain mirrored on the back of her skirts. He had younger sisters still in the schoolroom, so he knew about a young woman's monthly flow, but surely this was too much. Was it possible for a woman to lose so much blood every month and still survive? Unless, of course, the blood was not hers alone . . .

"Claudia," he said in a strangled voice, "Is that—are you—are you going to have a baby?"

She looked at the spreading stain on the shawl, and although her gaze was filled with sadness, it held nothing of surprise. "Yes," she whispered, then added sadly, "at least, I was."

* * *

March 1809
Somersetshire

Having posted his letter to London the next morning, Pickett had only to fill the hours until he might expect to receive a reply. He decided to begin his investigations with a visit to Tom's widow.

"Shall I come with you?" Julia offered, after being informed of his plans for the day. "I should not want to interfere, of course, but it would be quite proper for me to pay a call of condolence. I was married long before Papa hired poor Tom, but I remember him well as Lord Buckleigh's stable hand, for he would take charge of my horse every time I rode over the downs to visit Claudia."

Pickett shook his head. "Thank you, my lady, but I think I had best make this call alone."

Her face fell, and he resisted the urge to change his mind. He had reason to believe her family might be more deeply involved than she knew, although at the moment he failed to see exactly how this connection might dovetail with murder. Until he received a reply to his letter, he thought it best to keep his wife at a distance from his investigations. It was curious, in a way; he'd never had anyone to confide in except for his magistrate, who had never expected to be told every detail of his investigations, much less the minutiae of his life. Before he had met Lady Fieldhurst, he had never realized he was lonely. Ironically, now that he had made up his mind not to confide in her, he realized how much he had come to treasure an intimacy that went far beyond the physical.

"Very well, John, if that is what you wish." Her crestfallen expression brightened as a new thought occurred to her. "I know! Mama intends to take a basket to Tom's widow and children tomorrow afternoon following the inquest. Shall I accompany her, and report back to you anything she says—Tom's wife, that is, not Mama—that I believe may be significant?"

"An excellent notion," he said, relieved to grant her this

innocuous involvement in the case. She might even discover something useful; it would not be the first time. "By the bye, don't fret if I haven't returned in time to take a nuncheon with you. I may stop by the Pig and Whistle after I leave Tom's house. If so, I'll get something to eat there."

Julia heaved an exaggerated sigh. "I see I am going to dwindle into one of those unfortunate females whose husbands spend all their time in taverns," she said mournfully.

Pickett caught her about the waist and pulled her close. "I think you know better than that," he said, and bade her a lingering farewell.

As Tom had a wife and family, the groom did not live above the stables like many a bachelor of his profession, but had a modest house at the edge of the village. Although the cottage was small, it was neat and well-kept, with curtains at the tiny windows and fresh thatch on the roof. Pickett knocked on the door, and a moment later it was opened by a boy of about ten who stared at him with mingled fear and suspicion.

"Good morning," Pickett said. "May I see your mama?"

The boy's eyes narrowed warily. "Who wants to know?"

"John Pickett."

"You're from up at the big house."

Sir Thaddeus's house was surely not the only big house in Norwood Green. Nor, for that matter, was it likely to be the largest, for Lord Buckleigh's ancestral home was almost certainly bigger. However, Pickett correctly assumed that to the boy, the "big house" meant the one where his father had been employed. He nodded.

"I am married to Sir Thaddeus's daughter, but I am also a Bow Street Runner, from London. If your mother will allow me, I should like to try and discover who m—" Murder was such a harsh word, too harsh, surely, for the ears of a child mourning his father's violent death. "—who did this terrible thing to your papa."

To Pickett's surprise, the boy shut the door in his face. He stood there debating whether or not to knock again when it was opened once more, this time by a female with a baby on her hip and a toddler clinging to her skirts. She must have been very nearly Julia's age, but Tom's widow, while not unattractive, looked older, worn down as she was with labor and childbearing and, now, the death of her husband. Pickett wondered what would happen to the family, now that its breadwinner was gone.

"Mrs.—" Too late, Pickett realized he had never heard the groom's last name. "Tom's wife?"

"Aye. My Tommy says you'rre goin' to discoverr who killed his fatherr," she said with the burred "r's" so prevalent in West Country speech.

"With your assistance, ma'am, I would like to try."

"Come inside, then."

Pickett did so, stooping to pass through the low doorway. He found himself in a square room that served as both sitting and dining room, not unlike the larger of his own two rooms in his Drury Lane bachelor lodgings. Here, however, a woman's touch was evident, from the pewter plates neatly arranged on a shelf above the table to the bright rag rug before the fireplace, upon which two more children played, both of them younger than Tommy but older than the clinging toddler who hindered his mother's steps.

She sat down on one of the two mismatched chairs placed before the fire, and gestured for Pickett to take the other. He did so, and immediately one of the two children got up from the rug and waddled over to his chair, leaning against his knees and gazing up at him with unconcealed curiosity.

"What a fine fellow you are," said Pickett, although in fact he had to guess at the gender of the child, who still wore long skirts. "My name is John. What's yours?"

"Billy," said the child, and Pickett breathed a sigh of relief at having not given offense to a little girl. The boy raised his arms and Pickett, correctly interpreting this gesture, picked up the child, settled young Billy on his lap, and tried not to think of the children he would never have with Julia.

"First, Mrs.—" There it was again, his ignorance of the woman's name. Fortunately, she saw his dilemma and took pity on him.

"Pratt. Martha Pratt."

"Mrs. Pratt, let me say how sorry I am for your loss."

Martha Pratt gave a cursory nod, and Pickett could hardly blame her. She was left alone with five children and no visible means of support; words, however well meant, had no power to assist her.

"Have you any idea why anyone might do such a thing to your husband? Had he any enemies, or was there perhaps someone who might fancy himself with a grudge against him?"

Mrs. Pratt shook her head. "No, sir, not that I know of. In fact, things was goin' right well for us. See that bonnet?"

Pickett, not quite sure what Mrs. Pratt's millinery had to do with anything, nevertheless followed her gaze to a flower-bedecked bonnet of plaited straw hanging from a peg near the door.

"Tom come home with that for me just three days ago—paid five shillin's for it, and it still almost a full month till quarter day! I scolded him for a spendthrift, but he said all our money worries was about to be over. I thought maybe Sir Thaddeus had given him a rise in his wages, but Tom just laughed and shook his head." Her face clouded. "I wonder if it would be wrong of me to wear it to his funeral, it bein' so cheerful and all."

"I think he would be pleased to know you liked his gift well enough to honor him by wearing it," Pickett said, and was rewarded by a weak smile.

"To honor him. Aye, that's what I'll do."

"But about this money your husband expected to come into," Pickett said, steering the conversation back into more productive channels. "He gave no indication as to its source? An inheritance, perhaps, or a new business venture?"

She shook her head. "No, nothin' like that. Whatever it was, it was a secret, and one he were right proud of." She sighed and ran work-worn fingers through the toddler's curls. "I guess we'll never know now."

Privately, Pickett was not ready to concede defeat on

that point just yet. "I realize this is painful for you, but can you tell me about your husband's last days? Places he went, people he might have seen?"

"That's easy, leastways the place is. After dinner he liked to look in at the Pig and Whistle. He weren't a drunkard, mind," she added quickly. "It's just, well, a man who works all day wants to relax, and that's not easy with a houseful of chillurn underfoot."

Pickett wondered if the departed Tom would have been as understanding, had his wife expressed a similar desire for time away from her children, and decided probably not. Still, he suspected that, like Lady Runyon where Claudia was concerned, Martha Pratt would not be receptive to any implied criticism of her own departed loved one.

"And had he gone to the Pig and Whistle on the night before last, Mrs. Pratt?"

"Aye, it was always his habit of a Saturday."

"What time did he return?" Even as he asked the question, Pickett realized it was probably useless, as there was no clock in evidence on which Mrs. Pratt might have read the time.

She hesitated for so long that for a moment Pickett wondered if she intended to answer at all. "I guess you might as well know, for you're sure to find out," she said at last. "Truth is, Tom never come home at all that night. Here I was mad as fire, thinkin' he was with that Sadie, and he was probably dead all along!" Her voice broke and she dabbed her eyes on one corner of her apron.

"Sadie?"

"She what works at the Pig and Whistle. She's always had an eye for a good-lookin' man, mind. Calls herself a barmaid, but *I* could give you another name for her!"

Pickett did not doubt it, but had a feeling that the name she had in mind would not be suitable for the children's ears. She had given him a couple of promising leads, however, so after encouraging her to send word should she recall anything that might shed light on her husband's mysterious windfall, he took his leave and turned his steps in the direction of the Pig and Whistle.

The tavern was an ancient brick building whose broad bow window gave an excellent view of the main thoroughfare through the village. This, and the fact that it also housed the posting inn, led Pickett to believe that its regular patrons would be aware of almost anything that went on in Norwood Green or its environs. He opened the door and went inside. At a table near the fire, a gaggle of older men looked up at his entrance, their conversation suspended in mid-sentence. In one corner, apparently waiting while his horses were changed, a bored dandy sat nursing a tankard and rebuffing the advances of a dark-haired damsel whose low-cut bodice threatened to spill her charms all over the gentleman's table—a circumstance, Pickett reflected with some amusement, which would no doubt disconcert the gentleman a great deal more than it would the female. If he were a betting man, he would take any odds that this was Mrs. Pratt's despised rival, Sadie.

He took a seat at a table near the window, and a moment later the young woman abandoned with a huff of annoyance her fruitless pursuit of the dandy, and flounced across the room to Pickett's table.

"What'll you have, ducky?" she asked in accents far from refined.

Pickett ordered a pint of the local ale, and a moment later she returned with the foam-capped beverage and set it before him on the table with a *thunk*.

"You're not from around here, are you?" she asked, leaning one hip on the table and looking him over with an appreciative gleam in her eye.

"No, I'm just visiting." Then, since he hoped to get information from her without being obliged to fend off unwanted advances, he added, "As it happens, I'm on my wedding trip."

"Weddin' trip?" she guffawed, drawing the attention of everyone else in the place. "I wouldn't have thought Norwood Green was a likely place for a honeymoon."

Pickett grinned somewhat sheepishly in acknowledgment. "No, but my wife's family lives hereabout."

Her eyes widened in recognition. "I know who you are! You're that Bow Street man who's married Sir Thaddeus Runyon's daughter!"

"His younger daughter, Julia," Pickett said with a nod, thinking he had been correct in supposing that not much escaped the notice of those at the Pig and Whistle.

"Brave man, aren't you?" she asked, chuckling.

"Am I?" He stiffened. "Why should marriage to Mrs. Pickett require any degree of bravery?"

Although he had hoped to stay in her good graces in

order to acquire information, he was not about to let her or anyone else slander his wife with impunity. He was conscious of a certain satisfaction at seeing the barmaid squirm uncomfortably.

"No special reason, I'm sure," she demurred hastily. "Only, well, one hears things about her and her first husband—"

"One hears nasty rumors, in London just as in Norwood Green. This murder of Sir Thaddeus's groom, for instance. I'll wager there is no shortage of theories about that."

"No, for there hasn't been anythin' like that to happen here since that business with Sir Thaddeus's other daughter —the older one, Miss Claudia—back in '96."

Pickett was more interested in what had happened to Tom, but since the subject of Claudia Runyon had come up, he decided he might as well learn what he could about the Runyons' "ghost."

"Yes, what happened to Claudia Runyon?" Pickett asked, then added quickly, "I knew there was some scandal, but my in-laws don't talk about it, and of course I don't like to upset them by asking."

"I should say not!" Quite uninvited, she plopped down on the seat opposite and leaned forward to disclose in a conspiratorial whisper, "Whatever they may say about wild animals, everyone here knows that poor Miss Claudia— although she was milady Buckleigh by then—why, she was killed by the vicar's son!"

"Who, Major Pennington?" Pickett exclaimed, feigning shocked revulsion. He suspected her of exaggerating—

certainly there had been nothing in Jamie's reception at church to suggest that "everyone" believed him guilty of murder—but he had no desire to still the barmaid's tongue by challenging the accuracy of her assertions, so long as those assertions did not concern his wife.

"Aye, though he hadn't yet joined the army, mind you, so he was still young 'Mr. Pennington' back then. He'd been in love with her ever since she left the schoolroom, and when she married Lord Buckleigh, he took her off and killed her in a jealous rage!"

"I was under the impression that her body had never been found," observed Pickett.

"No doubt he threw her into a gorge—no shortage of those up in the hills, you know. What's certain is that they quarreled over tea, for there was broken china flung all over the place, and then when her horse come back to the big house without her, a search party went out, but all they found was her weddin' ring lyin' on the ground, and her shawl caught on a bush. All bloody it was, too," she added with a decisive nod, as if this damning evidence quite clenched the matter.

"Does it not seem a bit, well, odd, that having had such a row in the drawing room, she should decide to leave the mess behind and go out riding?"

"As to that, well, I'm sure I couldn't say," she admitted grudgingly. "I don't pretend to understand the ways of the Quality."

"And now Sir Thaddeus's groom has been found dead," Pickett said, seeing there was nothing new to be learned about the mysterious disappearance of Claudia, Lady Buckleigh. "It would appear the Runyons have had more than their share of trouble."

"Aye, some are sayin' the family is cursed, what with their older daughter dyin' like that, and then their younger—well, but you know all about that, don't you? Still, it seems to me that any curse would strike the family itself, not their servants."

Pickett could find nothing to argue with in this assumption and, having no great faith in curses in any case, decided to try a different approach.

"About this groom, Tom Pratt: were you acquainted with him?"

The barmaid sat up and eyed him belligerently. "What's that supposed to mean?"

Pickett gave her a look of wide-eyed innocence. "I only assumed that, given the popularity of the Pig and Whistle, there must not be many people in the village unknown to you."

"Well, that's true," she admitted, unbending slightly. "Tom did come in here three or four times a week, and almost always on Saturday night. And no wonder, him havin' a nagging wife and a houseful of brats."

The groom's children had not seemed particularly bratty to Pickett, nor had Martha Pratt seemed like a nag; in fact, if the flowered bonnet was anything to judge by, Tom Pratt had been quite devoted to her. He knew better than to make this observation aloud, however. "And this past Saturday? Did he seem, I don't know, different in any way? Fearful of his life, perhaps?"

"No, indeed! In fact, he was happier than I'd seen him in many a long day. Come into money, he had, or was about to—buyin' drinks for everyone in the place and spendin' like a drunken lord."

"And he didn't say where his sudden good fortune had come from?"

She shook her head. "Several folks asked him, but he just shut his mummer and wouldn't say a word." Her expression grew pensive as a new thought occurred to her. "There was one thing that was curious, though. As the drink flowed more free, the toasts got more and more rowdy. At one point Tom raised his mug and said, 'To milady Buckleigh, the founder of our feast!' It was that odd, since her ladyship had only just returned from her honeymoon and hadn't done nothin' yet, nor planned to, so far as I'd heard."

"Could he have been toasting the memory of the first Lady Buckleigh, perhaps?"

"Maybe," she said doubtfully, "but it sure didn't sound like it."

"Still, if he was drunk—"

"Oh, he weren't fallin'-down drunk, only about half seas over," she said.

"Perhaps he—"

"*Sadie!*" From behind the bar, the taverner bellowed at his errant serving maid. "Sadie, quit hobnobbin' with the customers and get to work, girl!"

Sadie rolled her eyes and got up from the table.

"I beg your pardon," Pickett said. "I've taken too much

of your time."

"Any time, ducky," she said, waving away his protests. She leaned down (giving Pickett an unobstructed view of her rather formidable cleavage) and whispered, "And listen here: any time you get tired of a 'lady' and want a 'woman,' you just come and ask for Sadie!"

Having reduced Pickett to blushing incoherence, she strutted across the room with much swaying of hips.

9

*Which Features an Inquiry
into the Death of Tom Pratt*

H e had withdrawn from her, Julia reflected, and she was not quite sure why. It was not that her husband was brusque, or even neglectful; in fact, when he had returned from the village he had kissed her with all the tenderness she might have wished. And yet there was something troubling him, something he refused to share with her. She felt a wholly irrational annoyance with Tom Pratt for getting himself murdered and thus intruding upon what was supposed to have been their wedding trip. At least, she assumed it was Tom's murder on his mind; better that, she supposed, than the discovery of her four hundred pounds per annum or, worse, their visit to the nursery and the brutal realization that he would never have children of his own. After a morning spent with Tom's widow and her brood, however, it would have been hardly surprising if his thoughts had taken such a turn.

Pickett's curious preoccupation continued into the

evening, to such an extent that even her mother noticed it. "The boy has no conversation to speak of," Lady Runyon complained under her breath, when her belabored attempts to engage him in dinnertime conversation evoked only mono-syllabic replies.

"No doubt this inquest is on his mind," Sir Thaddeus noted. "Tell me, Mr. Pickett, what can we expect upon the morrow?"

Pickett sat up straighter, roused at last from his reverie. "I will be very surprised if the jury returns anything other than unlawful killing by person or persons unknown." He glanced at Julia. "I'm sorry you had to be the one to find him, my lady. I wish you were well out of this."

She gave him a reassuring little smile. "It's all right, John. At least I shall only be giving evidence. It is not as if I myself were on trial."

"I should think not!" Sir Thaddeus declared, bristling. "Don't know why my word can't be sufficient. After all, we both saw the same thing. And so I told Buckleigh, be he son-in-law or no."

"Lord Buckleigh doesn't make the rules, Papa," Julia pointed out.

"In general, the more witnesses there are, the better," Pickett said. "One may notice something another did not."

Lady Runyon shuddered delicately. "I refuse to have murder discussed at the dinner table," she announced. "Tell me, what do you think of the new Lady Buckleigh? I found her to be a rather colorless little creature myself, and can only wonder at Lord Buckleigh's finding her an acceptable replacement for our poor Claudia."

"I doubt his lordship sees her as a 'replacement,' Mama," Julia protested. "After all, he waited more than a dozen years to marry again."

"A pretty little thing, but timid as a mouse," Sir Thaddeus put in. "Merchant's daughter, of course. I daresay she's afraid to open her mouth for fear of saying the wrong thing."

All eyes turned to Pickett, and he hesitated, weighing his options. As he saw it, anything he said would be held against him. If he were to praise Lady Buckleigh's bashful beauty, it would no doubt be perceived as a slight against her predecessor; any denigration, on the other hand, would be seen as presumption on his part for criticizing his betters.

"I think," he said at last, "that I would do well to follow Lady Buckleigh's example and refrain from comment."

Sir Thaddeus gave a bark of laughter. "Wise man, Mr. Pickett!"

"Wise, indeed," Lady Runyon agreed. "What a pity you could not have acquired this wisdom in time for the Brantleys' dinner party."

This home thrust was delivered with a hint of a smile, however, which Pickett felt to be a good sign—the first he had received since making her ladyship's acquaintance. "Yes, ma'am," Pickett agreed with feeling. "I flatter myself that I rarely make the same mistake twice, so I shall hope to do better next time."

"For my part," Julia observed, "I should be pleased to see more people err on the side of kindness. It seems to me that most social *faux pas* result instead from those trying to put themselves forward in some way."

"Alas, too true," conceded Lady Runyon. "One has only to think of Lady Buckleigh's mother for proof. I blushed for poor Lord Buckleigh at the wedding, for her manners were positively common! Whatever your sins, Mr. Pickett, at least no one could call you *encroaching*."

"Thank you, your ladyship," Pickett murmured, catching his wife's eye and giving her a wink.

After dinner, the family repaired to the drawing room, where Julia was persuaded to entertain on the pianoforte. She recruited Pickett to turn the pages of her music (prompting Lady Runyon to admit grudgingly, when pressed by her husband, that they did make a handsome couple, seated side by side on the bench with their heads together, although she could not quite like the way Mr. Pickett braced himself with one hand on the back of the piano bench lightly touching Julia's hip, which in Lady Runyon's opinion was tantamount to a public embrace), and in this manner the family passed a desultory evening until the butler arrived with the tea tray. As the inquest was to begin promptly at nine the next morning, they did not linger afterwards, but sought their respective bedchambers to prepare themselves for the morrow's unpleasantness.

"John, is something troubling you?" Julia asked as soon as they had reached the bedroom and closed the door behind them.

"Why do you ask?"

"That is *not* an answer," she said sternly. "You seem distracted and, oh, I don't know, distant in some way."

"Your mother paid me what might be interpreted as a compliment," Pickett said. "Truth to tell, I don't know quite what to make of it."

Julia smiled, but refused to be diverted. "Yes, I don't doubt it, but your curious preoccupation had begun long before then. Tell me, is something wrong?"

"Not wrong, precisely, just—puzzling."

"Something to do with Tom's death?"

"Perhaps. I'm not quite certain yet."

She sat on the edge of the bed and patted the mattress invitingly. "If you would care to confide in me, I should be glad to listen."

"I wish I could, my lady, but I dare not just yet. If I should tell you, and then I should be wrong"—he shook his head—"as soon as I know for certain, I'll tell you, I promise. But even so—" He broke off abruptly.

"Even so what?" she prompted.

"Even so," he said with a sigh, "you may not like it."

* * *

The foursome arose early and walked together to the village, Sir Thaddeus and Lady Runyon leading the way while Pickett and Julia brought up the rear. Pickett wore the black tailcoat he'd bought a year earlier for giving evidence at the Old Bailey in London, and Julia had chosen the most sober of the gowns she had packed for the journey. In fact, this peach-colored creation was not very sober at all in spite of its brown velvet piping and matching spencer, but she could not have worn black even if she had anticipated the need for it: during their week of newly wedded bliss in

140

Pickett's Drury Lane flat, she had piled all her black mourning gowns onto the grate in a symbolic (if expensive) gesture he had wholeheartedly approved. He himself had set the match.

He smiled a little at the memory and she, seeing the slight twitch of his lips and assigning a wholly erroneous interpretation to it, said drily, "I'm glad one of us is enjoying this."

He shook his head. "Nothing of the sort, my lady. I was just recalling why you aren't wearing black, like your mother." He bent a sharp look down at her. "Are you worried about the inquest?"

"Not worried, precisely, but I can't deny that it does bring all the ugliness following Frederick's death back to mind. But it will not be so bad this time." She gave him a brave little smile. "After all, this time I have you."

"You had me then, too. You just didn't know it."

She had known he had admired her, of course; she could hardly have failed to do so, for he'd had a habit of becoming rather endearingly incoherent in her presence. Still, she had no objection to a bit of lighthearted flirtation with her husband to distract her thoughts from the unpleasant duty that lay before her.

"Did I, indeed?" she asked, peeping coyly up at him from beneath her lashes.

He flexed his arm, giving a little squeeze to her hand as it rested in the curve of his elbow. "From the moment I first saw you."

"You'd best stop that, Mr. Pickett," she scolded,

although the gleam in her eye said quite the opposite. "It cannot be proper for me to appear at a coroner's inquest blushing like a bride! What will the good people of Norwood Green think?"

"Perhaps they will recall that you *are* a bride," he pointed out, but forbore to continue this mutually satisfying conversation until they could do so in privacy.

For privacy was certainly not to be found in Norwood Green that morning. The entire village, it seemed, had turned up at the Pig and Whistle, where the inquest was to be held. Even Lady Runyon, whom Pickett had assumed would not wish to attend so vulgar a gathering, had insisted upon supporting her husband and daughter throughout the ordeal —her son-in-law, Pickett assumed, could fend for himself.

Still, he felt a pang of sympathy for Lady Runyon as they entered the tavern just in time to hear, in the silence that fell at their entrance, one villager chortle gleefully, "—Not this much excitement since that yaller-haired Runyon chit disappeared." The man was immediately shushed by his neighbor, but the damage was done. If anyone in Norwood Green had forgotten the Runyons' family history, they certainly remembered it now, and their interest in the new arrivals increased exponentially.

The Pig and Whistle had been transformed since Pickett's visit the previous day. Chairs had been arranged in a line against one wall, and here sat a coroner's jury of seven good men and true. The tables had been pushed against the opposite wall, and the remaining chairs arranged in rows. Most of these were full, save for a few in the front row reserved for those who were to give evidence, as well as those who were present in some official capacity: Lord Buckleigh, as Justice of the Peace, held a position of prominence, as did another man whom Sir Thaddeus pointed out to Pickett as the sheriff, and a tall, white-haired individual identified as the physician. Jamie Pennington, tight-lipped, sat next to his parents in the second row, while immediately behind him, Martha Pratt and her brood took up almost an entire row, with two children on each side of their mother while the youngest held pride of place on her lap. In the row behind her, Lady Buckleigh sat between a stout, ruddy-complexioned yet well-dressed man and woman who were almost certainly her parents. The rest of the chairs were taken up by the local gentry, many of whom Pickett recognized from the Brantleys' dinner party, while the overflow crowd sat on the tables or leaned against the walls. As he studied the widow and her wide-eyed, frightened children, it occurred to Pickett that in the unlikely event that Tom had played his wife false with Sadie the tavern maid, it was unlikely that Mrs. Pratt could have avenged herself even if she had felt so inclined: it would have been very difficult for her to commit murder with five children in tow.

As for Sadie, she had dressed for the occasion with what Pickett supposed passed for sobriety in her opinion, her low-cut bodice supplemented with a kerchief tucked into the neck. Apparently feeling his eyes upon her, she looked up at him and winked. Despising (not for the first time) his tendency to blush, Pickett turned away abruptly and seated himself in the front row beside his wife.

The principal players now having taken their places, the elderly coroner, Mr. Hughes, rose to his feet and delivered himself of a rambling and barely audible speech. By those few phrases which were comprehensible ("inquiry into the death . . . Tom Pratt . . . body found on Sunday last . . ."), the assembly was given to understand that the inquest was now underway.

". . . Now call . . . employer, Sir Thaddeus Runyon."

Sir Thaddeus, correctly interpreting this as his cue to take the stand (the stand, in this case, being a single chair positioned at the front of the room and turned so that it faced the crowd), heaved himself out of his chair and, after being properly sworn in, sat down in the witness's chair and regarded the coroner with a faintly combative stare.

"Well, Hughes, let's get on with it."

Far from being intimidated, the coroner's chest swelled, and his whole demeanor changed. The years seemed to fall away, and instead of the elderly man muttering under his breath, the barrister who once appeared before the Assizes seemed to emerge as from a long hibernation.

"Sir Thaddeus Runyon," he announced in ringing tones, "you were the employer of the deceased, were you not?"

Sir Thaddeus nodded. "Aye, that I was."

"In what capacity did the deceased serve you?"

"Dash it, Hughes, everyone in the village knows that!"

"Just answer the question, if you please."

Sir Thaddeus gave a huff of annoyance. "Oh, very well. Tom Pratt was my head groom."

"And how long had he served you in that capacity?"

144

There was a moment's pause while Sir Thaddeus performed a few mental calculations. "Two years. For the three years prior to that he was my stable hand, having come to me from Brantley, who'd taken him on in '96, after Lord Buckleigh let him go."

A murmur arose from the crowd as the old-timers recalled the strange disappearance of Sir Thaddeus's elder daughter. In the aftermath of the search that had turned up no sign of the girl but a gold ring and a blood-soaked shawl, a distraught Lord Buckleigh, having no one else he could hold accountable for the loss of his wife, had dismissed the stable hand who had saddled her horse and thus unwittingly allowed her to take the fateful ride that had ended her life.

"Silence, if you please!" commanded the coroner, and the crowd obeyed, however reluctantly. "Now, Sir Thaddeus, would you say Tom Pratt was a good employee?"

"Aye, I'd not have trusted my horses to him otherwise," the squire said.

"When did you notice that he was missing?"

"I didn't, really. It was my stable hand, Will, who said he'd not been in all day. Mind you, I thought that odd, and unlike him."

"Did you have any reason to suspect foul play?"

"No. I just reckoned he'd had too much to drink the night before, and was sleeping it off."

"You will now tell us how you came to discover his body."

Sir Thaddeus rubbed the side of his nose. "Well, now, after church, I went riding with my daughter and her husband—showing him about the place, you know—"

"This would be your younger daughter, Miss Julia?"

"It could hardly be my elder, could it?" growled Sir Thaddeus. "Of all the asinine questions! Anyway, as we approached the rise where my land abuts the Layton place, my daughter and I raced to the big oak that marks the corner of the property. I reached the oak first, and found the poor fellow lying there dead. I didn't have time to warn my daughter away, for she reached the tree immediately afterward."

"Describe, as nearly as you can remember, how you found the body."

"Dash it, man, I just told you!"

"You misunderstand, Sir Thaddeus. I want you to tell me what you saw—what the body looked like."

Sir Thaddeus scowled. "He looked like a dead man. His throat was cut, by gad! How do you think he looked?"

A smothered sob from the widow broke the silence.

"Beg pardon, ma'am," Sir Thaddeus said sheepishly, "but, well, there it is."

The coroner pressed on, undeterred. "How was he lying? On his belly, or on his back? Think, man!"

"On his back," Sir Thaddeus said decisively. "I could see his face, and the, er, wound."

"And he was already dead at that point?"

"Undoubtedly."

"Did you check to make sure? Feel for a pulse, for instance, or anything of that nature?"

"Why should I have done? I tell you, the fellow was

dead! There was blood all over the place. I was more concerned with shielding my daughter. She's seen too much of bloodshed over the past year."

"Thank you, Sir Thaddeus, you may return to your seat." Turning back to the crowd, he announced, "Miss Julia, er, Lady Fieldhurst—that is, Mrs. John Pickett, you will please take the stand."

Julia gave Pickett's hand a quick squeeze, then took her father's place at the front of the room.

"Mrs. Pickett," said the coroner after administering the oath, "you reside in London, do you not?"

"Yes, Mr. Hughes."

"You will please state your business in Somersetshire."

"I am visiting my parents."

"You are newly married, are you not?"

She inclined her head. "Less than a fortnight, in fact."

"Curious sort of wedding trip," observed the coroner.

"I say, Hughes!" Sir Thaddeus bellowed. "Are you suggesting my daughter came all the way from London to murder my groom? Why, she didn't even know the fellow!"

"Sir Thaddeus, I must ask you to be quiet. I am not suggesting any such thing." He turned back to Julia. "Is it true what your father says, that you did not know the deceased?"

Her brow puckered. "Not exactly. I do remember Tom Pratt being employed in Lord Buckleigh's stables, for I used to see him when I rode over to visit my sister. She was married to Lord Buckleigh, if you recall."

Every eye seemed to turn to where Lord Buckleigh sat

in the front row, his countenance as stiff and pale as if turned to stone.

"Yes, thank you, Mrs. Pickett," the coroner continued. "Now, would you say your father's account of the discovery of the body was accurate?"

"Yes, it was."

"Did you recognize the deceased?"

"No, for I had not seen him in many years."

"How many, would you say?"

"Not since my marriage—my first marriage, that is. Six years, almost seven."

"Very well. And having seen the body, what did you do? Did you perhaps faint? I am sure no one would blame you."

"I certainly did not! I beckoned to my husband to hurry and join my father and me."

"Why this eagerness for Mr. Pickett's company at such a time, Mrs. Pickett? If you will forgive me, the presence of a dead body hardly seems conducive to wedded bliss."

"My husband is a Bow Street Runner, Mr. Hughes. In fact, it was he who cleared me of suspicion in the violent death of my first husband. Had it not been for him, I should very likely have gone to the gallows. Can you suggest anyone whose presence might be more desirable in such circumstances as my father and I faced?"

"Let me remind you that I am the one doing the questioning, your ladyship—that is, Mrs. Pickett. Why, may I ask, did you have to beckon to him? Why did he not participate in this race?"

Julia frowned. "I fail to see what that has to do with anything."

"Nevertheless, you will answer the question, if you please."

You don't have to answer any question you don't want to, he had told her. While she had no desire to hold him up to public ridicule, she was sure her husband would tell her not to create suspicion where no need for it existed.

"My husband is London bred, Mr. Hughes," she said. "He has had little opportunity for riding."

"I beg your pardon, Mrs. Pickett. I was unaware that there were no horses in London."

A smattering of laughter greeted this remark, and Julia controlled her temper with an effort. "I should have said, rather, that Mr. Pickett has had little time for leisure, being occupied instead with keeping the King's peace."

"In other words, he has to work for his bread, is that correct?"

"Yes," she conceded. "Much like yourself, Mr. Hughes." *But he is worth a dozen of you,* she added mentally.

"Very well, then, let us have this Bow Street Runner of yours up here and see what he has to say. You may step down, ma'am." He turned to face the crowd. "Mr. John Pickett, you will please take the stand."

10

Which Brings the Inquest to a Conclusion

As Pickett rose and approached the chair vacated by
his wife, he felt a subtle shift in the general atmo-
sphere of the tavern. Everyone present seemed to sit up
straighter, a few even leaning forward in their seats as if
fearful of missing a single word. Pickett was not quite
certain whether they were interested in the evidence he was
about to give, or simply curious for a good look at the
plebeian specimen who had married the squire's daughter.
Curiously enough, now that every eye in Norwood Green
was upon him, he found it bothered him not at all. He knew
himself to be more experienced in the workings of the law
than anyone present (with the possible exception of the
coroner himself, but Pickett suspected the Old Bailey in
London saw depths of depravity that a lawyer in the rural
Assizes never dreamed of) and likewise more qualified to
offer testimony. The knowledge gave him confidence and,
had he but known it, his demeanor as he approached the
makeshift witness stand was such that more than one young

woman was forced to acknowledge with a pang of envy that perhaps Julia Runyon had not disgraced herself so very badly, after all. His eyes found hers as they met in passing, and he gave her the quickest of winks before seating himself in the chair that was still warm from her—

He wrenched his mind away from ideas wholly inappropriate for a court of law, and fixed his gaze on the coroner, who scowled at Pickett as if he could read his thoughts.

"You will state for the jury your name and direction, please," Mr. Hughes commanded.

"John Pickett of Drury Lane, London."

"You are, as your wife claims, employed by the Bow Street Public Office?"

Pickett nodded. "I am."

"For how long, if you please?"

"In my present position, almost a year and a half. In total, five years."

Mr. Hughes scowled again, regarding Pickett with suspicion. "You seem very young for such a position, if I may say so. How old are you?"

Pickett suppressed a pang of annoyance at yet another reference to his age, or lack thereof. "I will be five-and-twenty next week." He saw his wife's eyebrows lift slightly, and realized she had not known of his approaching natal day.

"A young man of promise, it would seem," observed the coroner.

"Or fortunate in my mentor," Pickett suggested.

"Tell me, if you will, of your own part in Sunday's

excursion. I understand you declined to race with your wife and father-in-law."

"It is a wise man who knows his own limitations," Pickett said with a hint of a smile.

The coroner nodded. "Just so. Describe for the jury your arrival on the scene."

"By the time I reached the tree that had been designated as the finish line, Sir Thaddeus had already dismounted, and was bending over what appeared from a distance to be a rock. I could tell at once that something had happened to distress my wife, and before I could ask her what was the matter, Sir Thaddeus informed me that his groom, Tom, was dead. Since I am not without experience in such matters, I took it upon myself to examine the body."

"You will describe your findings, if you please."

"Certainly." Pickett cast an apologetic glance at the groom's widow. It was perhaps a good thing that the infant on her lap had begun to whimper and squirm, distracting the woman from the grisly testimony he was obliged to give. "The body of Tom Pratt lay face-up in a pool of blood. His throat had been cut almost from ear to ear. I took the liberty of touching the man's wound, and found the blood dry. I saw no sign of a weapon, and so with Sir Thaddeus's assistance, I moved the body in order to look underneath it."

"And did you find anything beneath the body?"

Pickett shook his head. "No, sir, nothing."

The littlest Pratt began to cry in earnest. There was a stirring in the little assembly, and somewhat to Pickett's surprise, Lady Runyon stood and addressed a few whispered words to the widow, then took the child from her and carried the infant from the tavern, bouncing it in her arms and cooing consolingly.

"Now, Mr. Pickett," the coroner said, once the distraction was removed, "what did you do next?"

"I took the liberty of searching the man's pockets."

The coroner, it seemed, could not approve this course of action. "You appear to have taken a great many liberties, Mr. Pickett," he said, frowning.

"If there is a man in Norwood Green better qualified to do so, pray point him out to me, and I will beg his pardon."

"Yes, well, what's done cannot be undone, I suppose," Mr. Hughes grumbled. "Having made this search, you might as well tell us what, if anything, you found."

"I found a number of coins in his pocket, including guinea pieces totaling more than ten pounds."

A murmur of speculation greeted this pronouncement, as everyone in Norwood Green apparently had his or her own idea as to how Tom Pratt might have come by such a sum.

"Was there anything else?" the coroner asked.

Pickett shook his head. "No, although I looked quite thoroughly."

"I have the impression you had something particular in mind. What, exactly, were you searching for?"

"After Sir Thaddeus confirmed my own suspicions that a groom would be unlikely to carry so much money on his person, I looked for some explanation: a bill of sale, a blackmail note—"

It seemed the vicar's son was not the only one who could set the cat amongst the pigeons, Pickett reflected as pandemonium broke out. Unfortunately, this attempt to force the blackmail victim (if victim there were) into betraying himself by some manifestation of fear or guilt appeared doomed to failure. Most of the faces in the crowd seemed to register expressions of scandalized glee. His wife looked back at him with a worried question in her eyes while her father, seated beside her, scowled at this implied slur upon his household. Lord Buckleigh appeared bored with the whole procedure, while Lady Buckleigh followed the proceedings with a gaze more courteous than rapt, as she might regard a matter of local interest that in no way concerned herself. Major Pennington looked straight ahead, his brow puckered thoughtfully.

"A blackmail note?" Mr. Hughes echoed sharply, raising his voice to be heard over the hubbub. "Did you have any reason to suppose that Tom Pratt was blackmailing anyone?"

"When a man turns up dead with an unexplained amount of money upon his person, the possibility must always be considered," Pickett pointed out reasonably.

"Just answer the question, if you please," the coroner chided.

Pickett sighed. "No, Mr. Hughes, I had no reason to believe Tom Pratt was blackmailing anyone. How could I? I didn't know the man."

"That will be enough, Mr. Pickett," the coroner said, scowling. "You may return to your seat."

As Pickett rose from the witness's chair, a smattering of applause broke out and a few people even slipped out of the tavern, eager to be the first to spread the news that Tom Pratt had been up to some sort of skullduggery. It appeared the crowd was pleased with Pickett's performance, even though he suspected the coroner did not share their opinion.

"Will Mr. Robert McAdams please take the stand?" called Mr. Hughes.

The tall, white-haired man in the front row came forward.

"Mr. McAdams," the coroner said, after the oath was administered, "you will state your credentials for the jury, if you please."

"Other than the fact that I have treated all of them, and their families as well, at some point or other?" the new witness said with a hint of a smile. Seeing that the coroner was not amused, he continued in a more serious vein, "Very well, Mr. Hughes. I studied both anatomy and surgery at the University of Edinburgh, and trained in medicine under the eminent physician Mr. Geoffrey Woodford. I have practiced medicine and surgery in Norwood Green for more than thirty years."

"And you examined the body of Tom Pratt after it was fetched back to his house, is that correct?"

The physician nodded. "It is."

"Tell us, if you will, the results of that examination."

"Certainly. It was very clear to me that Tom Pratt died from a catastrophic blood loss following the laceration of the jugular vein."

The coroner nodded, as this was exactly what he had expected to hear. "And, in your professional opinion, is it possible that he could have inflicted such an injury himself?"

Mr. McAdams frowned. "Committed suicide, you mean? Impossible! Given the length and depth of the wound, any man making such an attempt would be dead, or at least unconscious, before he could finish the job."

"Did your examination yield any evidence of a struggle?"

The physician was silent for a long moment. "Not a struggle, no, but there were certain signs that may be interpreted to lend credence to the theory of willful murder."

"You will describe these signs for the jury, if you please."

"A shock of the victim's hair—"

"Mr. McAdams, it has not yet been established that Mr. Pratt was anyone's 'victim.' Refrain, if you will, from naming him thus."

"Very well, Mr. Hughes," the doctor said, acknowledging this command with a nod. "A shock of *Mr. Pratt's* hair stood up from his scalp, and when I examined his head for any sign of injury, I discovered that a small but significant amount of hair around it had been broken off, sometimes pulled out by the roots."

"Let me remind you that Mr. Pratt was in his thirties. A great many men begin to lose hair at that age."

"I am well aware of that, Mr. Hughes, for I was once numbered among them. But the hair loss that accompanies aging usually follows a particular pattern, thinning at the crown and receding from the forehead and temples. That pattern was entirely missing in this case."

"Very well, we will accept that Tom Pratt was not going prematurely bald. But have you considered that he might have been driven to tear his own hair out? After all, the man had five children."

A smattering of laughter greeted this suggestion, and all eyes shifted to Martha Pratt, who seemed to find nothing humorous in it.

Mr. McAdams sighed. "I suppose he might have done the damage himself. Or another might have stood behind him, seized his hair, and pulled, thus jerking his head back and giving better access to his throat."

"Perhaps, Mr. McAdams, but since the purpose of this inquest is not idle speculation, we will hear no more of it. You may step down."

The physician did so, to the obvious disappointment of the crowd, who had enjoyed his evidence almost as much as they had Pickett's. The next person called to give evidence was the dead man's widow, who issued sternly whispered instructions to her children before taking the chair vacated by the doctor.

"Your name, please?" the coroner requested.

"Martha Watkins Pratt," was the barely audible answer.

"You were married to the deceased for how long?"

"Eleven years come June."

"State for the jury, as well as you can remember, your husband's movements on Sunday."

"That I can't do, sir, for I never seen him on Sunday."

The coroner frowned. "Very well, then, what did he do on Saturday?"

"He went to work for Sir Thaddeus, same as always," she said, nodding in the direction of her late husband's employer. "He didn't come home after, but that weren't unusual, it being a Saturday. I reckoned he'd gone to the Pig and Whistle, but then he never come home that night at all."

"Was it unusual for him to remain out all night?"

"Oh yes, he always come home soon or late—in spite of certain folks tryin' to get him to stay," she added with a darkling glance at Sadie.

"I see," Mr. Hughes said, nodding. "Mrs. Pratt, did your husband have any enemies that you were aware of?"

She shook her head. "No, sir."

"And what of this money that was found in his pockets? Have you any idea of its source?"

"Beg pardon, sir?"

"Its source," the coroner repeated. "Do you know where he came by it?"

"No. I knew he'd come into money of a sudden, but he didn't say from where. I reckoned Sir Thaddeus must've give him a rise in wages. Right excited about it, he were. He even bought me this here bonnet without my even asking for it," she added, apparently feeling some explanation was required for her wearing such festive headgear on so solemn an occasion.

A murmur of feminine approval greeted this pronouncement, and one woman went so far as to poke her husband in the ribs and deliver a whispered scold. Pickett suspected the man would be shopping for a bonnet in the near future.

"Thank you, Mrs. Pratt, and may I say how sorry I am for your loss," the coroner concluded.

He allowed the widow to return to her seat, and called Sadie, the tavern maid, to take her place.

"You will please state your name for the jury."

"Sarah Cooper, sir, but everyone calls me Sadie."

"You work at the Pig and Whistle?"

"Yes, sir."

"Aye, but she earns more on her back!" called a masculine voice from the crowd, to much raucous laughter.

Mr. Hughes addressed the assembly in stentorious tones that would not have disgraced the Old Bailey. "Let me remind all of you that a man is dead. It is the purpose of this inquest to discover why. If you are incapable of conducting yourself in a manner befitting the occasion, I must ask you to leave."

As no one wanted to miss out on the most excitement Norwood Green had seen in years, a hush fell over the taproom.

"Now, Miss Cooper, I want you to recall, if you will, the night of Saturday last. Was Mr. Pratt among the customers at the Pig and Whistle that night?"

"Aye, he were," she said, nodding.

"Was there anything unusual in his behavior?"

"Aye, it were unusual, all right! He were buying drinks all 'round like he was King Midas himself."

"I see. And did he offer any explanation for this uncharacteristic generosity?"

"He said he'd come into money, and all his worries was over, but he didn't say how."

"What time did he leave that night?"

"Eleven o'clock. I remember particular, on account of he kept saying he had to meet someone at midnight. I thought it was an odd time to be making plans, myself."

"Odd, indeed," the coroner agreed. "Was he drunk?"

Her brow puckered in thought. "Not falling down drunk, only about half seas over."

"Dutch courage, perhaps?"

She shook her head, setting her ebony curls bouncing. "No, for he didn't seem afeared at all."

"Thank you, Miss Cooper. You may step down."

Once Sadie had returned to her seat, the coroner addressed the jury. "Let me remind you that this is not a trial. No one is being accused of murdering Tom Pratt, nor are you to make any speculations as to who might have done so. You will render a verdict of natural causes, accident or misadventure, suicide, or unlawful killing."

The seven men of the jury shuffled out of the taproom and into the adjoining private parlor, where they did not deliberate for long. Scarcely ten minutes had passed before the door to the parlor opened and the jury filed back into the room.

"Have you reached a decision?" Mr. Hughes asked.

The seven nodded, and one, a shopkeeper apparently designated the spokesman, said, "We have, sir. We find Tom Pratt the victim of unlawful killing by person or persons unknown."

11

*In Which Mr. and Mrs. Pickett
Pursue Separate Lines of Inquiry*

I must say, it all sounds rather disappointing," Lady Runyon said with a sigh as they set out across the village green. She had not returned to the inquest since taking charge of the youngest Pratt child, and it had been left for her husband and daughter to fill her in on the testimony she had missed, as well as the jury's verdict. "It seems to me that we know no more than we did before. What will happen now?"

Sir Thaddeus rubbed the side of his nose as he considered the question. "With all those children to feed, it's unlikely poor Martha Pratt can afford the expense of an investigation. I suppose it will all depend on Buckleigh, and I'm afraid the death of a groom won't hold that much interest for him, he being just returned from his honeymoon. I daresay the whole thing will be forgotten in a fortnight."

"Er, perhaps not," Pickett said.

Sir Thaddeus bent a sharp look on his son-in-law.

"What do you mean?"

"I told his lordship that I should be pleased to look into Tom Pratt's death. He seemed to have no objection, so . . ." He shrugged his shoulders.

"Why should you do such a thing?" demanded the squire. "Buckleigh may have just returned from his honeymoon, but by gad, you're still on yours."

"Yes, and the murdered man was connected with my wife's family," Pickett pointed out. "It seemed the least I could do, under the circumstances."

Sir Thaddeus regarded his son-in-law with something akin to approval. "I'm obliged to you, Mr. Pickett."

"What will happen to the man's family now?" Pickett asked. "Mrs. Pratt and the children, I mean?"

Sir Thaddeus sighed. "I suppose I'll settle some sort of pension on the man's widow, or offer the oldest boy a place in the stable. Either way, it won't approach the wages poor Tom was earning—to say nothing of whatever windfall the fellow thought he'd found."

"I shall take a basket to Martha Pratt this afternoon," Lady Runyon announced with the air of the Lady Bountiful, leading the pragmatic Pickett to wonder just how long she expected this contribution to last, given that it would have to stretch to feed no fewer than six mouths. "Julia, would you care to accompany me?"

"Yes, thank you, Mama," Julia said, exchanging a loaded glance with her husband. "John, if you have no objection—?"

"None at all," Pickett assured her. "I'm sure I can find

something to do with myself."

In fact, he already knew exactly what he intended to do, and only wished he might have done it twenty-four, or even forty-eight, hours earlier. And so, after Julia and her mother had set out for the Pratts' cottage, he changed back into his old brown serge coat and his own sturdy walking boots (reflecting as he did so that, since his introduction to his wife's family, he seemed to spend an inordinate amount of time changing his clothes), and set out for the gamekeeper's cottage he'd been obliged to abandon so precipitously on the day the groom's body had been discovered.

No smoke rose from the stone chimney today, nor was there any other sign of life. With a growing sense of fore-boding, he knocked on the door and, receiving no answer, turned the knob and found that the door opened in his hand. It was, he thought, almost as if someone had wanted him to come inside.

"Hullo?" he called into the stillness. "Is anyone there?"

There was no response, not even the muffled sound of movement in the loft above that he'd heard on that previous occasion. Just as before, he armed himself with the poker from the fireplace—it was not at all the done thing to bring a pistol along on one's honeymoon—and started up the stairs.

There was no interruption this time, from Major Pennington or anyone else. He reached the top of the stairs and found himself standing in a space minimally furnished as a bedchamber. A curtain of faded muslin hung in the single window, and an old iron bedstead with a thin mattress had been positioned beneath the eaves. A cracked and spotted mirror hung from a nail driven into a beam, and beneath it a pitcher and bowl of chipped porcelain stood on a rickety washstand. The furnishings were far from luxurious, but the cottage contained everything necessary for an extended stay.

Everything, that is, except the person who had lived here as recently as two days earlier. Whoever it was—and Pickett had his own suspicions about that—had cleared out, removing any personal effects that might have offered some clue as to the identity of the recent resident. Heaving a disgusted sigh, Pickett crossed the loft to the window and twitched the curtain back. From this height, he could look out across the downs over which he had ridden on Sunday afternoon with Julia and her father. Nearer at hand, he noticed a tree with a low-hanging limb near the front corner of the cottage, the churned-up ground beneath bearing signs of recent disturbance by a horse's hooves.

He turned away from the window and let the curtain fall, then drew up short. Just before the faded muslin had blocked out the sun, he had seen a brief flash of light on the boards of the floor. Without turning back to the window, he stretched his arm behind him and lifted the curtain. Sunlight shafted across the scrubbed planks, and there, near the top of the stairs, a tiny pinpoint of light gleamed. Fixing his gaze on the spot so as not to lose it, he released the curtain and slowly crossed the room until he found what he'd missed upon first entering the loft. He stooped and picked up a small metallic object that had fallen between the floorboards. It was a single golden earring from which a pearl dangled. He allowed it to roll this way and that in the palm of his hand, watching as the light from the window played along the gold wire.

"I could be wrong," he said into the stillness, "but I don't think gamekeepers' wages run to pearls."

* * *

Julia and her mother loaded Lady Runyon's basket onto the seat of the squire's dog cart and, with Julia at the reins, set out for Tom Pratt's cottage. They arrived to find Mrs. Pratt looking strained and weary—small wonder, Julia thought, after what she had endured over the last three days.

"That's right kindly of you, your ladyship," Martha Pratt told Lady Runyon, accepting the basket she offered. "Won't you come in?"

Neither Julia nor her mother wished to impose on the woman at such a time, but to reject her offer of hospitality would be perceived as a slight, as if they considered themselves too good for their present company. They entered the modest abode and took the chairs Mrs. Pratt indicated. The children were conspicuous by their absence, and Martha Pratt explained that they were in the loft above, taking their naps.

"I haven't yet thanked you for your help at the inquest, your ladyship," the widow continued once they were seated.

"It was no trouble at all," Lady Runyon assured her. "I was glad to be of assistance."

"My Sally usually isn't so fussy," Mrs. Pratt said by way of apology. "I can't think what came over her."

"Children seem to have a way of sensing when their

parents are distressed," Lady Runyon observed, then added with a little smile, "Besides having an instinct for knowing when they must be still and quiet, and doing precisely the opposite."

"Lud, yes," agreed Mrs. Pratt, her countenance lightening somewhat. "When I think of some of the things mine have done in church, I wonder Mr. Pennington hasn't barred the door against us."

There followed a series of reminiscences about the misdeeds of their various offspring, and Julia, although unable to enter into the conversation, had to admire her mother's way of finding common ground between two women of very different stations. As the conversation continued along these lines, however, she began to feel like an outsider. Her mother and Mrs. Pratt, for all their dissimilarities, belonged to a sisterhood of which she could never be a part. Now, as Mrs. Pratt poured into her mother's sympathetic ear her fears for her children's futures, Julia could not but be struck by the unfairness of it all. Here was Martha Pratt with five children to feed and no visible means of support, while she, Julia Pickett, had four hundred pounds per annum with which to provide for a child, and could not have even one.

"And the worst of it," concluded the widow Pratt, "is that they may never know what happened to their Papa. Whoever killed my poor Tom might never have to pay for his crime."

"I wouldn't be so sure of that," Julia spoke up at last. "Mr. Pickett is very good at his work, so I believe there is every chance that he will be able to discover who did this terrible thing to your husband."

The widow's response was not what she might have hoped. "I hope your man will watch his back," she said doubtfully. "We've all seen what this fellow is capable of."

It was an unfortunate observation. For the first time, Julia wondered if it was a mistake on her husband's part to let anyone know of his interest in the case. If the killer were to learn of his investigations, would he dismiss the Bow Street Runner on account of his youth (as others had done, to their sorrow), or would he feel compelled to eliminate a potential threat? The image of Tom's dead countenance with its staring eyes and slit throat loomed before Julia's consciousness, and she had a sudden and horrifying vision of her own husband meeting the same fate. Bile rose to choke her, and she scrambled to her feet.

"Pray—pray excuse me," she stammered, and all but ran from the cottage.

Outside the house, she paced the tiny garden, taking deep but ragged breaths, and considered her options. Once again it was borne in upon her that her husband's occupation was potentially dangerous. But his present commitment, she reminded herself, was not an obligation to his magistrate, Mr. Colquhoun, or even to the King, whose peace he was charged with keeping. Instead, it was a voluntary pledge.

Could she persuade him to give it up? She feared not, for quite aside from hoping to win her parents' approval, he seemed to consider himself under an obligation to them to obtain justice for their servant.

Failing in persuasion, could she perhaps seduce him into abandoning the idea? This approach might prove more effective, and would certainly be more pleasant to attempt, regardless of the result. Still, the fact that they were staying in her parents' house was undeniably problematic in carrying out such a strategy. No, her arguments would have to be limited to the verbal variety, and she admitted that they were unlikely to move him. He was not a gentleman born, but he had his own brand of honor, and it would certainly be satisfied with nothing less. She smiled a little at the thought, conceding that she would not have changed him even if she could.

Gradually she became aware of a soft whimpering sound, and realized she was not alone. She looked about for its source, and saw a small boy curled up behind a shrub growing beside the cottage door.

"I beg your pardon," she said. "I didn't see you there."

The boy made no reply, but sniffed loudly and wiped his nose on his sleeve.

"Was Tom Pratt your papa?" She knew the answer even as she asked the question, for the lad bore a striking resemblance to his mother.

"Yes'm, your ladyship."

Julia sat down on the front stoop. "Oh, I'm not a ladyship, not anymore. I'm a 'missus,' just the same as your mama." In a more serious tone, she added, "I'm sorry about what happened to your papa. I know you must miss him."

The boy nodded sadly. "Aye, I miss him, but he don't miss me none. He hated me, you know."

Julia was rather taken aback by this pronouncement, but quickly rallied. "He hated a fine big boy like you? How could he?"

"It's true," the lad insisted, but he crawled out from behind the bush and sat down on the stoop beside her, which she considered a good sign. "He yelled at me. That was the last time I ever saw him," he added, and a fat tear rolled down his round, smooth cheek.

She put a consoling arm about the boy's thin shoulders. "He may have yelled at you, but that doesn't mean he hated you. I suppose it seems very unfair, but sometimes parents are cross and out of sorts with their children for reasons that have nothing to do with the children themselves."

The child shook his head. "Papa wasn't cross and out of sorts. He was happy, saying as how we were gonna be rich."

Julia recalled certain evidence given at the inquest that morning, and wondered if the child might have stumbled upon something that could have a bearing upon his father's death. Certainly Tom would have lashed out at the child if he had unwittingly done something to put the man's newfound wealth at risk. "Rich? That must have made your father very happy indeed!"

The lad nodded. "Yes, ma'am, most days he was. But then I come into his and mama's room to fetch him for dinner, and he yelled at me. Told me to get lost, he did."

"How very odd," Julia murmured. "What was he doing when you came to fetch him?"

"Nothing, leastways not that I could see. He was just bent over the grate, like he'd just put something on the fire."

A bill of sale, or a blackmail note . . . Her husband's words at inquest came back to her. If this child had, however innocently, interrupted his father in the act of burning something incriminating, it could certainly have provoked a tongue-lashing.

"There it is, then," she declared confidently. "He could not have been angry with you, for there was nothing in your actions, or in his, to provoke such a response. Depend upon it, he was thinking about his sudden windfall, and trying to decide how best to spend it. Should he buy something frivolous, or spend it on something the family needs?"

"He'd just come in with a new bonnet for Mama," the boy put in.

"Was it the one she wore this morning? I noticed it, and thought how pretty she looked in it. But what if, after he'd bought a gift for your mother, he'd discovered that one of the shutters needed replacing, for instance, or the chimney should be cleaned? I can assure you, such things always happen at the worst possible times."

"You think Papa might have been worrying about that, and thinking he shouldn't ought to have spent the money?"

"Very likely, for grown-ups fret over the silliest things, you know. Why, your mama is quite probably worrying herself frantic about where you are at this very moment, when anyone can see that you are quite safe sitting here with me!"

He glanced rather guiltily behind him toward the rear of the cottage, leaving Julia to infer that he had made his escape through the back door.

"I don't want Mama to worry," he said.

"No, indeed! I should return to my bed if I were you, and dwell no more on those cross words of your father's. Think of happy times you had together instead."

"Yes, ma'am." The boy stood and, after a moment of awkward hesitation, leaned forward and planted a wet, smacking peck on her cheek. "Thank you, missus."

"You're very welcome."

Julia remained in the garden until she judged the boy must be safely back in his room, then re-entered the cottage, where she found her mother and Mrs. Pratt had not yet exhausted the subject of motherhood. Lady Runyon glanced up at her daughter's entrance, and something in Julia's face made her rise to her feet. "I fear we have trespassed on your hospitality much too long, Mrs. Pratt. I shall stop by from time to time to see how you and the children are faring."

"We'll be all right, your ladyship," the widow said. "It won't be easy, I know, having five mouths to feed, but I can't be sorry to have the children. Tom is gone, but at least I've got something to remember him by."

Julia and her mother said their goodbyes, and mounted the dog cart for the drive back to Runyon Hall.

"Julia, my dear, is something wrong? Have you taken ill?"

Julia shook her head. "No, Mama. That is, I felt unwell for a moment, but I am quite recovered now."

Her recovery suffered a setback when they reached the house and discovered that Pickett had gone for a walk from which he had not yet returned. Julia told herself she was merely impatient to report her findings concerning the Pratt child, but deep in her heart she knew better. *I hope your man will watch his back . . . We know what this fellow is capable of . . .* Martha Pratt's words echoed in her head, and were not entirely silenced even when Pickett came walking up the gravel drive some half an hour later. Still, it was not until they retired to their room after dinner that they had an opportunity for private conversation.

"I hope you were not too bored this afternoon, being left to your own devices while I was gone with Mama," Julia said apologetically. "What did you find to do with yourself?"

Pickett shrugged. "Oh, this and that," he said vaguely, then picked up the coat he had discarded and took something from its inside breast pocket. "Tell me, my lady, do you recognize this?"

She looked at the gold and pearl earring in the palm of his hand. "Why, yes, I do! It belonged to my sister. Did you find it upstairs?"

"In a manner of speaking."

"I confess, I am surprised. Papa gave a pair of them to Claudia for her eighteenth birthday. I had assumed she must have taken them with her when she married Lord Buckleigh. Shall you give it to Mama? I wonder if she will be pleased to have it, or wounded that Claudia did not find them worth taking with her to her new home."

"I would be obliged to you if you said nothing to your mother just yet," Pickett said.

Julia regarded him with a puzzled frown, aware that there was more to this simple request than he was letting on.

"Certainly, if that is what you wish."

"But tell me about your visit to Mrs. Pratt," he urged. "Did you discover anything of interest?"

She was well aware that he was trying to change the subject, but since she had indeed discovered something of interest, she was willing to let him have his way, albeit not without making him pay a price. Slowly and deliberately, she sat down at the dressing table and began plucking the pins from her hair.

"I think you may have been right when you suggested Tom may have been involved in blackmail," she said, regarding his reflection in the mirror. Briefly she described her encounter with the Pratt child, including the boy's conviction that his father had hated him, and how he had arrived at such a conclusion.

"And Tom was burning something?" Pickett asked sharply, wrenching his attention away from the sight of golden curls tumbling over bare white shoulders. "Did the boy say hair—*where*—it had come from?"

"No, for he didn't actually see his father putting anything on the fire," she reminded him. "Only that he was bent over as if he had been interrupted in the process of doing so. But what reason could anyone have for blackmailing a groom?"

"I think you have it backwards, my lady. I think Tom was the one doing the blackmailing."

She bristled at this assertion. "One doesn't like to think of persons one knows doing such a thing."

"One doesn't like to think of persons one knows being

173

murdered, either, but it happens—as you, of all people, should know. And how well, really, did you know Tom Pratt? What could anyone of your class truly know of his life, or of what demons might have driven him?"

"Yes," she said slowly, conceding the point. "Yes, I see what you mean. And the letter, or whatever it was that Tom was burning?"

Pickett considered the question. "It could have been a reply from his victim, telling him what he might do with his threat, but given what happened later, I should think it more likely that the victim agreed to his demands and offered to meet him at a particular time and place. And we both know what happened to Tom when he got there."

She shuddered at the memory, an involuntary move-ment that did nothing for Pickett's powers of concentration. "Poor Tom! If he did indeed do such a thing, it was very wrong, of course, but I can't help feeling a bit sorry for him, having his dreams of wealth for his family go so disastrously awry. Whatever he had discovered, someone wanted very badly for it to remain a secret."

"Yes, which brings us to the next question: what person or persons might Tom have come in contact with who would have secrets worth paying—or killing—to keep? I think we can eliminate your father's stable hand, Will, as a suspect, for he would be unlikely to have the kind of money that might tempt a blackmailer." Seeing the stricken expression on her face, he added in a gentler tone, "My lady? Julia, what are you thinking?"

"Papa goes to London twice a year. He calls them

business trips, but Mama says they are actually for—for amorous purposes." Seeing him nod in understanding, she exclaimed, "John! You knew?"

"I've known ever since I investigated Lord Fieldhurst's murder. Your father came riding to your rescue long before word could have reached him in Somersetshire. When I confronted him with the discrepancy, he admitted he'd already been in London, and what had brought him there. But," he added quickly, "if you're thinking Tom might have been blackmailing him over it, and been murdered for his pains, let me put your mind at rest. If, as you say, your mama already knew of his activities in the Metropolis, then the blackmail theory falls apart. Why would your father pay to keep a secret that his wife already knew?"

"Yes, but he didn't know that she knew." Julia slipped off her shoes, then lifted the hem of her dress to her knees, untied her garters, and began peeling off her stockings.

"Perhaps not," Pickett said, observing this operation with interest, "but if she knew that he didn't know that she knew, then—then—then—"

"Then what?" she prompted.

"Never mind," he said, and pulled her roughly into his arms.

"In any case," she continued a bit breathlessly, when she could speak at all, "it appears Papa knew that *you* knew, so that alone must be enough to absolve him."

Pickett was ready to consign Sir Thaddeus, Lady Runyon, and indeed the entire population of Norwood Green to the devil, but suspected his wife would not welcome further advances on his part until she'd had her say.

"Aside from the burning of what may or may not have been a blackmail note," he said, "did you accomplish anything else at the Pratts' house?"

"Well, I hope I was able to reassure the little Pratt boy as to his father's affections," she said, smiling at the memory. "Indeed, I believe I must have done, for I received a kiss on the cheek for my pains."

Pickett regarded her with mock severity. "And you think kissing witnesses is an acceptable way to conduct an investigation? I can see I'll have to keep a closer eye on you in the future."

"I didn't kiss a witness; I was kissed *by* a witness," she retorted playfully. "Why, John, don't tell me you intend to be *that* sort of husband! When you, of all people, must know that I have a decided partiality for younger men."

It was just as she had suspected: seduction was infinitely more enjoyable than argument, although she did not deceive herself as to its effectiveness. She supposed she should be relieved that he did not apparently believe her father to be implicated in Tom's death. Still, whether it was the memory of her mother's words regarding a wife's duty to see that her husband's needs were met, or the visit with the fatherless Pratt clan, Julia found herself lying awake long into the night, thinking of the children she and her husband would never have.

Something to remember him by . . . As he lay sleeping in her arms, she ran her fingers through his tangled brown curls and found the small spot on his scalp where the hair was just beginning to grow back in. This, along with the occasional headache, was all that remained of the attack that had felled him outside Drury Lane Theatre.

But what if the next attempt on his life should prove to be successful? The only thing that might make such a loss bearable was for her to have some part of him to keep—not a lock of his hair (she already had that, for the physician had allowed her to have the hair he'd cut away from the wound), but a living, breathing piece of himself to cherish. It was the only thing that might assuage her grief—and the only thing she knew she could never have.

There was another way, of course, but the child that would result would contain no part of herself. Would she want to be a mother under such conditions? Could she love such a child for its father's sake, or would she be unable to look at it without searching for some sign of the woman who had borne it?

You are worrying about nothing, she scolded herself mentally. He was perfectly safe. It was not as if he had never investigated a murder before. And yet murder in the Metropolis seemed so anonymous; such things were not supposed to happen here, among people she knew, in the place where she had grown up.

She wriggled closer to her husband, finding reassurance in the warmth of his breath against her face and the feel of his heartbeat, strong beneath her hand. But when she closed her eyes, it was Tom's face that swam before her, gruesome in death.

12

In Which John Pickett's Suspicions Are Confirmed

T he following morning was taken up with Tom Pratt's funeral, which Pickett attended along with Sir Thaddeus. The graveside service itself was uneventful, which was neither more nor less than he had expected. As far as his investigation into the groom's death was concerned, there was very little Pickett could do until he received a reply from his magistrate. He dared not act on his suspicions without some confirmation, for if he should prove to be mistaken, the whole of Norwood Green would think him a raving lunatic.

Julia, sensing his restlessness although she could only guess as to its cause, suggested they go for a walk and pay the promised call upon Miss Milliken, her former governess. He readily agreed, for in addition to the fact that he had no more productive use for his time, this outing would allow him to escape the critical eye of his mother-in-law, at least for a time. Lady Runyon, when told of their plans, did not protest the loss of her son-in-law's company, but requested her daughter to purchase for her a paper of pins from the village emporium. Julia acceded to this request, and set out for the village with Pickett in tow.

By unspoken consent, they did not discuss the solemn events of the morning. Instead, Julia kept up a steady flow of anecdotes from her childhood in which Miss Milliken had played a part. It was clear to Pickett that a deep bond of affection existed between the teacher and her former pupil— a circumstance which, upon their arrival, made the little governess's welcome (if it might be so called) all the more baffling. When the maid of all work announced them, Miss Milliken, seated on a worn sofa of crimson brocade, shot to her feet as if ejected from a catapult.

"My dear Julia!" exclaimed the little lady, twisting her handkerchief in arthritic hands as her gaze darted nervously about the room. "And Mr. Pickett. What a surprise to see you!"

"Why, Millie, how can you say so, when you invited us to call only three days ago?" Julia chided her, smiling. "Have you forgotten us so quickly?"

"Of course not! That is, I had not *forgotten*, precisely, but I had not expected to see you quite so—oh dear, how I do run on! Will you not—will you not sit down?"

She indicated the sofa she had just vacated, but with such obvious reluctance that the gesture would have been comical, had it not been so bewildering.

"No, we must not," Julia said, laying a restraining hand on Pickett's arm. "I see we have come at a bad time. We will return another day—tomorrow, perhaps, or the day after?"

"No, no," Miss Milliken insisted. "It is not a bad time at

all, merely that I am ill-prepared for company, and—"

"Company?" cried Julia in mock indignation. "Surely I cannot be considered that, Millie! But I would not want to put you to any inconvenience, so if you would prefer that we postpone our visit to a later date—"

"Not at all, my dear, I am delighted to see you, of course—"

"Yes, I can see that," Julia noted with tongue planted firmly in cheek.

Still, in spite of the little lady's obvious discomfiture, Miss Milliken appeared to be so mortified by her own ungraciousness that in the end Julia and Pickett were obliged to trespass upon her hospitality. They seated themselves side by side on the sofa and received the cups of tea which the governess poured with trembling hands.

"I suppose you were present at Tom Pratt's funeral this morning, Mr. Pickett," Miss Milliken observed, pouring a cup for herself. "A sad business, that. Tell me, what do you make of it?"

"It's too early to say as yet," he demurred.

A soft, scarcely noticeable vibration over their heads was more felt than heard, as if someone were crossing the floor of the room above. Before Julia could ask if she had other visitors, Miss Milliken rushed into speech.

"Very wise of you, Mr. Pickett, for it is dangerous to go jumping to conclusions." She pitched her voice at a volume which would have made Julia wonder if her former precep-tress were losing her hearing, had this apparent disability not been entirely lacking when they had encountered her outside the church only three days earlier. Given the suddenness of its onset, Julia suspected Miss Milliken had also heard that faint noise from overhead and was attempting to cover it— or, perhaps, was warning her mysterious guest that she was not alone. Poor Millie! Her futile efforts would have been amusing, had she not been in such obvious distress.

Julia decided to take pity on her. She set her cup back into its saucer still half full, and bethought herself of the errand she had promised to run for her mother. Pickett was quick to follow her lead, and as a result, they left the house scarcely more than five minutes after they had entered it.

"Well!" exclaimed Julia after the door was shut behind them. "What do you make of that?"

"I would say your Miss Milliken wasn't at all pleased to see us," Pickett said. "In fact, I think she would have denied us the house if she could have fabricated some excuse for doing so."

"Yes, indeed, which is most unlike her! In fact," Julia added, her eyes narrowing in suspicion, "if it were anyone but Millie, I should have said she was hiding her lover upstairs."

"Or someone else's," Pickett put in cryptically.

"I beg your pardon?"

He shook his head. "Never mind."

They called next at the emporium for the pins Lady Runyon had requested, having failed to reach any satisfactory conclusion regarding Miss Milliken's strange behavior. Julia selected a paper of pins and had taken them to the counter when she was hailed by a fellow customer.

"You—Miss Julia—Sir Thaddeus's other girl, isn't it?"

Turning, Julia saw a stout female in a frilled and be-ribboned white muslin gown more suited for a schoolroom miss than a woman of at least forty. Even as she recalled seeing this same female seated beside Lady Buckleigh at the inquest, Julia noticed Lord Buckleigh's young bride cowering behind her mother, blushing furiously as she raised anguished eyes to Julia's. Recalling her mother's words regarding the new Lady Buckleigh's parentage, Julia took pity on the girl and did not give the vulgar woman the set-down she deserved.

"Yes, I am Mrs. John Pickett, Sir Thaddeus's younger daughter," Julia said, lifting her chin and raising her eyebrows ever so slightly. "I fear I haven't had the pleasure, Mrs.—?"

Alas, Lord Buckleigh's new mama-in-law was impervious to hints. She seized Julia's gloved hand and pumped it heartily. "Mrs. Gubbins, ma'am, Edna Gubbins. This here's my daughter Betty, Lady Buckleigh."

"Lady Buckleigh." Julia dipped a curtsy, feeling rather sorry for the girl who was so ill-suited to fill her sister's shoes. "Of course I recall meeting you at Mrs. Brantley's dinner, although we had no chance to do more than exchange greetings. How do you do?"

"My Betty says your poor sister was the first Lady Buckleigh," put in Mrs. Gubbins before her daughter could answer.

"Hardly the first, Mama," protested the current holder of the title. "The barony has existed for centuries."

"Yes, well, Mrs. Pickett will know what I mean, for she used to be a 'ladyship' herself, or so I hear," continued Mrs. Gubbins, undaunted. "And here we were, thinking his lordship would never marry again, after having his heart broke! Mind, he'd been sniffing 'round my Betty ever since he met her at an assembly in Wells last September. I was afeared he'd try to give her a slip on the shoulder, and that's the sort of thing I don't hold with, nor never shall, be his lordship never so high and mighty! You could have knocked me over with a feather when he showed up at our doorstep one day asking Mr. Gubbins for our little girl's hand! I was that proud to think of my Betty as a 'ladyship', I nearly busted my stays!"

She laughed gustily at her own witticism, putting the aforementioned stays once more at risk. "As for you"—she turned to Pickett and wagged a stubby finger at him—"Betty tells me you cooked your goose right proper, offering to take her in to dinner right under Mr. Brantley's nose. Lud, I'll bet that put their noses out of joint! Still and all, it was right thoughtful of you, what with my poor girl feeling that out of place amongst the nobs, and I'm not sure but what I don't think the better of you for it."

"Er, thank you, ma'am," Pickett stammered.

"Aye, and what's more, I don't doubt my girl would have been happier sitting next to a good-looking young fellow like you, rather than a man old enough to be her father—although I don't say but what my Mr. Gubbins wasn't a handsome one back in the day, so mayhap that Mr. Brantley might have been quite a catch himself, back in his

183

salad days."

Julia, judging it time to put the two mortified subjects of this discourse out of their mutual misery, cast a sympathetic glance at Lady Buckleigh and was chagrined to discover her ladyship casting coy glances at Pickett beneath her lashes.

"And so you are visiting your daughter, now that she and Lord Buckleigh have returned from their wedding trip," Julia observed. "Tell me, Mrs. Gubbins, how long is Norwood Green to enjoy the pleasure of your company?"

"Lud, I don't know—until my girl gets settled into married life, I suppose. Oh, she knows how to hold house, mind you, but I'll not deny our own place was never so fine as Buckleigh Manor! Only fancy, his lordship's house has forty bedrooms! Why, one might sleep in a different room every night for a month!" Her chuckles died abruptly as she recalled her present audience. "But then, you already know that, for your own poor sister was once its mistress."

"Yes, but that was long ago," Julia assured her. "I'm sure all his friends must be glad Lord Buckleigh has found a second chance at happiness with your daughter."

"Aye, he's that happy, he's given her a free rein in redecorating the house," Mrs. Gubbins put in. "And since her father is a linen-draper, she'll not lack for materials to do the thing up right."

Julia made approving noises, but privately hoped Lady Buckleigh's tastes were more refined than those of her mother. "Tell me, Lady Buckleigh, do you plan to replace the carpet on the stairs? I remember my sister Claudia was always tripping over it."

"It's early days yet to be making plans," Lady Buckleigh demurred. "I should not want to offend the good people of Norwood Green by flaunting my rise in the world." Her speaking eyes appealed to Pickett to concur, and her mother, noting this, was quick to seize upon it.

"Aye, I'm sure Mr. Pickett there will agree with you, for you've a lot in common, have you not? I don't doubt the four of you will all become great friends. Although if rumor don't lie, your birth is rather better than Mr. Pickett's, my love. We may lack a fine pedigree, but Mr. Gubbins and I have always been what you'd call respectable."

"I fear Mr. Pickett and I will be fixed in London for most of the year," Julia put in gently but firmly. "And now, if you will excuse us, we must go before Mama begins to wonder what has become of us."

"Aye, you'll give our regards to your mama, will you not? Perhaps Lady Runyon will honor us one day by coming to take tea at Buckleigh Manor."

Julia returned a vague reply, then paid for her pins and all but thrust Pickett through the door before Mrs. Gubbins could think of any reason for detaining them. Once in the village's main street, she turned to her husband and found his shoulders shaking. Her lips curved upward in spite of her efforts to keep a straight face.

"What are you laughing at?" she demanded, having a very good idea of the answer.

"I was just picturing your mother and Mrs. Gubbins sitting down to tea together."

Julia rolled her eyes. "Oh, heavens! Can you imagine?

185

Now I understand why Mama took the news of Lord Buck-leigh's remarriage so hard. Her own daughter replaced with Mrs. Gubbins's child, of all people!"

"She does seem an odd choice for a man in his position," Pickett admitted. "Does his lordship need money?"

Her brow puckered as she considered the question. "Not that I am aware of. Not nearly so badly as he needs an heir, I should think. Perhaps," she added in a curiously flat voice, "perhaps he thought, given the Runyon girls' poor perform-ance in that area, that a girl from the merchant class might prove more fecund."

Pickett took her hand and drew it through the curve of his arm, "Or perhaps he fell so deeply in love with Betty Gubbins that such things as class no longer mattered."

"Impossible," she assured him, giving his arm a little squeeze. "No one does that."

"My mistake," Pickett murmured by way of apology. "You'll have to pardon my ignorance. Remember, my birth is not as good as Lady Buckleigh's."

"For which I am profoundly thankful!"

They returned to the Runyon house smelling strongly (as the butler later confided to the housekeeper) of April and May. This idyll was soon shattered, however, for while Julia went in search of her mother in order to deliver the pins, the butler approached Pickett with a folded and sealed paper.

"Begging your pardon, Mr. Pickett, but in your absence, a letter arrived for you from London."

"What, already?" Pickett exclaimed in some surprise. "The mail is faster than I had any right to expect."

"The letter did not come by post, sir, but was brought by a messenger on horseback."

Pickett's eyebrows rose, but he did not satisfy the butler's curiosity by offering any suggestion as to why such a means of transportation might have been deemed desirable. He merely accepted the letter with thanks and then took it up to the bedchamber he shared with his wife, taking care to shut the door before breaking the seal and spreading the single sheet.

"*My dear John,*" it read, "*I am pleased to know your introduction to your wife's family is going well, although I could selfishly wish you had found them less welcoming, if that would hasten your return to London. I have fulfilled the commission you laid upon me, and although I can't imagine the reason for it, I am taking the liberty of sending a reply by fast courier, assuming that your need is urgent and not trusting to the reliability of the post.*

To answer your question, Major James Pennington has indeed been accompanied on the Peninsula by his wife, who has followed the drum since first he purchased his commission in 1796. I regret that I could find no date for the marriage, nor any information on Mrs. Pennington's maiden name.

If you need anything else, please do not hesitate to ask. In the meantime, I look forward to the explanation which I trust will be forthcoming upon your return to Bow Street. Until then, I remain

Affectionately Yrs,
Patrick Colquhoun, Esq.

Post Scriptum: I don't know if it will be of any use to you in whatever mischief you have got up to, but Mrs. Pennington's given name is Claudia.

Pickett stared for a long moment at this last line.

"By Jove," he breathed, unconsciously echoing the favorite oath of his mentor, "I've got you."

13

In Which John Pickett Confronts the Major

M y lady, I must go out for awhile," Pickett told Julia when he met her going up the stairs as he was hurrying down. "I shall be back in plenty of time for dinner."

"John, what is the matter?" She had the distinct impression that he would have slipped out without telling her, had their encounter on the stairs not prevented him—indeed, that he would have preferred it so. "Is something wrong?"

His hand went instinctively to the pocket of his coat in which his magistrate's letter resided. "Not wrong, exactly. I can't discuss it at present, but I will tell you as soon as I return." He sealed the promise with a quick kiss, and made his escape before she could question him further.

"Coward," she muttered affectionately to his retreating back.

Upon arriving at the vicarage, Pickett asked for Major Pennington and was told, rather disappointingly, that the major was out.

"Ever since he has come back from the Peninsula, he

189

has been out more than in," Mrs. Pennington fretted. "Still, if you would care to wait, he always returns before dinner."

"Now, now, Mary," the vicar chided his wife, "James's whole aim in coming home was to see to his inheritance, and I don't doubt there is a great deal of work to be done there. With my sister's health so uncertain in her last years, I fear the place must be sadly in need of repair."

Pickett had a very good idea of where Jamie Pennington had gone, and he suspected the condition of the Layton estate had very little to do with it. Still, he resigned himself to making small talk with the vicar and his wife until the major returned. Thankfully, he had not long to wait until Jamie arrived, checking in the doorway at the sight of Pickett sitting in the drawing room.

"Ah, there you are, James!" exclaimed his father. "Here's Julia Runyon's young man been waiting for you this age."

"Not an age, surely," Pickett protested. "No more than ten minutes."

"I beg your pardon, Mr. Pickett." In spite of his conciliatory words, it seemed to Pickett that Jamie regarded him rather warily. "How may I be of service to you?"

"I would not want to bore your parents," Pickett said, although he felt certain the vicar and his wife would find the conversation anything but dull. "If there is somewhere we may speak privately—?"

"Of course. The garden is very pleasant this time of day, if you would care to take a turn?"

Jamie gestured toward the door at the rear of the house,

and Pickett followed him outside into a sunny quadrangle bisected with stone-paved pathways along which herbaceous borders blossomed in a riot of spring color.

"Now, Mr. Pickett, to what do I owe the honor of this visit?"

"I was wondering when I am to have the pleasure of being introduced to your wife."

Jamie regarded him with an arrested expression. "I fear you are laboring under some misapprehension, Mr. Pickett. I am not married."

"Quite so, Major. Perhaps a better question would be, when do you intend to tell the squire and his wife that their daughter is alive and well, and has spent the last thirteen years as your camp follower?"

In answer, Jamie Pennington doubled his fist and planted it squarely in Pickett's jaw, knocking him backwards into one of the flowering shrubs.

"I'll take that as a 'never,' " Pickett muttered, rubbing his chin.

"I suppose I must beg your pardon," Jamie conceded grudgingly, offering a hand to pull Pickett to his feet. "I am not in the habit of assaulting guests, but to hear the sweetest creature who ever drew breath described in such sordid terms—"

"Then you do not deny that Claudia Runyon—or, rather, Lady Buckleigh—is very much alive, and living under your protection?"

"No, damn you, I do not deny it! Nor, for that matter, do I owe you an explanation."

"Not me, perhaps, but what of my wife? What of Sir Thaddeus and Lady Runyon? You must be aware that they have mourned Claudia as dead for more than a decade."

Jamie grimaced, kneading the knuckles of his right hand in the palm of his left. Pickett took some satisfaction in the knowledge that he had in some measure given as good as he'd got. "I am aware of it," Jamie admitted. "Believe me when I tell you there was no other way."

Pickett glanced about him, taking in the neat house and its pleasant garden. "Your father seems to enjoy a comfortable living here, yet you gave up the opportunity to succeed him for the rigors of a military campaign on the Continent."

The major's lips twisted in a humorless smile. "I daresay the church would frown on one of its servants living in adultery with another man's wife."

"And in the meantime, Lord Buckleigh and that little Gubbins girl believe themselves to be legally wed," Pickett observed.

"If you expect me to sympathize with his lordship's plight, Mr. Pickett, you are wasting your breath."

"A divorce, then"—Pickett suddenly recalled a chance remark of Julia's earlier that afternoon, and drew in his breath as the truth dawned—"he was beating her, wasn't he? She told people she tripped over the carpet on the stairs, when in fact Lord Buckleigh was beating her."

"Yes. If she'd asked him to petition Parliament for a divorce, he very likely would have killed her." He gave a bitter laugh. "Are you picturing a romantic elopement by moonlight? It was nothing of the kind, I assure you. When I carried her away, she had a black eye, a fat lip, and a couple of cracked ribs. I ask you, Mr. Pickett, what would you have done in my place?"

Pickett thought of the dark days following Lord Fieldhurst's death almost a year earlier, when it appeared that Julia—Lady Fieldhurst, as she was then—would hang for her husband's murder. "I know a little of what it's like," he said slowly, "seeing the woman you love in danger and being powerless to protect her. If your actions had been an option for me, I'm not sure I wouldn't have done the same thing."

"It's those Runyon girls," Jamie said with a rueful grin. "They look up at us with those big blue eyes, and we poor devils are putty in their hands."

Pickett returned his smile, finding nothing to dispute in this observation. "I can only wonder that you brought her back to Norwood Green at all."

"I hadn't planned on doing so, but then my Aunt Layton died, and I was obliged to see to my inheritance. I could hardly leave Claudia alone in Spain, so—" He shrugged.

"So you put her up in the gamekeeper's cottage, where no one would know of her presence."

Jamie inclined his head. "As you say. And it would have been sufficient, had her sister not chosen the worst possible husband, so far as my purposes were concerned."

"There was no thought of pleasing you when we were wed," Pickett retorted with a grin. "But Claudia herself must shoulder part of the blame. My suspicions were aroused by a certain ghost prowling about the premises."

"I told her it was a bad idea," Jamie grumbled. "But having come this far, nothing would do but that she must see her parents and sister again. You gave her a rare turn when she opened the door of Julia's bedroom and found her little sister with a man in her bed!" He chuckled at the memory.

"No more than she gave me," Pickett said, recalling a somewhat later encounter in the nursery. "Who saddled the horses?"

"I beg your pardon?"

"When you made your escape with Claudia. Who saddled the horses?" Pickett asked again.

"Lord Buckleigh's stable hand, Tom—" He frowned. "Look here, Mr. Pickett, what are you suggesting?"

"There is considerable evidence that Tom Pratt was blackmailing someone—someone who killed him rather than continue to buy his silence. I've been at a loss to know what secrets a groom might have known that would be worth paying, or killing, to keep."

"It's true that I paid Tom rather handsomely for holding his tongue thirteen years ago, but he never made an attempt to extort more—and had he done so, I would have told him he might go to the devil! I am not ashamed of what we did. Besides," he added darkly, "if I were inclined to kill anyone, I would not have waited thirteen years—and believe me, Tom Pratt would not have been my victim of choice." Jamie bent and yanked up one of his mother's flowers by the roots, then began stripping it of its petals one by one, giving Pickett the impression that, given half a chance, he would gladly perform a similar operation on Lord Buckleigh's hide.

"Have you inspected the Layton stables recently?"

"No," admitted Jamie, blinking at this seeming *non sequitur*.

"I have," Pickett said. "I found a man's greatcoat drenched in blood."

"That in itself means nothing," Jamie pointed out. "Have you ever seen a mare give birth, Mr. Pickett? It's a messy process, I assure you."

Pickett shook his head. "Aside from the fact that the blood was fairly fresh while the Layton stables have been empty for years, the greatcoat was the sort that would be worn by a gentleman, not a stable hand."

"I see," Jamie muttered as the significance of Pickett's discovery began to dawn on him. "And he's planted it on my own property to try and incriminate me. Damn him!"

" 'He'?" echoed Pickett, certain that he already knew the answer.

"Look here, you must see that if I didn't kill Tom—and I promise you I didn't—there can only be one other person who would have reason to want the man dead. Here's his lordship just returned from his honeymoon and in need of an heir, only his first wife is still alive, so his new marriage is invalid and any children he has with the woman now calling herself Lady Buckleigh will be illegitimate, and thus unable to inherit. If you're Tom Pratt, with a wife and five children to support, who are you going to blackmail: me, or Lord Buckleigh? Who has the deeper pockets or, perhaps more importantly, the most to lose if the secret should come out? No, if you ask me, Claudia's clandestine presence in the vicinity is no more than an unfortunate coincidence. It was his lordship's return, not hers, that spawned this whole scheme of Tom's."

"I hope you're wrong," Pickett said with a sigh, "but I'm afraid you're probably right."

"You hope I'm wrong?" demanded Jamie. "If you had seen Claudia that day, as I had, you would know hanging is too good for his lordship. Are you really so dazzled by a man's rank that you can't see his true worth—or lack of it?"

Pickett bristled in indignation. "I am hardly dazzled by rank! Remember, I'm married to a viscountess," he added for emphasis, conveniently ignoring the fact that he was only just beginning to feel comfortable addressing his aristocratic bride by her given name. "But I'm not at Bow Street any-more, and no longer under my magistrate's authority. When I have sufficient evidence, I'm going to have to apply to the local Justice of the Peace for an arrest warrant."

"Yes, what of it?"

"I daresay you're unaware of it, having been absent for so long," Pickett acknowledged, "but the local Justice of the Peace is Lord Buckleigh."

Jamie let out a long, low whistle and collapsed onto a nearby bench. "In other words, he'll get off scot-free. Some things never change!" he added bitterly.

Pickett shook his head. "Not if I have anything to say to the matter. I told Sir Thaddeus I would look into Tom's death since the murder touched my wife's family. Given Claudia's involvement, my sense of obligation has increased exponentially. Unfortunately, Lord Buckleigh knows of my interest in the case. In fact, I asked his permission to pursue it." He slapped his forehead at the realization of his own naïveté. "Of all the idiotic—I even agreed to keep him informed as to my progress!"

"Don't be too hard on yourself, Mr. Pickett. After all, you had no reason to suspect him at the time. The question is, what will you do now? It seems to me you'll have to tell him something."

Pickett pondered for a long moment. "It is a constant irritant to me that I'm often assumed to be incompetent because of my age, or lack of it. I wonder if I can turn it to my advantage."

"How so?"

"I'm going to question his lordship regarding Tom's murder. No, not about Claudia—I think it best if I don't betray my knowledge of her existence, at least for the nonce—but I can ask him about his acquaintance with Tom, and have him account for his movements on Saturday night after the Brantleys' dinner."

Jamie did not hold out much hope for this examination. "What do you think to accomplish by that, other than setting up his back?"

"Exactly that. He may berate me as an imbecile—in fact, I expect he will—but it's always possible that, finding himself under suspicion, he'll become rattled and betray more than he intends."

"I wouldn't count on it, if I were you," Jamie predicted grimly, idly lashing his boot with the denuded flower stem he still held. "Lord Buckleigh is a cool customer, I'll grant him that much. I only hope you don't turn up under a tree with your throat slit."

Pickett shook his head. "I don't think there's much chance of that. He'll not want to do anything that might lend credence to my suspicions, and my death would only attract the sort of attention he would most wish to avoid. No, better from his perspective to give me a sharp set-down for my pretensions and put it about that I'm incompetent." In a more serious vein, Pickett asked, "You do realize, don't you, that I have to tell Julia? I refrained from doing so until I was certain, but now—" He shrugged. "I can't keep such a secret from my wife."

"I suppose it can't be helped," Jamie acknowledged without enthusiasm, "but I would be obliged to you if you'll say nothing to her parents just yet."

"You need have no fears on that account," Pickett said with feeling. "I wouldn't have that task if you paid me! I don't envy you when Lady Runyon finds out. But if I know anything at all about Julia, she's going to insist on seeing her sister."

Jamie nodded. "Claudia, too, for that matter. If you'll bring Julia to the gamekeeper's cottage tomorrow morning, I can promise the pair of you a warmer welcome than you received today."

"Very well, but will that give you time to remove her from Miss Milliken's house without anyone being the wiser?"

"Now, how the devil did you know about that?" Jamie demanded.

"I'm sure Miss Milliken is a very nice lady, and genuinely attached to her former pupils, but as a co-conspirator, you could hardly do worse! Her every word betrayed her, while as for her demeanor, let's just say that even if I had not already been suspicious, her agitation alone would be enough to make me so. Best get Claudia away from there with all possible speed. Oh, and you may tell her that I found her earring."

Jamie shook his head in bewilderment. "I confess, I'm rather glad to have you on our side, Mr. Pickett. And to think," he added, with a hint of regret for what might have been, "under different circumstances, you might have been my brother."

14

In Which Two Sisters Are Reunited

The walk from the vicarage was accomplished all too quickly, as Pickett tried to form some sort of plan for the inevitable conversation with his wife. How did one break the news that a beloved sister, presumed dead for more than a decade, was alive and well and living in sin with the vicar's son? *My lady, I have some good news and some bad news* . . . No, that wasn't it. He was still groping for the right words when he reached Runyon Hall. He darted a furtive glance into the drawing room (letting out a sigh of relief at finding it empty), then went upstairs to put off his hat and gloves.

It was a tactical error. His wife sat in the wing chair beside the fire, and although she held a book in her hand, it was obvious that her mind was not on the printed page. He wondered how long she had been lying in wait for him.

"At last!" she exclaimed, rising eagerly at his entrance. "I have been—good heavens, John! What happened to you?"

He put up a hand to stroke his tender jaw, where he had

no doubt a bruise was beginning to form. "A little gift from Major Pennington."

"Jamie *struck* you?" she demanded, her bosom swelling in righteous anger.

"Yes, but I'm not sure I didn't deserve it," Pickett confessed, gratified nonetheless at her indignation on his behalf, let alone the interesting effect of this emotion on her anatomy.

"I wish you will tell me what it is all about! I have been waiting this age!"

He tossed his hat and gloves onto the bed and took her in his arms. "I missed you, too," he said, deliberately misinterpreting her.

"Of course I missed you," she insisted, although she gave him the most perfunctory of kisses, "but you must know I have been positively agog with curiosity!"

Something in his expression must have given him away, for her smile faltered, and when she spoke again, it was in a very different tone. "What is the matter, John? Have you found Tom's killer? Is it someone I know?"

He shook his head. "No, it isn't that. Sit—sit down, Julia."

He took her hand and drew her down to sit beside him on the edge of the bed. She raised her eyebrows in ironic expectation, even as she recognized there was no amorous light in his eyes.

"John?" she said again. "What is wrong?"

"Not—not wrong, exactly, but"—he took a deep breath—"you must prepare yourself for a shock, my lady.

It's about your sister, Claudia. She isn't dead after all."

Her expression hardened. "If this is some sort of a joke, I must tell you I fail to see the humor in it!"

"You must know I would not joke about such a thing. I assure you, Claudia is alive and well, and has spent the last thirteen years following the drum under the protection of Jamie Pennington."

She snatched her hand from his and leaped to her feet. "How dare you say such a thing? How dare you sit there and accuse someone you never even knew of—of lying to her family and—and committing adultery—and living in sin— and—and—" Her voice rose in volume and pitch with each of the purported charges.

"You said yourself that she was no saint," Pickett reminded her.

"I said she was not the saint that Mama made her out to be. I never said she was a woman of—of *loose morals!*"

Pickett might have reminded his wife that, on the night they had first met, she had been on the brink of engaging in an illicit liaison of her own, but apparently there was a difference in having a discreet *affaire* and openly living with one man while legally wed to another. It seemed there was a great deal about her world that he did not understand, but a finely honed instinct for self-preservation cautioned him against pointing out this discrepancy. With a sigh of resignation, he stood and folded her in what was meant to be a comforting embrace—or as comforting as one could be, while holding a lady who stood as stiff and straight as a ramrod. "I'm sorry to have to break it to you like this.

Believe me, I wouldn't say such a thing without sufficient proof."

" 'Proof'?" She raised her head and looked up at him, her blue eyes flashing with anger. "What 'proof' can you possibly offer? It's a wicked lie!"

"I have a letter from Mr. Colquhoun, who made inquiries at the War Office on my behalf, and I've just come from the vicarage, where I had the tale from Major Pennington himself." There was also the fact that he had seen—and kissed—Claudia in the nursery upstairs, but this, he decided, could wait until another time.

"*Jamie* said that?" she said wonderingly, detaching herself from his embrace. "Then I suppose there must be no denying it."

Pickett frowned. "In fact, you consider his word more reliable than mine."

"On any other subject, no," she said hastily. "But you never knew Claudia, whereas Jamie adored her, and would never—at least, I *thought* he would never—oh, how could they do such a wicked thing?"

"Perhaps not so wicked after all, once you know the whole story."

He had been uncertain as to just how much of her sister's history Julia should be told, but he knew now that nothing less than the whole truth would suffice. And so he recounted it all, from Lord Buckleigh's cruelty to Jamie Pennington's gallant rescue and the years since.

"Oh, poor Claudia!" she breathed at the end of this recital, and there was no hint of condemnation in her voice.

"Jamie asked that your parents not be told, at least not yet," he cautioned her.

"Good heavens, no! Mama would never understand! But now that I know she is alive, and here in Norwood Green—John, I must see her!"

"And so you shall, tomorrow morning." He took her hand and raised it to his lips, glad to be restored to her good graces. "I knew you were going to say that."

* * *

They left the following morning in some haste, eager to make their escape before Lady Runyon could inquire as to their plans for the day. They need not have wondered, however; Julia's mama was not so fond of her son-in-law as to question his absences. They did not ride, but set out on foot (a fact that probably pleased Lucifer as much as it did Pickett), and reached the gamekeeper's cottage half an hour later. Just as before, a curl of smoke rose from the stone chimney.

"So you were right in thinking someone was staying here!" Julia exclaimed, having readily forgiven her husband in the light of the coming reunion.

"Yes, except for the one day I came to investigate, when she was safely tucked away with Miss Milliken."

"Poor Millie! No wonder she was so distressed by our visit. I wonder Jamie should ask such a thing of her!"

"I daresay he had no one else he could trust, and he knew very well that I would be coming to get a closer look at that cottage, for he had already interrupted me at it once. The major and I have been playing a very nice game of cat and mouse—and I, for one, am glad it's over, for he makes a formidable opponent."

She gave his arm a squeeze. "I suspect he would say the same about you."

They had reached the cottage door by this time, and Pickett gave the knock he and the major had agreed upon. The door swung open, and Jamie Pennington stood in the aperture, grinning at them with his boyish smile.

"Thank God! Claudia has been beside herself for the last hour and more! Won't you come in?"

He stepped back and threw the door wide. Pickett handed Julia over the threshold, and watched the scene unfold as his wife beheld the sister she had believed dead for thirteen years. In the center of the room stood a blonde woman in her early thirties, the same woman he had seen in the Runyon nursery. In the sunlight streaming through the windows, the resemblance between the two ladies was even more pronounced, the major difference (saving that of their ages) being the light dusting of freckles across the elder's cheekbones, a relic of her years on the sun-drenched Peninsula.

"Claudia?" Julia's voice broke on the single word.

"My dear little Julia! How you've grown!"

As if by unspoken agreement, they both moved forward at once, to meet, embracing, in the middle of the room.

"Oh, how I've missed you—"

"—Thought of you every day—"

"—Could have sent word—"

"—Dared not tell anyone—"

They were both talking and crying at once, and Pickett, feeling very much *de trop*, glanced rather helplessly at Jamie. Major Pennington rolled his eyes expressively, then jerked his head in the direction of the door. Pickett correctly interpreted this gesture to mean that their presence was no longer needed nor even desired, and followed his host outside.

Alone with her sister, Claudia cupped Julia's face in her hands and subjected her to a long, searching look. "Just look at you, all grown up and married!"

"Married for the second time, in fact," Julia confessed with a shaky laugh.

"Yes, we knew, of course, about your marriage to Lord Fieldhurst—and about what followed, although the London newspapers were weeks old before they reached us. You were constantly in my thoughts, although I dared not inquire too closely for news lest anyone wonder about my interest and become suspicious." She made a wry grimace. "We didn't do so well with our brilliant marriages, did we?"

"No, but although Fieldhurst could be rather beastly, he never reached the depths of cruelty that Lord Buckleigh did. John told me everything, and—oh, my poor Claudia, I only wish I had known! Perhaps I might have helped you."

"You were only fourteen years old," Claudia pointed out. "What could you possibly have done?"

"I could have told Mama—"

Claudia gave a bitter laugh. "Having a devoted husband of her own, Mama has no idea what a prison an unhappy marriage can be. She would have told me I was not doing

206

enough to please Buckleigh, that if only I would try harder, everything would come out right."

Julia, having heard a very similar version of this speech herself, could not dispute it. She allowed her sister to lead her to the worn horsehair sofa, where they sat down side by side with hands clasped. Julia looked about her at her sister's living quarters with disfavor.

"And you have been staying *here* while Jamie stays at the vicarage with his parents?" she asked in tones of deepest revulsion, quite forgetting her own blissful days in a shabby little flat in Drury Lane.

"It is no worse than some of the houses where we were billeted in Spain," Claudia said, then continued brightly. "But tell me about this new husband of yours! I gather the marriage is of very recent date?"

Julia nodded. "Only two weeks. And you might as well know that I have quite sunk myself in the eyes of Society, for John is a Bow Street Runner. In fact, it was he who kept me from going to the gallows for Fieldhurst's murder."

Claudia's blue eyes, so like her sister's, grew wide. "A Bow Street Runner? I can imagine what Mama had to say about *that!*"

"Yes, I daresay you can," Julia said, making a face. "I console myself with the knowledge that her opinion of John will greatly increase when she reflects that he and I, at least, are legally wed! But *you*, my dear! I always knew you and Jamie belonged together, even when I was a girl. But how can you bear it, living in a way that goes against everything you have been brought up to believe is right?"

Claudia gave a bitter little laugh that held no trace of humor. "I have very little choice. Believe me, if there were any way for us to be married, we would have seized upon it thirteen years ago. In fact, it has been so long that I some-times forget"—she blinked back tears—"I forget we are not truly wed. Jamie is everything a husband should be, and everything Lord Buckleigh was not."

"I didn't mean to make you cry, dearest, and you know I want only the best for you. But—if you should have children—"

"There is always that risk, of course. And while we have tried to be very careful to avoid such a thing, we have not always been successful."

Julia's eyes grew round. "Claudia! You *do* have children?"

"One child—a daughter." The child's ambiguous legal status did nothing to dim the glow of maternal pride in her face. "And perhaps I am biased, but I think she is an excep-tionally beautiful little girl."

"But—where is she?"

Claudia's glow was extinguished, and her expression grew pensive. "We could not keep her with us, of course. The rigors of following the drum are not for children. Jamie arranged for a farm family not far from here to take her in, and of course we send money every month for her support."

"I think we saw her!" exclaimed Julia. "After church last Sunday—Mama even noted the resemblance!"

"Mama?" Far from being gratified, Claudia sounded disturbed by this revelation.

"Oh, not that she suspected for a moment that the little girl might be yours—how could she think such a thing, when she believes you to be dead?—but she said the child reminded her of you at the same age. I confess it surprised me, for I thought she looked like Jamie. In fact—" Recalling exactly what she had thought, Julia broke off, blushing.

"In fact, you thought Jamie must have made a very lively time of it on his last leave," Claudia finished for her, smiling. "I warned him how it would be, for she looks just like him!"

"But Claudia, what will you do?" Julia asked in a more serious vein. "The war will not last forever, and sooner or later, you must come back home."

Claudia shook her head sadly. "Not to Norwood Green. Not ever again. Indeed, I never expected to have even this brief visit. I wish we might take up residence at Greenwillows, and keep our daughter with us, but it cannot be, not so long as Lord Buckleigh lives. Jamie intends to sell the property and buy something far away, perhaps in the north, where no one will know us. We must of necessity live very quiet lives, but at least we could be together, all three of us, as a family."

Julia leaped up from the sofa and began to pace the floor in agitation. "It all seems so unfair! You are forced to go into hiding, while Lord Buckleigh is still received everywhere." She paused in her perambulations to bend a pointed gaze upon her sister. "I suppose you have heard that he has married again?"

"Yes, Jamie told me, but I am not bitter. Jamie and I are

very happy together, and if I think of Buckleigh's new wife at all, it is only to pity the poor girl with all my heart." She sighed. "I know too well that she has purchased her high position at a terrible price. If she doesn't know it yet, she will learn soon enough."

The cottage door opened and Jamie entered, followed by Pickett.

"I hate to break up the party," he said, "but I must return to the vicarage before Mama and Papa begin to wonder at my long absence."

"So soon?" Claudia turned to Pickett. "You will bring her back again one day, won't you?"

Pickett promised to do so, and after a protracted and tearful farewell, Claudia released Julia into his care. They left the cottage and walked for some distance in silence, before Julia asked abruptly, "Tell me, John, does Claudia's reappearance have any connection with Tom Pratt's death?"

He took her hand and raised it to his lips. "You, my lady, are a great deal too astute for my peace of mind! I suspect her *reappearance* was no more than an unfortunate coincidence. But as for her *existence*, and Tom's knowledge of it—yes, I think it very likely."

"Then—surely not *Jamie*—?"

"I don't think so," he assured her. "Oh, I wondered the same thing myself, at first, but as the major himself pointed out, who had the most at stake? If the groom hoped to blackmail someone, who would make the most promising target: a cavalry officer who would be out of Tom's reach most of the time, or a nobleman who had just contracted a bigamous marriage in the hopes of begetting an heir?"

"Then *Lord Buckleigh* killed Tom?"

"I would stake my reputation on it—although whether I will ever be able to prove it may be quite another matter."

"Perhaps you'd better drop the investigation entirely," she said urgently. "It seems you cannot win, and if his lordship should guess that you suspect him—"

"He won't have to guess; he's going to know." Pickett stopped and swung 'round to face her, capturing her other hand in his. "Don't you see, my lady, too much is riding on this. If his lordship is guilty—and if I can prove it—then he will be executed, and your sister and Jamie will finally be free to marry."

"It is just as I always suspected: you, my dear, are a hopeless romantic." She stood on tiptoe to emphasize this accusation with a kiss, then added with a sigh, "Still, this is not turning out to be the wedding trip I had hoped for."

"This is what I do, Julia," he pointed out. "Even if Tom Pratt had been a total stranger, I would have felt an obligation to do whatever I could to assist. But as matters stand now, knowing of his connection to your family's history—"

He broke off with a shrug, and she did not press him further. His sense of duty—perhaps a legacy from the magistrate who had rescued him from a life of crime, perhaps an atonement for those early years—was one of the things that made him the man he was.

"It would be good if Claudia and Jamie were able to marry at last," she acknowledged. "John, it has been wonderful, seeing Claudia again, but emotionally taxing all the same. I don't think I can face Mama just yet. Must we go back at once?"

Pickett was nothing loth, and so after partaking of a nuncheon in the Pig and Whistle's private parlor, they spent a very agreeable afternoon wandering about the village, Julia pointing out to Pickett various landmarks from her childhood. It was while they were admiring the church, parts of which dated from the fourteenth century, that they were interrupted by the vicar, Mr. Pennington, who insisted that they accompany him back to the vicarage. Here Julia watched with dread which gradually changed to admiration as her husband allowed himself to be presented to Jamie and the two men exchanged pleasantries quite as if they had not just spent the entire morning in one another's company.

"I was on tenterhooks the entire time, for fear one or the other of you would let slip something and betray us all," she scolded him after they had said their goodbyes to the Penningtons and set out for her father's house. "But it is my belief that you were enjoying yourself thoroughly. So was Jamie, for that matter. I am persuaded the two of you are cut from the same cloth."

Pickett laughed, but did not deny the charge. It was not until they were halfway across the long stretch of meadow that separated Runyon Hall from the village that she grew pensive, and finally broached the subject that had been preying upon her mind since her conversation with Claudia.

"They have a child, did you know?"

"Who?"

"Claudia and Jamie. They have a daughter."

He tucked her hand into the curve of his arm, and they resumed their trek. "Yes, the little girl outside the church last Sunday. Jamie told me while you and Claudia were enjoying your reunion."

She had wondered fleetingly what they would find to talk about; apparently they'd found a great deal. "It seems rather unfair, doesn't it? Even trying not to, they managed to have a child, whereas I, on the other hand—"

"Pray do not distress yourself, my lady—"

"No, hear me out, John! I have given it a great deal of thought, and I have come to realize that you must not be robbed of the opportunity to have children merely because I am—lacking—in that area. You are in a better position than my first husband, for where Frederick required a legitimate heir of the body, you have only to locate a willing female and—and—and you may be sure that I would love any child of yours as if it were my own," she concluded miserably.

The silence from the man at her side was deafening, but she dared not look at him to gauge how this proposal was being received; from looking him in the eye it was only a very short step to imagining him in the arms of another woman, and there, she feared, her resolution would fail her.

"Am I to understand," he said at last, with great deliberation, "that you are *encouraging* me to take a mistress?"

"Only for as long as it takes for you to get her with child," she said hastily. "We must be very clear on that point."

"Oh, of course," he agreed drily.

213

"There are a couple of other conditions that I must insist upon as well."

"I should love to hear them," he said, although there was that in his voice that suggested otherwise.

"First, I should prefer that the woman have brown hair and brown eyes, as much like your own coloring as possible. That way, if the child should happen to resemble its mother, I should still see you, and not her, when I looked at it."

"I see. And the other condition?"

"That the woman must not be Lucy," she said, naming the Covent Garden strumpet who'd had designs on John Pickett's virtue long before she, Julia, had ever met him. It would be too galling, to have won that particular battle only to lose the war.

"In that case, I'm afraid the deal is off, for you must know it has always been my life's ambition to bed Lucy." Pickett stopped in his tracks and seized his lady by the shoulders. "How is it possible for an otherwise sensible female to spout such arrant nonsense? Have I ever given you the slightest indication that I wanted children on such terms?"

"I—I didn't mean to make you angry—"

"I am not angry!" Pickett insisted with such vehemence that two sheep looked up from grazing, no doubt filled with admiration at so calm and reasonable a demeanor. "I am wounded to the quick by the knowledge that you hold what we share so cheaply as to consider it transferable to anyone else who happens to have the right body parts!"

"No, no! Indeed, the very thought of you lying with

214

another woman makes me ill! But recently I have been forced to recognize that in denying you the opportunity to have children I have done you a disservice."

His eyes narrowed as a possible explanation presented itself. "Have you been talking to your mother, by any chance?"

"No, not about that," she answered quickly. "I could not discuss such a thing with Mama! But when she told me about Papa's trips to London, she did say that it was a wife's duty to see that her husband's needs were met—"

"If you were meeting them any better, I wouldn't be able to walk," said Pickett, with a reminiscent gleam in his eye. "My lady, I'm well aware that a fellow like me should never have a wife like you in the first place. In the usual way of things, I never should have even crossed your path, much less aspired to marry you. Yes, I always thought I would want children one day—what man does not? But if being childless is the price I pay for such a stroke of good fortune, I consider I made a very good bargain, for I want no other woman but you."

There was only one answer she could make to such a declaration, and so she made it. "But John," she said at last, emerging breathless and disheveled from a protracted embrace, "if anything were to happen to you, I should have nothing, no part of you, to remember you by."

"Nothing is going to happen to me, my lady," he assured her.

"So says the man who was coshed over the head less than a month ago!" she scoffed. "I have lost one husband to violent death already; is it so inconceivable that I should lose another?"

"I'm not a betting man, but I should think its having happened once would decrease the odds of such a thing happening again."

"Perhaps it might, if my second husband did not insist upon going about looking for trouble," she pointed out with some asperity. "I don't like Lord Buckleigh, John. I didn't like him when I was a child and he was courting Claudia, and now, knowing what I do, I like him even less."

"I'm not fond of him myself," Pickett said, "but as you said yourself, Lord Buckleigh holds all the cards in this particular game. He may try to discredit me, but if he were to make any attempt against my life, he would only lend credence to my suspicions. In fact, we have one another at a stalemate—and I intend to be the one to break it. And as for you having something to remember me by," he bent to whisper in her ear, "is there any chance we might slip away upstairs immediately after dinner?"

The answer to this hopeful query proved to be a resounding "no."

"There you are!" Lady Runyon exclaimed upon their return. "Where have you been all afternoon? Just after you left, we received an invitation to dine with Lord and Lady Buckleigh tonight. Lady Buckleigh keeps country hours—most unfashionable, but what can one expect, with such a mother?—so we will sit down to dinner at five. You'd best go upstairs and change, both of you, for Papa has ordered the carriage for four o'clock."

The Picketts, man and wife, exchanged looks of mutual regret before heading upstairs to change their dress and prepare for whatever the evening might bring.

15

In Which John Pickett Makes His First Move

A t promptly four o'clock that evening, the Runyon contingent piled into the squire's carriage and set out for Lord Buckleigh's elegant Palladian mansion. Pickett could have wished for more time in which to decide on just how he should approach his lordship; it was, after all, not every day that he was faced with the prospect of notifying his primary suspect of his progress in the investigation. He derived what comfort he could from the knowledge that his mother-in-law took no more pleasure in the night's entertainment than he did himself.

"And when I think that the last time I sat at Lord Buckleigh's table, my dear Claudia presided over it as hostess," sighed Lady Runyon. "While as for that shockingly vulgar creature who is his mother-in-law, well, what I shall find to say to her, I'm sure I don't know!"

"If you feel that way, Mama, I wonder you didn't make our excuses," Julia said.

"Oh, how I longed to do so! But it must have been

considered appallingly rude. I suspect the new Lady Buck-leigh feels quite inferior to her predecessor, and so for her to be on terms with the family of her husband's first wife can-not but ease her way." She sighed again. "I suppose we owe Lord Buckleigh too much to deny his new wife this small courtesy."

Julia's jaw tightened, and Pickett, catching her eye, frowned a warning. Julia obediently held her tongue, but as he handed her down from the carriage a short time later, she whispered, "Even if Lord Buckleigh did not kill Tom, I shall never forgive him for his treatment of Claudia! How am I to sit at the same table and exchange pleasantries with him, when I could tell Mama and Papa *such* things?"

"You will do it in just the same way you faced down your London acquaintances while they speculated behind your back on whether or not you killed your husband," Pickett reminded her.

"Yes, but I was certain of my own innocence," she reminded him. "Besides, I had a devoted advocate, if you will recall."

His hand tightened on hers. "You'll always have that."

"Come along, Julia, Mr. Pickett," Lady Runyon called from the portico, where the butler stood at the front door ready to announce them. "We must not keep Lord and Lady Buckleigh waiting."

Julia made a droll face for her husband's benefit, then picked an infinitesimal speck of lint from his lapel, took his arm, and allowed him to escort her up the stairs in her parents' wake. A few minutes later, they were shown into an elegantly appointed drawing room whose Grecian-inspired furnishings retained no trace of the violent scene enacted there almost thirteen years earlier. Lord Buckleigh stood near the fireplace with one hand resting on the mantel, presenting a chiseled profile to anyone entering the room. His youthful bride perched stiffly on the edge of her chair, looking like a bird ready to take flight at any moment. The red-faced, middle-aged man they'd seen at the inquest and identified as Lady Buckleigh's father sat beside her, mopping his brow and looking woefully out of place. In fact, the only one of the Buckleigh party who looked completely at ease was Mrs. Gubbins. Once again dressed in a gown better suited to a much younger woman, she leaned back on a sofa with one leg thrown over the other to expose chunky ankles encased in pink-clad stockings.

"Well, well, here's the squire and his family!" she announced before the butler could do so, uncrossing her legs and heaving herself to her feet. "I met your daughter and her husband in the village yesterday, you know, but as for the rest of you, I haven't yet had the pleasure—"

"In that case, you must allow me," his lordship put in smoothly, effectively silencing his mother-in-law. "Sir Thaddeus, Lady Runyon, Mr. and Mrs. Pickett, may I present Lady Buckleigh's parents, Mr. and Mrs. Horace Gubbins? I'm sure I need not introduce my wife, for you will remember her from the Brantleys' dinner party." The rather pained glance he directed at Pickett made it clear that the presentation of Lady Buckleigh was not the only memorable event of that night. "Mother Gubbins, as you have surmised, this is

Sir Thaddeus and Lady Runyon, and Mr. and Mrs. John—you did say it was John, did you not?—Pickett."

The men shook hands, and although Lady Runyon could not quite bring herself to curtsy, she dipped her head, all the while maintaining the sort of repulsed yet fascinated eye contact with Mrs. Gubbins that a rabbit might display when confronted with a cobra. The dinner itself was no better, for it was inevitable that such an ill-assorted group of people would find little to say to one another. Pickett found himself wondering about Lord Buckleigh's courtship of his unlikely bride, and decided that if he was made uncomfortable by the obvious vulgarity of his new in-laws, it was no more than he deserved.

"And now, Mr. Pickett, I would like to know a bit more about you," said Mrs. Gubbins, when the reliable topic of the weather had been exhausted. "I'm sure I don't exaggerate when I say you're an odd sort of husband for a ladyship to have—are you still a ladyship, ma'am, or a mere missus, like me?"

A missus, thought Pickett, *although, thankfully, nothing like you.*

"Now, Edna," Mr. Gubbins chided his wife, "I'm sure anyone might say the same thing about our Betty marrying his lordship."

"That's what I mean," insisted Mrs. Gubbins, undaunted. "You, Mr. Pickett, seem like the sort of man who might have had our Betty, if she hadn't caught the eye of our dear Lord Buckleigh." She simpered at her son-in-law seated at the head of the table.

"Unfortunately, a grand title don't always make a great match," put in Sir Thaddeus, leading Pickett to wonder how much he knew about Claudia's marriage until the squire expounded upon this theme. "Lord Fieldhurst, you must know, ran himself to ground and got himself killed for his pains, and dam—er, dashed near took our Julia along with him. She might have gone to the gallows for his murder, had it not been for Mr. Pickett, here."

"Is that so?" Mrs. Gubbins bent a keen gaze on Julia. "I hope you didn't make such a poor match out of gratitude, my dear, for it rarely lasts."

Up came Julia's chin. "No, indeed! Mr. Pickett is widely admired for his cleverness, and has solved many a case where it appeared the miscreant would go free. Why, just recently he was rewarded by the Russian government for his efforts on behalf of the Princess Olga Fyodorovna on the night of the Drury Lane Theatre fire."

Pickett felt himself blushing, even as he saw his chances of lulling Lord Buckleigh into complacency fading. "It sounds much less impressive when one considers that my 'efforts' consisted mostly of getting myself coshed on the head," he protested.

"I'm sure you are too modest, Mr. Pickett," Mrs. Gubbins insisted. "I daresay you see many interesting things in your line of work—more interesting than Mr. Gubbins there, for although he makes a pretty penny, the life of a linen-draper is far from exciting."

"It's certainly surprising, the depths to which men can sink," Pickett agreed, seeing his opportunity. "Why, just recently I learned of a case where a man so abused his poor wife that she was forced to escape with her life. And did the man show any remorse over his ill treatment of her? Why, no! In fact, he made a bigamous marriage with another female."

There was a moment's shocked silence, broken by Sir Thaddeus, who asked, "Did the fellow know his first wife was still living?"

"I have wondered that myself, sir," Pickett said.

"It is easy to judge the actions of others when we don't know all the facts," observed Lord Buckleigh. "Perhaps he was desperate for a son to inherit his title."

Pickett's eyebrows rose. "Have I said there was a title?"

"*Touché*, Mr. Pickett." His lordship smiled thinly. "I suppose it is only human nature to assume that others' situations must reflect our own. Because I am in need of an heir, I must think it a priority for any other man as well."

"In fact, my lord, you are quite right," acknowledged Pickett, lifting his wineglass and taking a sip. "There was a title—a barony, if I understand it correctly."

"But how appalling for the poor second wife!" exclaimed Lady Runyon. "No doubt she believes herself to be legally wed to this baron, when in fact she must be quite ruined if the truth of her situation were known."

"Yes, indeed," agreed Mrs. Gubbins, unconsciously putting the squire's lady in the surprising position of finding herself in agreement with the vulgarian. "If anyone treated a child of mine so shabbily, *I* should know how to deal with him!"

"I am sure no one could blame you, Mrs. Gubbins," Pickett said, then, having made his point, judged it time to turn the subject. "But I cannot accept your suggestion that your husband's work must be dull when compared to mine. One tends to think of brandy when the subject of smuggling arises, but I believe there are more than a few bolts of silk for sale in England that never paid a tariff, are there not, sir?"

"Aye, that there are, and for those of us trying to ply an honest trade, they wreak havoc on the prices," said Mr. Gubbins, much gratified. He found himself wishing his daughter might have married just such a fellow as this—aye, a level-headed young man to whom he might have bequeathed his business one day, not a high-falutin lordship around whom a man couldn't make a move without fearing he was setting his foot wrong. Not that Lord Buckleigh ever said anything, but he had a way of looking at one with that nose of his stuck in the air that said more than any words. Granted, Mrs. Gubbins didn't seem to take any notice, and little Betty was over the moon at being a ladyship, so if his women were happy, he supposed he must be, too.

At last (and only after receiving a nudge from her mother), Lady Buckleigh gave the ladies the signal to withdraw, and the gentlemen remained at the table for post-prandial port. Conversation between the men was desultory, and Pickett had the impression that his host was merely going through the motions until he could tactfully break up the little party—a suspicion that was confirmed when they rose to join the ladies.

"I should like a word with you, Mr. Pickett," his
lordship said, and the glint in his eye gave Pickett to
understand that he was unlikely to enjoy the encounter. "Sir
Thaddeus, Mr. Gubbins, I'm sure you will make our
apologies to the ladies."

Mr. Gubbins dared not contradict his son-in-law in
anything, and Sir Thaddeus saw nothing to wonder at in his
lordship's desire for a *tête-à-tête*, being aware of Lord
Buckleigh's request that Pickett keep him abreast of his
progress in the matter of Tom Pratt's death. Therefore both
men agreed to this arrangement, thus leaving Pickett to his
fate.

"If you will join me in my study, Mr. Pickett, we may
be more private," Lord Buckleigh said, and led the way from
the dining room down the corridor to a square chamber
decorated according to masculine tastes in rich wood and
leather, with curtains of bronze-colored velvet hanging from
its tall windows. He waved Pickett toward a nail-studded
armchair, then seated himself behind his long mahogany
desk. Pickett felt rather like a recalcitrant schoolboy
summoned before a stern tutor; indeed, it was only the
realization that this was exactly what his lordship intended
him to feel that allowed him to resist an uncomfortable
impulse to squirm.

"You have not yet approached me to request an arrest
warrant," was Lord Buckleigh's opening salvo. "Am I to
understand by this omission that you have not yet discovered
who killed Sir Thaddeus's groom?"

Pickett paused to consider his lordship's question for a

long moment before answering. "Let us say, rather, that I have not yet uncovered sufficient evidence to prove it to a jury's satisfaction."

Lord Buckleigh's eyebrows lifted slightly. "A cautious answer, Mr. Pickett, and no doubt a wise one."

"I do have a few questions to ask you, my lord, if I may."

"Anything I may do to speed you in your quest for justice is, of course, yours to command," the baron assured him with a wave of one well-manicured hand.

"It has come to my attention that before Sir Thaddeus hired him, Tom Pratt worked in your own stables, is that correct?"

"Yes, what of it?"

"When did he leave your employ, and why?"

Lord Buckleigh picked up a penknife and idly turned it to and fro in his hand, watching the play of firelight on the blade. If his intention was to recall to Pickett's mind the sight of Tom Pratt's throat slit open from ear to ear, he succeeded admirably. "When? That would have been the summer of '96, if memory serves. As for why, I suppose your own father-in-law would know that better than I. If you have learned anything about Sir Thaddeus at all, you will have noticed that he thinks very highly of his horses, and would spare no expense for their care. I suppose he must have been impressed with Tom Pratt's skill, and offered him a higher wage than he earned on my payroll."

"Summer of '96," Pickett echoed thoughtfully. "Almost thirteen years ago. That would put it right around the same time the first Lady Buckleigh disappeared, would it not?"

Lord Buckleigh lifted his head and looked down his nose at Pickett, his light blue eyes like chips of ice. "My good fellow, is it possible that you have the effrontery to interrogate *me*? What the devil could a mere stable hand possibly have to do with my wife's disappearance?"

"Perhaps nothing," Pickett acknowledged. "Or perhaps he knew things about that disappearance that made him judge it safest not to remain in your employ."

Chuckling under his breath, Lord Buckleigh shook his head wonderingly. "I must say, you have quite an imagination, Mr. Pickett. Even if I were inclined to hold a stable hand responsible for the loss of my wife, is it likely that I would wait thirteen years to exact my revenge upon him?" His lordship tossed the penknife aside and leaned forward over the desk, his face dark, his voice low and menacing. "Make no mistake about this, Mr. Pickett: in London you may be regarded as something of an *enfant prodige*, but amongst these old County families, you are nothing but a jumped-up mushroom who contrived by hook or by crook to marry above himself. If you make any attempt, even the slightest, to besmirch my name, it will go very, very ill with you. Do I make myself clear?"

Pickett, refusing to be intimidated, looked him squarely in the eye. "Perfectly, your lordship."

"Excellent." Lord Buckleigh rose to his feet with feline grace, once again the congenial host. "Now that we understand one another, I suggest we join the ladies."

227

16

In Which a Trap Is Set

H e didn't even bother to deny it, except for a token protest against my effrontery in daring to question him," Pickett recounted bitterly the following morning.

He and Julia had made another trek to the gamekeeper's cottage, and Julia now sat beside her sister on the worn horsehair sofa. Jamie stood next to the fireplace leaning his broad shoulders against the mantel, while Pickett paced the floor and considered his next move.

"As you said, Major, he's a cool customer." He gave a short, humorless laugh. "And why not? Even if I could produce indisputable evidence tomorrow, I can hardly ask him for a warrant to arrest himself—and he knows it."

"Then Buckleigh will never have to pay for his crimes," Claudia said with a sigh of resignation. "Some things never change."

Pickett took another turn about the room, his chin sunk in his hand. "Perhaps not, at least not where Tom Pratt is concerned," he said slowly. "But if he felt threatened, if he

228

felt compelled to take some new action, and if there were witnesses on hand to catch him in the attempt . . ."

"John, you are not thinking of accusing him publicly!" Julia exclaimed.

He shook his head impatiently. "No, for I don't think it would do the least bit of good if I did. He would merely laugh it off and dismiss me as—I'm quoting here—'a jumped-up mushroom from London' who married above himself."

"But he threatened you! Surely he would not have done so unless he thought he had something to fear from you."

"I am convinced he only thought to frighten me into dropping the investigation. I don't believe he would take any action against me, for he is persuaded I don't represent a great enough danger to make it worth the risk. But if there were someone whom he had a very real reason to fear, someone whom he judged it necessary to remove by whatever means . . ."

Jamie frowned. "What are you thinking, Mr. Pickett?"

Pickett did not answer, but turned instead to the sofa where Claudia sat. "I hate to ask such a thing of you, Lady Buckleigh—"

She shuddered in distaste. "Pray do not call me by that despicable name! 'Claudia' will do."

"Claudia, then. Lord Buckleigh knows you are alive, thanks to Tom Pratt, but if he were to discover that you were right here in Norwood Green, and that you intended to make your presence known—"

"No!" Jamie's shoulders came up off the mantel. "No,

229

I'll not have it! I won't let you put Claudia in danger."

"She's been in danger ever since Lord Buckleigh learned of her existence," Pickett pointed out.

"He's quite right, Jamie," Claudia concurred.

"Yes, and his lordship may well come here looking for her anyway," Pickett said. "We may consider ourselves fortunate that his in-laws' presence has placed demands on his time, else he might have done so already. After all, I told him I believed there was someone living here."

"Why the devil did you do that?" demanded Jamie.

"I had no reason to suspect him at the time. After all, he is the Justice of the Peace. He'd just given me permission to investigate—given it rather reluctantly, too, now that I think of it—and asked to be kept informed as to my findings. How was I to know he was trying to pump me? Besides," he added in growing indignation, "if certain persons hadn't insisted on being so mysterious when I tried to investigate that day, and had told me plainly of the danger his lordship posed, I might have been forewarned against him."

"I'd only met you the night before!" protested Jamie. "Why should I have trusted you?"

"Boys, boys! Play nicely," chided Claudia, with a twinkle in her eye. She looked up at Pickett. "Tell me, Mr. Pickett, what do you want me to do?"

"If you could send for Lord Buckleigh, arrange for him to come here," Pickett said, ignoring Jamie's noise of protest, "the major and I would be just out of sight, both of us armed—you do have a pistol I can borrow, do you not, Major?—if you make it plain to him that you have had enough of hiding, he would have to do something to get rid of you permanently—"

"What he means is that Buckleigh will try to kill you," Jamie interrupted. "I tell you, Mr. Pickett, I won't allow it."

"Perhaps *you* will not, Jamie, but *I* have taken no vows to obey you, at least not yet," Claudia reminded him. "As it happens, I have an old score to settle with his lordship, and he may be surprised to discover that I am no longer a frightened and bullied young girl. But what excuse should I give, Mr. Pickett? Not blackmail, surely, for that has already been tried—I know! I shall ask him to petition Parliament for a divorce! He could not agree, for to do so must be to acknowledge that his first wife is still alive, and his marriage to that girl is not valid."

Jamie scowled. "That should certainly provoke him." He turned to Pickett. "I am more accustomed to giving orders than following them, but since it appears Claudia is determined on this course, I must do all I can to ensure its success. Where shall we position ourselves? I don't see that this place offers many vantage points where we might hide and still keep his lordship covered."

Pickett cast his gaze about the small room, and recognized the force of Major Pennington's argument; the furniture was insufficient to hide anything larger than a cat. The loft would conceal them adequately, but it would also put Lord Buckleigh out of range of their pistols. A narrow door in the back wall offered a possibility; Pickett strode across the room to open it, and discovered a second room which served as a kitchen. He stepped into the kitchen and closed the door behind him, then put his eye to the narrow gap between the door and its frame. He could see Claudia and Jamie, but of Julia there was no sign, even though she sat next to her sister on the sofa. The other side of the door, the hinged side, presented a slightly different view. From this vantage point he could see Julia, and Jamie's left arm and shoulder, but Claudia was blocked from his sight by the wooden panel.

He opened the door again. "We can conceal ourselves behind the door, but the angle is not good. If we're to have a clear shot at his lordship, he'll have to be standing directly in our line of vision, which will be narrower than I could wish for." He looked at Claudia. "If we were to calculate the lines and mark them off on the floor, do you think you could keep him from moving beyond them?"

"No, we can't leave that much to chance," Jamie protested. "We'll have to use the window."

Everyone turned to regard the single window in the wall adjacent to the front door. It was not promising, hung with thin muslin curtains that stopped fully three feet above the floor.

"I'm sure Lord Buckleigh won't notice a bulge behind the curtain, never mind the fact that the window has grown legs," Pickett said, his voice dripping with irony.

"No, he won't, for he won't see them," the major replied. "We'll make a thicker curtain from the counterpane on the bed upstairs, one that goes all the way to the floor. I'll fashion a rod that will stand out farther from the wall, making a sort of embrasure behind it."

"Can you do that?" Pickett asked, impressed in spite of himself.

"I've been in the army for almost thirteen years," Jamie reminded him. "If I've learned anything during that time, it's how to improvise."

"But what of Claudia's bed?" Julia protested. "She'll be cold, with no blankets."

"You forget that Claudia is an experienced campaigner. She's endured discomforts far worse. Mind you," he added, giving Pickett a stern look, "I still don't like it."

Pickett nodded in understanding. "I know you don't like it, Major, but I promise you, we shall take every precaution to see that no harm comes to your wife."

Jamie's frown was erased, and when he spoke again, it was in a very different voice. "Thank you for that, Mr. Pickett."

"For what?"

"For calling her my wife."

Pickett shrugged, suddenly self-conscious. "I call it as I see it, Major."

* * *

By the time Pickett and Julia left the cottage half an hour later, all the plans were in place. Alas, one little detail had not yet been addressed, one of which Pickett was unaware until the pair of them were walking across the downs toward Runyon Hall.

"One thing still puzzles me," Julia said. "What will I do?"

"What do you mean?" asked Pickett, all at sea.

"While Claudia is confronting Buckleigh and you and Jamie are tucked away behind the curtain with pistols trained on him, where will I be?"

"I don't know," he said, rather taken aback by the question. "I suppose you'll be with your parents, doing whatever it is they're doing that day."

"John!" She stopped in her tracks and wheeled about to face him. "You cannot mean to leave me out of it!"

"That is exactly what I plan to do! My lady, we're talking about a confrontation with a murderer! Do you really think I would expose you to that?"

"You didn't think twice about exposing Claudia!"

"That's different."

"Oh?" Her voice could have frozen water. "In what way?"

"She's rather more closely involved than you," he pointed out. "After all, the man is her husband."

"And I am her sister!"

"And you are my wife." Seeing that this tracing of the family tree was getting them nowhere, he tried a different approach. "The whole purpose of this meeting is to provoke his lordship into making an attempt on Claudia's life. He is unlikely to do so with her younger sister present."

"But I could hide, like you and Jamie," she said coaxingly. "I know the window is not large, but I don't take up much room."

She didn't. In fact, she fitted rather nicely beneath his arm, with her hair just brushing his chin— "That isn't the point," he said, putting aside an all too distracting train of thought. "I won't put you in unnecessary danger."

"You told Jamie that Claudia would be perfectly safe!"

"Yes, with both him and me looking out for her. But if you're there, I won't be thinking of Claudia, at least not entirely. If you're there, my first priority will be your safety, not hers."

Her expression softened. "That's very sweet of you, John, but perhaps I could stay in the loft, well out of harm's way—"

"My mind is made up, Julia. Unlike Claudia, you *have* taken a vow to love, honor, and obey. I don't intend to abuse the privilege, but I'm afraid I must insist that you obey me in this."

She opened her mouth to voice an indignant protest at such high-handed treatment, but the words stuck in her throat. It was just as she had told her mother: he was no boy, this young man she'd married. He would not allow himself to be browbeaten, not threateningly by Lord Buckleigh, nor even lovingly by herself. And strangely enough, she discovered she preferred it that way.

"Very well, if you insist," she conceded reluctantly. "I suppose it would be just as well for me to stay behind this once, lest Mama or Papa become too curious about where we have been going every morning. But you must promise to tell me all about it the moment you return!"

He captured the finger she had jabbed into his chest and raised it to his lips. "Every word," he said, and hand in hand they resumed their journey.

17

In Which a Trap Is Sprung

T hey were in position a full fifteen minutes before ten
o'clock the next morning, the time appointed for the
meeting. Jamie, having exchanged his scarlet regimentals for
country tweeds, stood shoulder to shoulder with Pickett in
the alcove created by the thick makeshift curtain, from
which vantage point they could observe the proceedings
through strategically placed slits in the fabric. These had
been Jamie's idea. In fact, it seemed to Pickett that, once
resigned to the scheme, the major had taken charge of the
entire operation; apparently Jamie had not exaggerated when
he'd said he was more accustomed to giving orders than
following them. Still, Pickett supposed he could hardly
blame Major Pennington: if it had been his own wife who
was being dangled as bait to catch a murderer, he doubted he
would be content to leave the details to a comparative
stranger, either.

"I wish he would hurry," Claudia complained. Through
the slits in the curtain Pickett could see her sitting on the

worn sofa, pleating the folds of her skirt with nervous fingers. "I just want to have it over with."

"Claudia, my love, you must be quiet. We can't risk Lord Buckleigh hearing, should he come upon us unexpectedly."

Although Jamie's voice was gentle, Pickett could feel the tension emanating from the man at his side. He suspected they all shared Claudia's sentiments, even if they were not at liberty to discuss them.

And so they waited in silence until finally, after what seemed like hours even though it could not have been more than ten minutes, a firm knock sounded against the wooden front door. Pickett and Jamie exchanged a look, and cocked their pistols.

"Come in," Claudia called in a steady voice, her inner turmoil betrayed only by the compulsive smoothing of her skirts.

The door opened, and Lord Buckleigh entered the room, every inch the rural aristocrat in a russet tailcoat, buckskin breeches, and topboots. "So it's true," he said, confronting at last the wife he had not seen in more than a decade. "It has been a long time, Claudia."

She rose gracefully at his appearance, but did not move forward to greet him. "Not long enough, in my opinion."

"And yet, you sent for me, not the other way 'round." His long, appraising gaze took in her still-youthful figure, her blonde hair untouched by gray, her golden, sun-kissed skin. "You look well, my dear."

"Do I?" she asked, mildly surprised. "I daresay it must

be the lack of bruises."

The familiar irritation crossed his face, and she willed herself not to flinch instinctively, as she had in the old days. She was not a terrified girl any longer, and although he was still legally her husband, he had no real power over her, not anymore. There was a man concealed behind the curtain—two, in fact—who would make sure of it.

"Surely you haven't approached me after all these years merely to bandy words over some perceived grudge," Lord Buckleigh complained.

Jamie's pistol arm twitched at this cavalier attitude toward his lordship's ill treatment of Claudia, and Pickett laid a restraining hand on his sleeve.

"No, not to bandy words, but to make a request." She took a deep breath and clasped her hands tightly together at her waist. "I want you to petition Parliament for a divorce."

If she had hoped to disturb his oppressive calm, she had the satisfaction of knowing that she succeeded, if only for a moment. "A divorce? Why the devil should I?"

"Because I am weary of hiding. I am ready to move forward with my own life, and I'm sure you must be, as well. I understand you have taken another wife, Buckleigh. I wonder, what would she say if she knew her marriage to you was invalid? I am credibly informed that you never bothered to have me declared legally dead."

"No, for although I was almost certain you were dead—your shawl was found in the gorge, you know, covered in blood—there was always the possibility that you had merely flown, and had drenched your shawl with the blood of a rabbit or a squirrel to put me off the scent. I dared not take any legal action for fear it would flush you out of hiding, wherever you were."

" 'Fear,' Buckleigh? You, afraid of me?" She gave a snort of derision. "I wish I might have been there to see it!"

He scowled at the interruption. "I found a wealthy merchant's daughter, one whose parents were too enthralled at the prospect of their child's marrying into the nobility to quibble at a thirteen-year-old scandal. I'm fifty years old, you know. I need an heir." His face darkened as a new thought—or rather an old one, long forgotten—occurred to him. "There was a child, Claudia. He would be about twelve years old by now. *What have you done with my child?*"

"Can you not guess?" she asked with a bitter laugh. "The blood you found on my shawl was all that remained of your heir. I hope you gave it a proper burial."

"Damn you!" He started toward her, and Pickett was forced to seize Jamie's arm to restrain him. "You did it on purpose, didn't you? You rid yourself of my child so you might be free to run off to God knows where!"

She shook her head in mingled amazement and resignation. "You haven't changed, have you, Buckleigh? Nothing is ever your fault. Someone else is always to blame, and that someone was usually me. May I remind you that you kicked me in the abdomen that day? *You* did this, Buckleigh. You killed our child as surely as if you had slit its throat, just like you slit poor Tom Pratt's."

If Lord Buckleigh heard this last accusation at all, he did not react to it, so filled with rage was he at the first one.

"You're lying!"

"By all means, believe that if you must, but it won't change the truth."

"Let me remind you, Claudia, that you are still my lawfully wedded wife," his lordship ground out through clenched teeth. "It's not too late for me to get an heir on you, and by God, I've a mind to do it!"

He seized her arm and flung her onto the sofa. Although she fought like a madwoman, he pinned her down with one knee on her skirts while he fumbled with the fall of his breeches. Behind the curtain, Jamie swatted Pickett's hand off his sleeve as if he might a fly. He pushed the hammer of his pistol back and tossed it aside, then advanced upon Lord Buckleigh. During his thirteen year absence from Norwood Green, the scales of time had tipped in Jamie's favor. Where he had once been a mere stripling trying to protect a young lady against a grown man, Major Pennington was now in the prime of life and battle-hardened into the bargain, while Lord Buckleigh had passed his fiftieth year. Jamie grasped his lordship by the collar of his coat and the seat of his breeches, and lifted him bodily off his struggling wife.

"I believe it is time you were leaving, my lord," said the major, shouldering the door open and dumping Lord Buckleigh unceremoniously onto the front stoop.

"Well, well, look at the brave soldier, hiding behind the curtain and lying in wait for an unarmed man," Lord Buckleigh said with a sneer, picking himself up and dusting himself off with as much dignity as he could muster. "As for you, Claudia my dear, I suppose I shouldn't be surprised to learn that you've spent the last thirteen years whoring for the vicar's son."

Far from being shamed by this accusation, Claudia lifted her chin in a manner strongly reminiscent of her younger sister. "No, indeed! Why should you be surprised, when you all but threw me into his arms? Why should I not commit the sin of which I had so long been accused? Jamie and I may not be legally wed, but he has been a better husband to me than you ever were!"

" 'Husband'?" scoffed his lordship. "Call yourself his wife all you wish, my dear, but I know you for what you really are. Oh, and as for my divorcing you so that you might marry the vicar's brat, know this: you are my wife 'until death do us part.' And who knows? The death that eventually parts us may not be mine."

"Is that a threat, Buckleigh?" Claudia asked.

"No, merely an observation that life sometimes takes unexpected twists." He gave her a long look with something surprisingly like regret in his eyes. "I did love you, you know."

There had been a time, more than a dozen years earlier, when such an assertion would have had her begging his pardon with tears of remorse. But in the intervening years, she had seen firsthand how a man was supposed to treat the woman he loved, and so she had no difficulty now in recognizing Lord Buckleigh's attempt at manipulation for what it was. " 'Love,' Buckleigh? You will pardon me for observing that you had strange ways of showing it," she said, then closed the door on his lordship and sagged against it, burying

241

her face in her hands.

Jamie was beside her in an instant, gathering her into his arms, and Pickett, emerging from behind the curtain, thought he had never seen a man and woman who belonged more completely to one another.

"Well?" the major asked, regarding him with a faintly accusing lift of one eyebrow. "Any other bright ideas from the boy genius?"

Pickett bristled at the injustice of this charge. "I don't see how you can blame *me* for the plan's failure, when *you* were the one who abandoned your post!"

"I suppose that, if it were *your* wife being assaulted by her first husband, you would merely watch and take notes," Jamie retorted.

"No," Pickett said thoughtfully. "No, I probably would have shot him."

"And so I might have done, but for one little detail."

"What was that?"

"A Bow Street Runner stood ready at hand to charge me with murder," Jamie pointed out.

Pickett grinned ruefully at him. "I doubt I could have brought myself to do so, given the circumstances."

"*Now* he tells me!" Jamie groaned aloud to no one in particular.

"Mr. Pickett is an honest and honorable man," Claudia told her beloved. "Perhaps it is just as well that you did not put him in the position of being forced to compromise his principles."

She was smiling now, albeit somewhat shakily, and

Pickett realized with some admiration for the major's methods that this was exactly the result Jamie had been pressing toward ever since she had shut the door on her husband. Perhaps he should make a note of it in his occurrence book, under the heading "How to Handle Women." After all, he was a married man now; he needed all the help he could get.

"His sins against you are undoubtedly great, Lady—er, Claudia, but I would prefer that he be executed in accordance with the law," Pickett told her. "The two of you have suffered enough without Major Pennington being held responsible for his death, even if only in the court of public opinion."

"So what will you do now, Mr. Pickett?" she asked.

He sighed. "I wish I knew. I suppose I could question Lady Buckleigh—Miss Gubbins, that is—provided I could get her away from her mother. Perhaps she saw or heard something without realizing its significance at the time, something that might connect Lord Buckleigh with Tom Pratt's murder."

"But would she be willing to give evidence against him?"

Pickett shrugged. "Who knows? If she believed he had tricked her into a bigamous marriage, she might be only too happy to see him get his comeuppance. I'll try to see her this afternoon, but my first priority must be letting Julia know that you"—he turned to look at Claudia—"are unharmed. She was not at all happy at being left behind, you know."

"I don't doubt it!" Jamie said, grinning. "I wonder if I

243

can prevail upon you to take the long route back through the village and stop in at the vicarage long enough to deliver a message."

"Of course," Pickett agreed, and the major clapped a hand to his shoulder and walked with him as far as the door.

"Let my parents know that I won't be coming home tonight," he said, lowering his voice to a conspiratorial murmur. "I can't be sure Lord Buckleigh won't return, now that he knows where to find Claudia. I won't leave her alone until I've removed her to a safer location."

"Very well, but what excuse will I give them?"

"I dare not claim an invitation to dine with the Runyons, for fear Mama would blow the gaff to Lady Runyon. Wait, I have it! You may say that I ran into old friends at the Pig and Whistle—Mama dislikes the place, on account of a certain tavern wench who is rather too accommodating—and have accepted an impromptu invitation to stay the night."

"But your lack of a valise—" Pickett protested.

"If she asks, remind Mama that I have campaigned in Spain, and can get by with very little." He frowned as the sound of a gunshot echoed in the distance. "And mind you watch out for poachers! Greenwillows has been without proper game management for far too long, and it appears the natives are getting bolder."

Pickett agreed to these instructions and, after saying his farewells to both Jamie and Claudia, set out on his way. He did not retrace his steps across the downs toward Runyon Hall where his wife waited, but instead turned down a narrow, overgrown path that would eventually widen into a cart track before it finally gave onto the main street of the village. He had not gone far along the path when a splash of color caught his eye, and he recognized the russet of Lord Buckleigh's coat lying in the grass, its autumnal hue contrasting sharply with the bright greens of spring. Even from a considerable distance, it was clear that the coat still contained his lordship's person. Recalling the scene he had witnessed only minutes earlier, Pickett was much inclined to follow the biblical example of the priest and the Levite and thus pass by on the other side; the urgings of duty, however, overrode those of inclination, and reluctantly he strode forward to offer whatever aid he might.

This, he discovered when he reached his lordship, was little enough, for Lord Buckleigh was far beyond any earthly assistance. The baron lay flat on his back with his left arm flung out to his side, and his right clutching at his chest. His once-pristine cravat was liberally splattered with blood which trickled down his splayed fingers to run in rivulets onto his buff-colored waistcoat. Between the middle and ring fingers could be seen the jagged edges of a small round hole in the waistcoat. His lordship's glassy eyes stared expressionlessly up at Pickett, who could not help feeling a certain sense of satisfaction that Claudia need fear nothing from this man ever again.

Eager to return to the gamekeeper's cottage to bring Claudia the news, Pickett began to turn away when a curious bulge beneath Lord Buckleigh's coat drew his eye, and he bent to flip the cloth back. Tucked into the waistband of his lordship's breeches was a pistol.

The brave soldier, lying in wait for an unarmed man . . .
Lord Buckleigh had not, perhaps, been quite so helpless as
he had led Jamie to believe. But no, Pickett thought with
growing conviction, if his lordship had had access to a pistol
at the time, he surely would have threatened Jamie with it,
even if he hadn't actually used it. It must have been just as
he had said: he had come unarmed to the meeting with
Claudia, being fully confident of his ability to overcome
with his fists any obstacle she might have presented. After
all, he'd had no trouble doing so in the past.

He withdrew the pistol and sniffed the barrel, wrinkling
his nose at the acrid scent of burned powder. The gun had
been used, and recently; the only logical conclusion was that
the person who had shot his lordship had then planted the
weapon on his person. Pickett was not quite sure whether
this was a stroke of genius, or a display of incompetence. If
the killer had thought to make the death look like a suicide,
then he had failed miserably: setting aside the improbability
that anyone would attempt to commit suicide by shooting
himself in the chest, he would be dead long before he could
tuck the weapon neatly away in his waistband. No, this was
no suicide, but a murder—and one done by a person from
whom his lordship perceived no threat, for there was no
indication that Lord Buckleigh had attempted to elude, much
less overpower, the shooter.

As for the gun itself, Pickett was no expert on firearms;
fortunately, there was a man nearby who would probably be
much more knowledgeable than he, and who would have his
own reasons for taking an interest in his lordship's death.

Thus Pickett was doubly impatient to return to the game-keeper's cottage, and within minutes was standing on the front stoop and pounding on the door.

"Back so soon, Mr. Pickett?" Jamie's expressive face registered surprise as he opened the door. "Is something wrong?"

"That depends on your point of view," Pickett said, glancing past him into the room where Claudia had just risen from the sofa. "I've just come from Lord Buckleigh. He was apparently shot as he walked back along the path toward the village. Ma'am, your husband is dead."

"Dead?" Claudia turned quite pale, and groped for the back of the sofa for support. "Are you sure?"

Pickett nodded. "Quite sure."

"Then I'm free," she murmured to herself in disbelief. "After all these years, I'm finally free."

"But not for long." Reaching her in two strides, Jamie took her hand and dropped to one knee before her. "My Lady Buckleigh," he said, looking up into her dazed countenance, "will you do me the infinite honor of bestowing upon me your hand in marriage?"

In answer, she cradled his head to her bosom and burst into overwrought tears.

18

The Return of Lady Buckleigh

I shall send to London for a special license as soon as I return to the vicarage," Jamie promised Claudia, in between kissing her and drying her tears.

Pickett cleared his throat, feeling very much *de trop*. "If you are headed back to the village, Major, I wonder if I could persuade you to come and have a look at the weapon."

"Certainly, Mr. Pickett, if you feel you need assistance. Although I must point out that I am a cavalry officer, and therefore more knowledgeable of sabers than I am of firearms." He released Claudia with obvious reluctance. "I will return for you as soon as I am able."

She clung to his sleeve. "Surely you don't intend to leave me here!"

"He is dead, my love," Jamie reiterated. "You need fear nothing from him ever again."

"That's just it. I have to see him. I have to!"

"He's not a pretty sight," Pickett cautioned her.

"Perhaps it's just as well," she said with a shaky smile.

"At least I'll know he is truly dead."

Jamie shook his head. "Claudia, I don't think—"

"No, Major, let her come if she wishes," Pickett said. He smiled at his sister-in-law. "They're tougher than we realize, these Runyon girls."

Jamie, having seen the gently reared Claudia Runyon survive the abuse of a brutish spouse and then endure the rigors of following the drum, could hardly dispute this observation. And so the three of them set out down the path, and soon arrived at the place where Lord Buckleigh's body lay.

"Well, he is certainly dead," noted Claudia, with only the slightest of tremors in her voice. "I cannot rejoice in his death, but nor can I regret it. In fact, I feel—nothing. It is rather like awakening from a nightmare, and discovering that none of it was real."

"That's all it was, then," Jamie said, his arm tightening briefly about her waist before he released her and knelt beside the body. He sniffed at the gun, just as Pickett had, then turned it over in his hands. "This was almost certainly the murder weapon, Mr. Pickett, but I daresay you've already deduced that. It's one of Manton's—you can see his maker's mark here—hullo, what's this?"

"What have you found?" Pickett asked, leaning closer for a look.

"Lord Buckleigh's crest. He had it carved into the stock." He held it out so Pickett might see. "In fact, this is one of a pair of dueling pistols he ordered from Manton shortly after he married Claudia. I remember when he bought them, for he made a point of showing them to me. I suppose you can guess why," he added cryptically.

Yes, Pickett could imagine his lordship taunting his vanquished rival, daring a young man barely out of his teens to challenge him to a duel. But Jamie had won in the end, and that without firing a shot. Which, of course, raised the question: if Jamie had not fired it, then who had?

"Do either of you know where his lordship kept his firearms?"

Claudia nodded. "There is the gunroom where his hunting weapons were stored, but he kept the dueling pistols in his study, for he was immensely proud of them." She gave a rueful smile. "Or such was the case thirteen years ago. I daresay his habits may have changed in the interim."

"It is safe to assume, then, that only someone in the household would have had ready access to them," Pickett reasoned.

"I suppose so."

"Wait." Jamie raised a hand in protest. "Are you saying you intend to try and discover who did this?"

"Wouldn't you like to know, yourself?" Pickett asked, surprised.

"Yes, but only so that I might shake his hand," retorted Jamie. "If you knew who killed him, would you charge him with murder?"

"I could do no less," Pickett pointed out. "I have a duty—"

"Half an hour ago, you said you could not bring yourself to charge me if I'd shot him!"

"To save Claudia from assault, yes, but as far as I can

tell, Lord Buckleigh was doing nothing but walking back home. Look about you: no signs of struggle, of trauma —the man was simply minding his own business."

"For all you know, he was already planning his next attack on Claudia!"

"But we can't know that, can we? Yes, his lordship was a bounder and a cad, but even bounders and cads are entitled to justice under the law."

Claudia tucked a hand through each man's arm. "I suggest, gentlemen, that we not stand here quarreling, but lay our plans. Mr. Pickett will have to break the news to that poor little creature who believes herself to be Buckleigh's wife, while as for us"—she turned to address Jamie—"I confess I am ready to come out of hiding. Shall we inflict ourselves on your parents, or mine?"

"Neither," Jamie declared. "Or both, depending upon how one looks at it. You, my dear, are returning to your father's house until the vows can be said, while I—"

"May we not stay together?" Claudia protested. "In the gamekeeper's cottage, perhaps, until a room at Greenwillows can be prepared for us?"

"Live together without benefit of clergy?" Jamie exclaimed in tones of deepest revulsion, although his eyes twinkled. "My dear Lady Buckleigh, you shock me to the core!"

"It is not as if we have not been doing exactly that for the last thirteen years!"

"Yes, but then we had no other choice," Jamie said in a more serious vein. "We have a choice now, and I intend to see that everything is done openly and aboveboard. Anything less would be dishonoring to you, my love."

"Perhaps, but"—she looked down at the dead man at her feet, and shook her head as if to clear it—"I have dreamed of this moment for so very long. Now that it is here, I—I don't quite know what to do. I'm frightened."

Pickett, having met her mother, saw nothing surprising in this confession. "I think it would be best if the major was not present, at least not at first."

"No, indeed!" Jamie and Claudia spoke as one.

"In fact, I think we might do best to put it all in my wife's hands."

"Julia?" Claudia's brows lowered skeptically. "Are you sure?"

"Your little sister has grown up in your absence," Pickett reminded her. "Have you a bonnet with a veil, or something else similarly concealing? Major Pennington and I will walk with you as far as Runyon Hall, and I'll have the butler fetch Julia. She can break the news gently to your mama while the major accompanies me to Buckleigh Manor. By the time we return, Lady Runyon will have had time to accustom herself to the situation."

"What he means," put in Jamie irrepressibly, "is that he hopes the fireworks will be over."

Pickett regarded him with raised eyebrows. "Of course, if you would prefer to break the news to her ladyship yourself—"

"On the contrary, Mr. Pickett, having won the fair maiden, I find myself filled with a burning desire to obtain justice for my vanquished foe. I will accompany you."

"Am I to understand, Major, that after having met Bonaparte on the field of battle, you are afraid to face Lady Runyon?"

"Bonaparte never had to admit to Lady Runyon that he'd been living in sin with her daughter," Jamie retorted. "No, Mr. Pickett, you are in need of a lieutenant, and I offer myself in your service. I am yours to command!"

* * *

And so it was that, a short time later, Pickett and the major arrived at Runyon Hall accompanied by a woman heavily veiled in a black lace mantilla of the sort worn by Spanish ladies. If Parks, the butler, was at all surprised by the appearance of this female, he hid it admirably, pausing only for the briefest of moments before asking if he might take her wrap—an offer which she declined with a vehement shaking of her head.

"Ah, Parks," Pickett addressed the butler, "will you send Mrs. Pickett down to me?"

"Er, Miss Julia is in the drawing room with her ladyship," said Parks, gesturing toward a door across the hall. "Shall I announce—?"

"By no means! You may tell Miss Julia that her husband has need of her here."

With a last, dubious glance at the veiled lady, Parks took himself off to obey this behest. A moment later Julia came hurrying to meet them. Pickett was relieved to note that Parks did not accompany her; apparently the butler had the good sense to know when discretion was required.

"Yes, John, what is—*Clau*—" She broke off abruptly as Pickett put a finger to his lips in an urgent plea for silence. When she spoke again, her voice was little more than a whisper. "Claudia, what are you doing here? John, Jamie, do you think this is wise?"

"It's been a busy morning, and I haven't time now to tell you all the details," Pickett said in like manner. "Suffice it to say that Lord Buckleigh is dead. No, Jamie didn't kill him," he added quickly, seeing her wide-eyed gaze slew from him to the major.

"Then—who did?"

"We don't know, at least not yet. Major Pennington is going with me to inform Lady Buckleigh—or Miss Gubbins, rather—and Claudia is finally coming out of hiding. I need you to break the news to your mother."

"I shall be only too glad to do so! But—oh dear, it will be a delicate task, won't it?" She glanced at her sister, or as much of her as might be glimpsed through the layers of black lace.

"Yes, it will, which is why I would not entrust the task to anyone but you," he said.

Her lips curved in a warm yet knowing smile. "Flatter me all you like, John, but I shall still demand a full explanation upon your return."

"You shall have it, too," he promised, giving her a quick kiss before turning to Jamie. "If you're ready, Major, we'll be on our way."

After they had gone, Claudia took her sister's hand and let out a long breath that stirred the lace concealing her features. "I suppose we'd best have it over with."

Julia gave her hand a squeeze, then led the way into the drawing room. Parks hovered inconspicuously in the corner and, upon receiving a speaking look from Julia, quickly made himself scarce, closing the door softly behind him.

"What is this all about, Julia?" Lady Runyon asked, regarding the veiled figure with narrowed eyes. "Who is this person?"

Julia dropped to her knees before her mother's chair and took Lady Runyon's frail hands in hers. "You must prepare yourself for a shock, Mama. It's just that—she's come home, you see."

Recognizing her cue, Claudia pushed back the folds of her mantilla. "It's good to see you again, Mama."

"*Claudia?*" The arthritic fingers tightened convulsively on Julia's. In the next instant, Lady Runyon was on her feet and embracing her long-lost elder daughter. "Oh, my dear child, my precious girl! We thought you dead!"

"I know, Mama," Claudia said through her own tears. "But as you can see, I am very much alive, and—and with your permission, I should like to come home."

"*My* permission? I can deny you nothing, my darling, but surely it is Lord Buckleigh whom you should ask. Oh dear, and he has taken another wife! Whatever will he say when—but you have been gone for *thirteen years*, my love! Where have you been all that time?"

"Yes—I know—I am sorry for it, Mama, but—but I have been with Jamie. He—he carried me away."

Lady Runyon released her firstborn, but only so that she

might cup Claudia's face in her hands and look into her eyes. "He *carried you away?* I'm sure I shouldn't wonder at it, for he always resented Lord Buckleigh. Thank God you were able to escape at last!"

"No, no, Mama, it wasn't like that at all," Claudia protested, tears giving way to shaky laughter at the very idea of the vicar's son kidnapping her and holding her against her will for more than a decade. "His was no evil intent. In fact, he—he rescued me. From Buckleigh."

Lady Runyon's hands dropped abruptly to her sides, and she stepped backwards as if stung. "Claudia! Do you mean to tell me that all this time, while we mourned you for dead, you have been living in sin with that Pennington boy?"

Julia, who had feared that the joyful reunion might take just such a turn, rose to her feet and moved protectively to her sister's side. "If we are to talk of sin, Mama, perhaps we should be speaking of Lord Buckleigh. Surely you have not forgotten all those Sundays that Claudia came to church with bruises on her face, having tripped on the carpet covering the stairs! You said yourself—more than once, if memory serves —that she should have it replaced before she did herself a serious injury. It was not the carpet at fault, Mama, it was Lord Buckleigh. *He* was the one who needed replacing!"

"Is this true, Claudia?" Lady Runyon demanded, bending a keen gaze upon her daughter.

Claudia nodded. "Yes, Mama. He had done it many times before, but the last time was by far the worst. Jamie was coming to have tea with me on the day before he was to return to Oxford. When Buckleigh found out, he flew into a jealous rage."

"Then—the tea things scattered all over the floor—?"

"That was Buckleigh's doing, not Jamie's. When he found me—Jamie, that is, not Buckleigh—I had a black eye, a swollen lip, and two cracked ribs. And shortly after we made our escape, I"—her voice cracked at the still-painful memory—"I suffered a miscarriage."

"You were expecting a child?" Lady Runyon's face crumpled at the discovery of this lost grandchild. "Why did you not tell me?"

"I had not known for very long myself. I had thought—hoped—that my condition might offer some protection from Buckleigh's increasingly violent outbursts, but I was mistaken. He even made the vile suggestion that the child was not really his."

"Oh, but to elope—" protested her mother.

"Believe me, Mama, it was not what we would have chosen—either of us—but we had no alternative."

"You should have come to me instead!"

"Why?" Claudia asked with a trace of bitterness. "So that you might tell me it was my own fault, that I should try harder to please him?"

"I'm sure I never would have—" Lady Runyon began, then caught Julia's eye and abandoned this argument, apparently remembering, just as Julia did, a recent conversation in which she had said something very similar. "But you let us believe you were dead!"

"I know." Claudia blinked back tears. "I am sorry for it, Mama, but there was no other way. I could not risk

257

Buckleigh finding us out."

"If only you had told us, your father could have talked to Lord Buckleigh, could have given him a very stern warning that we would not allow him to mistreat our daughter, no matter how lofty his position."

Claudia shook her head. "Talking would have paid no toll—quite the reverse, in fact, for I have no doubt he would have felt himself justified in punishing me for betraying him." She took her mother's hand and was somewhat encouraged to note that, although Lady Runyon did not return the pressure of her fingers, neither did she snatch her hand away. "Mama, I know this is hard for you to accept, but this is no shameful little *affaire* between Jamie and me. We have loved each other all our lives, and on the day we eloped, we made vows to one another—and meant them just as sincerely as if we had spoken them in church."

"But you had already made a vow to your husband, for better or worse!"

"I know all about the 'worse' part," Claudia said, suppressing a shudder at the memory. "But it seems to me that there was also something said at our wedding about Buckleigh's responsibility to love his wife as Christ loved the church and gave Himself for it. If I broke my marriage vows—and I can hardly deny having done so—then Buckleigh had broken his own vows to me long before."

"Perhaps, but one does not negate the other," insisted Lady Runyon. "As for what Lord Buckleigh will say when he finds out—"

"He won't say anything," Julia put in. "Lord Buckleigh

is dead—and no, Jamie didn't kill him," she added, anticipating her mother's next question.

"Jamie and I are to be married as soon as he can obtain a special license," Claudia said. "Until then, I should like to return home, if I may."

"Your 'home' is Buckleigh Manor!"

"Which currently has another mistress in residence," Claudia pointed out.

"Yes, well, I do not wish to appear unsympathetic, my dear, for I can see things have been most uncomfortable for you. But surely you must see—the impropriety of it—I could never hold my head up at church—"

"Mama!" Julia exclaimed, aghast that her mother's sense of decorum meant more to her than the return of her long-lost daughter. "If you will not allow Claudia to stay here, then I shan't stay, either. John and I shall remove to the Pig and Whistle, and we will take Claudia with us."

A murmur of voices came from beyond the drawing room door, and it burst open to admit Sir Thaddeus. "What the devil is going on here? First Parks will hardly allow me to enter my own drawing room, and now—" He broke off abruptly at the sight of Claudia. "My girl! My little girl!"

The squire wept openly as he gathered his daughter into his arms.

"It seems that Claudia has spent the last thirteen years living adulterously with that Pennington boy," his lady informed him.

"Indeed, it is true, Papa, but it was not by choice." Claudia explained about the beatings, concluding, "Jamie was persuaded that Buckleigh would kill me sooner or later, and so he took me away."

"In fact, he did what your own father should have done," the squire grumbled when she had finished. "By God, when I get my hands on his lordship, I'll—"

"It's all right now, Papa. Buckleigh is dead, and Jamie and I will be married as soon as may be." She smiled apologetically. "The last thirteen years notwithstanding, Jamie refuses to live with me any longer until the marriage is solemnized. I had hoped to stay with you and Mama until the arrangements are made, but since Mama dislikes the notion—"

"Nonsense! Why should she?" He bent a fierce look upon his wife.

"Adultery, my dear—" protested Lady Runyon. "The scandal—"

"And where is Jamie to stay in the meantime?" he demanded of Claudia.

"He will continue at the vicarage."

"There it is, then, Caro! If the vicar can survive the scandal, I don't see why we shouldn't."

"Yes, but Jamie is their son, and it is different for men," Lady Runyon objected feebly. "Besides, however little I may approve of his actions, Jamie at least has no living wife—"

"Jamie's 'actions,' as you call them, might not have been necessary if Claudia had felt she could confide in us," Sir Thaddeus growled. "No, by God, it was left to a damned Bow Street Runner to tell me how things stood between Julia and Fieldhurst. I'll not repeat the same mistake. Claudia must not suffer any longer for our lack of understanding."

"But what will they say in the village? I have always tried to set a virtuous example—"

"Why should we care what they say? Saving for Lady Buckleigh, you are the highest ranking female in Norwood Green, and I daresay most of the villagers will look to you for their example. Seems to me that if you let it be known you accept Claudia and Jamie back with open arms, no one else would dare say or do anything to offend you." He scowled fiercely at her. "On the other hand, if you can't find it in your heart to do so, I suppose the Pig and Whistle can house one more."

"Thaddeus!" she gasped. "You would leave me?"

"It's a funny thing about paragons of virtue, Caro. I'm sure they are very admirable from a distance, but they're damned difficult to live with."

Lady Runyon took a quavering breath. "Very well," she said with obvious reluctance. "You may stay, Claudia, but only until the vows are said—if you are quite certain they *will* be said," she added darkly, muttering something under her breath about the need for buying a cow when one is already getting the milk for free.

"We have waited thirteen years for the opportunity to marry," Claudia assured her. "We shan't wait a moment longer than necessary. That is all we ever wanted, you know—to come back home and live openly as man and wife at Greenwillows with our daughter."

Here, it seemed, was a fresh blow for her ladyship. "Daughter? You have a child out of wedlock?"

"Not out of wedlock, Mama, for I was married, just—just not to the father of my child."

"You have seen her, Mama," Julia put in. "The little girl at church. You said she reminded you of Claudia, and you were quite right."

"That beautiful child—she is my granddaughter?" Lady Runyon breathed, clearly overcome at the idea that the wages of sin should yield such precious dividends.

Claudia nodded. "We could not keep her with us in Spain, so as soon as she was weaned, Jamie arranged for the wife of a fellow officer to convey her to Mr. and Mrs. Turner so that they might raise her along with their own children. I knew we could rely on their discretion—one has only to look at her to know who sired her, although even they do not know who her mother is—and I knew they would be good to her. I could not bear to give her to a stranger." Her voice cracked on the words. "Although she must know the truth of her parentage someday—Norwood Green is too small a village to allow of its remaining a secret—I want her to think of her father as a hero, as indeed he is. I should hate to have to explain to her how we came to be estranged from her grandparents."

"It's true that the poor mite should not suffer for her parents' actions, for she never asked to be born," Lady Runyon acknowledged, visibly weakening. "And so I have a granddaughter! What, pray, is her name?"

"Can you not guess, Mama?" Claudia asked gently. "Her name is Caroline."

With a sob, Lady Runyon buried her face in her

handkerchief and wept, her shoulders shaking so violently that Sir Thaddeus felt compelled to put his arms around her and pat her awkwardly on the back. He looked over her head at his daughters, and the three expelled sighs of profound relief.

Claudia had come home at last.

19

In Which John Pickett Encounters
Resistance from an Unexpected Source

P ickett and Jamie left Claudia to Julia's care, and soon reached the Palladian mansion which, it appeared, would soon stand vacant, and would remain so until the next in line to the title could be discovered. But this, thankfully, was not their problem. Theirs was the more pressing (and far more delicate) task of informing the widow that, firstly, her husband was dead; and that, secondly, she was no widow after all, for she had never really been a wife.

Pickett lifted the polished brass knocker and let it fall, and a moment later it was opened by the butler, who goggled over Pickett's shoulder at the sight of the one person he had never expected to see darken Lord Buckleigh's doorstep.

"I'm afraid his lordship is out—" he began.

Pickett cut him short. "Yes, we know. I wonder if we might see your mistress."

The butler inclined his head. "If you will come inside, I shall inquire."

He took himself off, and returned a moment later with the information that Lady Buckleigh and her mother would receive them in the drawing room. Pickett had not bargained on the presence of Mrs. Gubbins, but decided it might be a good thing if she were present; after all, Miss Gubbins was about to receive a considerable blow—two of them, in fact. She might want her mother's support. They followed the butler to the door of the drawing room, where he announced, "Mr. Pickett and Major Pennington, ma'am."

The two ladies sat side by side on the striped satin sofa, the younger wearing a crisp morning gown of figured muslin, the elder a walking costume and sturdy half-boots whose dew-bespattered kid uppers (to say nothing of the damp patches beneath the wearer's arms) bore testament to her morning constitutional. Lady Buckleigh—or rather, Miss Gubbins—rose gracefully and bobbed a curtsy. "Mr. Pickett. And Major Pennington," she added with a chill in her voice that led Pickett to wonder just what Lord Buckleigh had told his bigamously wedded bride about Jamie's rôle in the loss of his first wife.

"Come in, come in," bellowed Mrs. Gubbins jovially, once again usurping her daughter's rôle as hostess. "We've just rung for tea. Betty, my dear, you'll have to send the butler back for extra cups."

Pickett quickly demurred. "We'll not impose on your daughter's hospitality, ma'am. In fact, we have come on a sad errand." Turning to the young woman who believed herself to be Lady Buckleigh, he said, "I am sorry to inform you that your—that is, that Lord Buckleigh is dead."

"Dead?" Betty Gubbins's face turned first white and then red, and her voice rose on a note of hysteria. "But he can't be! He was in perfect health only this morning!"

"It is true, nevertheless. I discovered him lying on the path between here and the gamekeeper's cottage on the Greenwillows estate." He paused, but if he had hoped for some hint of guilt from the young woman, he was doomed to disappointment. "I'm afraid he was already beyond any assistance I might have been able to render."

"Oh, but *dead!* Mama, what shall I do?" She burst into noisy sobs.

"There, there, my pet." Mrs. Gubbins cooed, gathering her daughter to her bosom. "Your papa may not be a lordship, but he's a very warm man, you know, and he'll see that you never want for anything."

"If I may make a suggestion," Pickett said, "you might want to send a few of the servants to bring the, er, to bring his lordship back home. Also, a message to the coroner would not go amiss."

"The coroner?" Betty Gubbins lifted her head, revealing tear-drenched eyes that now sparkled with indignation. "Surely you cannot mean to suggest that my husband was murdered?"

"That will be for a coroner's inquest to decide, ma'am. Although a tragic accident might be just within the realm of possibility—but *only* just—all the evidence points to willful murder."

"But why should anyone do such a thing?" she demanded, her gaze shifting accusingly to Jamie. "Perhaps

Major Pennington can tell us."

"Nonsense!" put in Mrs. Gubbins. "Depend upon it, my pet, it is nothing but a tragic accident. I daresay some poacher saw him moving through the trees and shot him, thinking he was a deer."

Pickett regarded her curiously, his expression unreadable. "Did I say he had been shot, Mrs. Gubbins?"

"Of course you did!" the woman insisted, as her daughter stepped backwards out of her arms to regard her with mounting horror. "You said you'd discovered him lying on the path, and that he'd been shot dead!"

"I said I'd discovered him lying on the path, and that he was already dead, but I did not say how he had met his end. I wonder how you knew that, unless you had seen him yourself—or, perhaps, shot him yourself?"

"Nonsense! Why, I've been right here with Betty all morning!" She turned rather wild eyes on her daughter in a silent plea for confirmation.

"Your clothes suggest otherwise," Pickett observed, looking down at her damp half-boots, "and the fact that you have not yet changed indicates that your return to the house was quite recent." Never before had he thought the near-constant clothing changes demanded by Society might prove to be useful.

"Why, you—you—" Mrs. Gubbins sputtered, turning quite purple in the face.

"It was interesting, too," Pickett continued, "that when comforting your daughter, you said her father would take care of her. You never said anything about his lordship, about her widow's jointure."

"Because he never really married her, the blackguard! Oh, he came a-courting with flowery words and a fancy title, but all the while he was still wed to that Runyon girl! I may not be a 'ladyship,' Mr. Pickett, but I wasn't born yesterday. When you told that tale at dinner, I had no trouble putting two and two together and getting four."

"Yes, and you told us you would know what to do to any man who served your daughter such a turn, did you not?" he recalled, not entirely without sympathy.

"If you're thinking I regret what I did now that I've been caught, I'm afraid you're fair and far off! I confronted his high-and-mighty lordship that same night after Betty had gone up to bed, and he laughed in my face. Told me if I didn't want to see my daughter utterly ruined, I'd keep a still tongue in my head. You may call it murder, Mr. Pickett, but I say he had it coming to him, thinking he could play such a trick on my girl just because her father didn't have a fancy handle attached to his name. Why, I'll wager he never would have treated a lady of his own class so shabbily!"

"Don't bet on it," muttered Jamie.

"Oh, Mama, how could you be such a fool?" shrieked Betty, her veneer of gentility abruptly stripped away. "Now I'll never be a 'ladyship'!" With this pronouncement, she burst into gusty sobs.

Pickett sighed. "This is a bit irregular, what with it being the Justice of the Peace who is dead, but I think you had better come with me, Mrs. Gubbins."

The faint click was nearly inaudible, drowned as it was

by Betty Gubbins's moans, but Pickett heard enough to make him turn—and find himself staring down the barrel of Jamie's pistol.

"What the devil—?"

"I'm sorry, Mr. Pickett, but Mrs. Gubbins isn't going anywhere except to Bristol, where she may board the next ship for America," Major Pennington informed him.

Setting his hands on his hips, Pickett regarded his mutinous lieutenant with more exasperation than fear. "You'd shoot your own brother-in-law?"

"You're not my brother-in-law yet," Jamie reminded him with a grin. "As for shooting you, I couldn't bring myself to kill you—aside from the fact that Julia would never forgive me, I quite like you for your own sake, you know."

"I wish I could say the same for you!" retorted Pickett.

"You're talking a bit rashly for someone with a gun trained on him," Jamie responded in like manner. "No, Mr. Pickett, I wouldn't kill you, but a ball in the leg would hinder you sufficiently to give Mrs. Gubbins ample time to escape. I'm afraid it wouldn't do much to enhance your honeymoon, either," he added apologetically.

"But you volunteered to assist me! We're on the same side!"

Jamie shook his head. "Not entirely. You are driven by a sense of duty to justice and the Crown, whereas my motivation is rather more personal. The man had beaten Claudia black and blue on more than one occasion, and I am delighted to see him get his comeuppance at last. The fact

269

that he met it at the hands of a woman lends a pleasing symmetry to the whole business. In avenging her daughter's ruination—and Claudia's mistreatment at the same time, although she did not know it—Mrs. Gubbins has made it possible for Claudia and me to marry at last. Is it likely that I would allow her to hang for it?"

"You do realize I could have you charged as an accessory after the fact?"

Ignoring this threat, Jamie turned to the still-sobbing Betty Gubbins. "Come, girl, hush this caterwauling and help your mother pack her bag! Only one, mind you, ma'am, and carry only the barest essentials for a month-long sea voyage. I can't hold Mr. Pickett at bay indefinitely, you know, for the man is my brother-in-law, or near enough as makes no odds."

Responding, perhaps, to the major's air of command, Mrs. Gubbins hurried from the room with her daughter hard on her heels, the latter vowing to accompany her mother, since she could (she said) never hold her head up in England again.

Their footsteps clattered up the stairs, and as the sound grew fainter, Major Pennington addressed his captive. "It is not as if she is going utterly unpunished," he pointed out. "She is obliged to leave everything behind, to try and begin again in a country half a world away. It is not so very different from being transported, when you think of it."

"Transportation is for thieves, not murderers," pointed out Pickett, who had cause to know, having seen his own father thus sentenced.

"Surely some allowance must be made for the fact that Mrs. Gubbins had considerable provocation," Jamie argued.

"Perhaps, but that was for the courts to decide, not you."

"And what chance would she, a merchant's wife, have had against an aristocrat? Can you honestly tell me that hers would have been a fair trial?"

They might have debated this point indefinitely, had not the Gubbinses, mother and daughter, appeared in the door of the drawing room, each of them struggling with a bulging portmanteau.

"I don't know how to thank you, Major—" Mrs. Gubbins began.

"Never mind my thanks," interrupted Jamie, waving impatiently toward the door with his gun. "Just get you gone."

"Yes, sir! At once, sir!" Mrs. Gubbins and her daughter hurried to the large front door, reaching it just as it opened to admit Mr. Gubbins, who had spent the morning fishing in the stream below the house. "Horace! Thank God! Have you any money on you? Give it to me at once!"

"What? Shopping again, Edna?" asked Mr. Gubbins, withdrawing a roll of bank notes from the inside pocket of his coat.

"Betty and I must away to Bristol. Dear, *dear* Major Pennington will explain everything!" She snatched the money from her befuddled spouse, gave him a quick kiss on the cheek, and made for the stables, shrieking for the coachman as she and Miss Gubbins made their escape.

But if Mr. Gubbins thought his wife's behavior puzzling, there were still greater surprises in store for him. For as the merchant reached the drawing room, he drew up short on the threshold at the sight of Major Pennington holding Sir Thaddeus Runyon's son-in-law at gunpoint.

"Look here, what's toward?" he demanded.

Jamie, judging it time to release his hostage, lowered his pistol. "I'm sorry to tell you, sir, that your wife has shot Lord Buckleigh, and been obliged to flee before Mr. Pickett here could haul her off to the roundhouse."

"What, my Edna? Nonsense! Why should she do such a thing?"

"She did it in defense of your daughter, who has been shamefully used." Jamie briefly recounted the story of Lord Buckleigh's bigamous marriage.

At its conclusion, Mr. Gubbins gave a sigh. "Well, I can't say I liked his lordship above half. I'm sorry for Betty, mind, for she was that pleased to be a 'ladyship,' but I'm plump in the pocket, if I say so myself, and what with her being my only child, she won't lack for men willing to marry her with no questions asked. Not any lordships, I trow, but that's no great loss, in my opinion."

"And what of yourself, Mr. Gubbins?" Pickett asked. "Will you continue here, or join your wife and daughter in America?"

"Oh, once she writes to me with her direction, I'll send my wife sufficient funds to see her through until I can settle my affairs here and follow her across the water. Although," he added with a lurking twinkle in his eye, "between you and

272

me and the lamppost, I may not be in any great hurry."

With these words, Mr. Gubbins took himself off, leaving Pickett and Jamie alone to pick up the threads of their interrupted debate.

"I should go after her, you know," Pickett said with a marked lack of enthusiasm. He supposed his return to London would be further delayed while he appeared at yet another inquest; he did not envy the coroner and the constable the task that lay before them, what with the Justice of the Peace being dead and his self-professed killer on board a ship bound for America. He was thankful he had no obligation to report such an outcome to Mr. Colquhoun; his magistrate would certainly have choice words for any of his men who bungled a case so badly.

"Perhaps you should, but I suspect you won't, for you know justice when you see it." In a bracing tone, Jamie added, "Come, Mr. Pickett, even had he lived, Lord Buckleigh never would have paid the price for killing that groom. Neither he nor Tom were fool enough to leave any correspondence that could have been traced back to the blackmail scheme, but even if you'd had a mountain of evidence against him, it would have made no difference; his lordship's position as Justice of the Peace put him beyond your reach. If you had continued with your investigation—and I quite see that your own integrity would not have allowed you to do anything else—you would have achieved nothing, only put a large blot on an otherwise distinguished career. Mrs. Gubbins dispensed the justice that you could not. In a way, she did you a favor. And speaking of favors," he added in a lighter tone of voice, "I have one to ask of you."

"It seems to me that you are hardly in a position to be asking me anything!" retorted Pickett, not entirely placated even though he could not deny the truth of Jamie's words.

"Perhaps not, but I shall ask, nevertheless. I wonder," Jamie said, grinning as he offered his hand, "if you will do me the honor of standing up with me at my wedding."

Pickett struggled with himself, then smiled and took the major's proffered hand. "The honor is all mine—my brother."

EPILOGUE

Which Ends, as It Began, with a Wedding

T he guest list was of necessity small, consisting only of the bridal couple's immediate families, but it was one of the happiest weddings ever to take place in the ancient stone church in the village of Norwood Green. Mr. Pennington presided over the nuptials of his only son as Major James Pennington, resplendent in scarlet regimentals, at long last married his childhood sweetheart, Claudia Runyon Buckleigh. The bride did not wear white—it would hardly have been suitable, given the fact that she had buried her first husband less than a fortnight earlier—but looked radiant nonetheless in apricot silk, with a mantilla of ivory-colored lace draped over her golden hair.

The bridegroom's mother (whose maternal feelings might have been said by the more rigid of her husband's parishioners to be stronger than her moral scruples) beamed upon the couple, while Lady Runyon held her little granddaughter on her lap and more than once sought furtive recourse to her handkerchief. Sir Thaddeus blew his nose loudly as the vicar pronounced the two man and wife, and

Pickett and Julia, standing at the altar in attendance upon the bridal pair, exchanged fond glances over the heads of the kneeling couple as they recalled their own recent exchange of vows, and the rôle they had unexpectedly played in this one.

At the conclusion of the brief ceremony, Major and Mrs. James Pennington signed the church register and made what was intended to be a discreet exit through a side door. In this, however, they were thwarted, for news traveled fast in Norwood Green, and by this time everyone in the village was aware not only of young Lady Buckleigh's long-ago elopement with the vicar's son, but of the perfidy of his lordship that had driven her to so desperate a flight. And so it was that, when the church door was flung open to permit them egress, Jamie and Claudia were met with loud cheers from the villagers and a shower of flower petals from the children, most prominent among whom were the Pratt youngsters. Fortunately, Jamie had anticipated that the people who had known both him Claudia all their lives would be forgiving once the truth was known to them, and was prepared for this reception. He dug his hand into his pocket, withdrew a handful of coins, and tossed them into the air, then made a hasty exit with his bride while the villagers scrambled to retrieve these riches.

For the Pratt family, there was greater wealth still to come: Jamie had determined to settle at Greenwillows with his wife and daughter, and in appreciation for Tom Pratt's long years of silence (a silence which, he suspected, had finally been broken only by the groom's concerns over providing for his growing young family), he and Claudia had decided to invest the money from the sale of his commission, using a portion of the interest to provide for the young Pratt children and, when the time came, to establish them in whatever trades they might choose.

The formalities having been completed, the two families repaired to the squire's house for the wedding breakfast, where they feasted on bride-cake, spiced negus, and every other delicacy that Lady Runyon could contrive on short notice. However irregular the circumstances of her elder daughter's second nuptials, she was resolved to throw over the union the cloak of her own respectability in the hope that, as her husband had predicted, the villagers would follow her own example and accept the newlyweds as a proper married couple.

At last the final toasts were drunk, and Major and Mrs. Pennington prepared to depart for their own home. Jamie picked up little Caroline Pennington (who, exhausted by the festivities and liberally smeared with cake crumbs, had fallen asleep on the sofa) and settled her in his arms, with her coppery head resting on his shoulder. As impatient as they were to keep their daughter with them, Jamie and Claudia were resolved to return her to the Turner farm every evening for a time, in order to make the transition as easy as possible for her.

Lady Runyon kissed the child's smooth round cheek and, after a moment's awkward hesitation, presented her own cheek to her newly minted son-in-law.

"Thank you for taking care of our Claudia," she told

277

him. "I know you did the best you could."

He bent to kiss her papery white cheek. "Believe me, ma'am, I considered it a privilege to do so." He turned to the squire. "I hope you won't hold it against me, sir."

"Nonsense!" Sir Thaddeus pounded him heartily on the back. "I only wish I'd known—but I suppose that's all water under the bridge. Welcome to the family, son."

Pickett was next in line. "Well, Mr. Pickett—look here, may I call you John? After all, we are brothers-in-law"— receiving an affirmative nod, Jamie continued—"I hope there are no hard feelings."

"None at all," Pickett assured him, shaking the Major's free hand.

"You've got a good man there, Julia," Jamie said, stooping to kiss his sister-in-law. "I'm not sure you could have found a better."

"Nor am I," Julia said with a smile. "Claudia, I wish I might stay and become better acquainted with my niece, but John has been too long away from Bow Street already. You will make Jamie bring you to London, won't you? We can take little Caroline to Astley's Amphitheatre, and the Royal Menagerie, and—oh, everywhere!"

Claudia, who had been following her husband down the line embracing each member of her family in turn, promised to do so, and the two sisters bade each other a fond (if tearful) farewell. And then the newlyweds were gone, and the other newlyweds, Mr. and Mrs. John Pickett, turned to one another.

"I suppose we'd best be on our way if we want to make

Reading before dark," Julia told her husband.

"Yes, and before the driver is as drunk as a wheel-barrow," Pickett agreed.

He was quite right in this assessment. The post chaise they'd sent for earlier that morning had arrived, and its driver was now cooling his heels downstairs in the servants' quarters, where the household staff was having its own celebration unhindered by Lady Runyon's notions of propriety.

"Mr. Pickett, I fear I owe you an apology," said his mother-in-law, offering her hand. "Little as I may like the match, at least you married our Julia in all honor."

Blushing at this unexpected praise, Pickett took her hand. Ironically, now that he had won some measure of approval from his wife's mother, he found he could not accept it, not at the expense of another man. He shook his head. "Ma'am, I don't think you could find a more honor-able man than Jamie Pennington, or one more completely devoted to your daughter." He glanced down at Julia, and grinned sheepishly. "Your elder daughter, that is."

"Well, Mr. Pickett, I stand in your debt." Sir Thaddeus took his hand and pumped it heartily. "First you saved our Julia from the gallows, and now you've given us Claudia back."

Pickett shook his head. "Jamie deserves the credit for that, not I."

"Still, if you hadn't fixed Buckleigh as Tom's killer, his lordship would still be alive and well, and Claudia still in hiding."

The foursome strolled out onto the front portico, where the post chaise stood with their bags strapped to the boot. After a final round of goodbyes, Pickett would have handed Julia up into the vehicle, but Sir Thaddeus stopped him.

"One moment." The squire stepped forward and withdrew a folded rectangle of paper from the pocket of his coat. "I know you fellows work on commission, so here's a little something for you."

Pickett shook his head. "I'm sorry, sir, but I can't accept this."

"Why the devil not?" demanded Sir Thaddeus, scowling fiercely.

"Because—" Pickett broke off with a shrug. "I hope you will pardon the presumption, sir, but because you're family."

Sir Thaddeus was silent for a long moment, during which the frown lines on his brow cleared, and he regarded his low-born son-in-law with something akin to approval. "Well said, Mr. Pickett." He glanced toward Julia, waiting beside the post chaise. "Take care of my little girl."

"I intend to," Pickett promised.

The squire nodded, satisfied. Pickett handed Julia up into the post chaise, and the driver raised the step and closed the door. A minute later, they were heading down the long drive toward the road that would take them back to London.

Alone with her husband, Julia let out a long breath and turned to regard Pickett with eyes shining. "I must say, it was not the wedding trip I had expected, but I thought it went rather well, all things considered."

He said nothing, but yawned widely. Before they had left the wedding breakfast, she had reminded him of the effect on his injury of being bounced over bad roads, and insisted on dosing him with laudanum for the journey. It was beginning to take effect. She saw that yawn, and slid to the end of the seat so that he might lie down with his head on her lap.

"Still," she continued, "it will be good to return to London, will it not?"

To this he readily agreed, recalling fondly those nights spent in his Drury Lane flat with no in-laws to impress or ghostly interruptions to investigate.

"It seems an age since I have resided in Curzon Street." She stroked his brown curls with loving fingers. "I confess, I have long been impatient to get you under my own roof."

Curzon Street. Not his flat, but her town house, complete with servants and all the trappings that four hundred pounds per annum—*her* four hundred pounds per annum—could buy. "My lady—Julia—" he said pensively, holding his eyes open with an effort, "—we were happy in Drury Lane, were we not?"

"Mmm, blissfully so." Her lips curved in a satisfied smile at the memory. "Still, I am ready to return to real life, aren't you?"

That is *my real life*, he thought, but before he could put voice to the words, the laudanum took hold, and he fell asleep in his lady's arms as the carriage bowled eastward, toward London and the new life that awaited them there.

SHERI COBB SOUTH

But wait! There's more!

The next book in the series, *Mystery Loves Company*, is scheduled for January 2018. In it, Mr. and Mrs. John Pickett are back in London, where they're forced to confront the realities of their unequal marriage. Will their love be strong enough to survive? (Oh, and there will also be a mystery to be solved.)

In the meantime, you can get a sneak peek at their homecoming in the short story (yes, another one!) "Finders Weepers," available for free download. Here's the link: http://dl.bookfunnel.com/6xx43qg1v7

About the Author

At the age of sixteen, Sheri Cobb South discovered Georgette Heyer, and came to the startling realization that she had been born into the wrong century. Although she probably would have been a chambermaid had she actually lived in Regency England, that didn't stop her from fantasizing about waltzing the night away in the arms of a handsome, wealthy, and titled gentleman.

Since Georgette Heyer died in 1974 and could not write any more Regencies, Ms. South came to the conclusion she would simply have to do it herself. In addition to her popular series of Regency mysteries featuring idealistic young Bow Street Runner John Pickett (described by *All About Romance* as "a little young, but wholly delectable"), she is the award-winning author of several Regency romances, including the critically acclaimed *The Weaver Takes a Wife*.

A native and long-time resident of Alabama, Ms. South recently moved to Loveland, Colorado.

She loves to hear from readers, and invites them to visit her website, www.shericobbsouth.com, "Like" her author page at www.facebook.com/SheriCobbSouth, or email her at Cobbsouth@aol.com.

CPSIA information can be obtained
at www.ICGtesting.com
Printed in the USA
LVOW08s0754100617
537658LV00001B/243/P

9 780692 729830